WARRIOR

A *FIRST TO FIGHT* NOVEL

NEW YORK TIMES & *USA TODAY* BESTSELLING AUTHOR

NICOLE BLANCHARD

Warrior

Copyright © 2015 by Nicole Blanchard

All rights reserved. No part of this publication may be reproduced, distributed or transmitted in any form or by any means, including photocopying, recording, or other electronic or mechanical methods, without the prior written permission of the publisher, except in the case of brief quotations embodied in critical reviews and certain other noncommercial uses permitted by copyright law.

Publisher's Note: This is a work of fiction. Names, characters, places, and incidents are a product of the author's imagination. Locales and public names are sometimes used for atmospheric purposes. Any resemblance to actual people, living or dead, or to businesses, companies, events, institutions, or locales is completely coincidental.

DEDICATION

To my OG readers who claimed Ben as their book boyfriend.
He was yours first.

CONTENTS

CONTENT & TRIGGER WARNINGS

Thank you so much for reading Warrior.

Before you dive in, please note this novel contains pregnancy, medical trauma / conditions, scenes of action, descriptions / acts of violence, military situations, and on the page spice.

Please mind the triggers and take care of yourselves.

Nicole

PART ONE

CHAPTER ONE

BEN

"I'm glad you were able to take some time to come see your momma before you took off again."

I wrap her into a bear hug, the kind I used to use to piss her off with as a kid because she'd always been so much smaller than me. "You saw me a few months ago." I kiss her hair and inhale the scent of her perfume. Something inside me hitches, but I shove it away. "Besides, I remember you yelling at me to get the hell out when I was eighteen. So, really, you're the reason I joined the Marines in the first place."

She laughs, but it's watery. I don't know what to do other than squeeze her a little tighter. She takes a deep breath and then pushes me away. We both ignore the fact that her eyes are still rimmed with red. "Get out of here. Jack's been calling all afternoon. I swear it's like the two of you are sixteen again."

I kiss her once more. "Save me some of the ribs and rice, woman."

"I'll fix you a plate before your father eats it all. Now go."

The creaky front door slams behind her and I hear her yelling at my dad about anything that will distract her from the fact that I am deploying in just a few days.

Ah, home sweet home.

My shoulders slump and I wipe off the smile I'd slapped on when the plane touched down in Jacksonville. A shrink would have a field day with my mental state, but it's nothing I haven't been through before, so I drown out those thoughts with our homegrown country station. The sooner I get to Jack's, the better. The last thing I need is to be alone in my head right now.

Driving around my hometown is a surreal experience. I clearly remember growing up here, going to school here, but the person I was then and the man I've become couldn't be more different.

I pull up to the lake house and momentarily contemplate passing on his offer to hang out when my eyes fall on movement in the doorway. My breath catches in my throat when I realize it's Jack's younger sister, Olivia. Her eyes meet mine and I realize I'm not the only one who's done some changing over the years I've been away. Was she always such a knockout?

My hands clench on the steering wheel until Jack appears in the doorway behind her as a much needed reminder that I should keep my distance. I hop out of the truck and make my way over to them. Olivia stays back with her arms wrapped around her waist as Jack walks over and gives me a one-armed hug.

"Good to see you, man," he says. "It's been way too long."

"Yeah," I say, my eyes still on Olivia. "It has."

"Do you mind helping Olivia with the food? I'll pull out the chairs and shit. Logan should be here soon."

"Sure, man. Whatever you need." I make it a point not to look at Olivia until Jack leaves the room.

She bites her lip and smiles. "C'mon, I'm making bacon wrapped shrimp. It's pretty awesome, I'm not gonna lie."

I chuckle. "I'm sure it is." I follow her in and immediately feel at ease. "God, this place hasn't changed at all."

Constructed just about entirely of wood, the house is really more of an expanded cabin with floor to ceiling windows that look out over the pristine surface of McCormick Lake. Through them I can see Jack wrestling with the patio furniture. I squint my eyes at the dark figure beside him.

"Holy shit, is Sofie out there, too?"

Olivia turns from the fridge, a package of bacon in her hands. "Yeah, she didn't want to miss your big homecoming and I managed to convince Jack to be on his best behavior."

I glance back at them and note their hostile postures. "Yeah, I'm not sure how long that's going to last."

She places a bunch of ingredients on the counter and looks out the window only to shrug them off. "Who knows with those two? Here, will you rinse these off for me?"

I move across the kitchen to her side at the sink. The dress she's wearing brushes my leg and my body warms. She smiles up at me and all I can think is, *Oh, shit.*

We're interrupted by the sound of the back door to the patio slamming. "I'm going to strangle that girl, Liv," Jack says, grabbing a beer from the fridge. He motions toward me and I nod.

"Relax. You can control yourself for a couple hours," she tells him.

"I doubt it," he replies cryptically. And fuck if I don't have the same thought.

When Jack leaves again, I should put a careful distance between us, but I don't. Instead I move to her side and lean against the counter. "So how have you been?" I ask, knocking my shoulder into hers playfully.

"Oh you know, busy as hell. How about you?"

"Same."

"Well, I'm glad you were able to make it. I don't think I've seen you since before you left for boot camp." She flicks a glance up at me and the memory of our one and only kiss feels like a physical presence. She blushes and then looks back down.

"My mom was about to kill me for staying away for so long. War I can handle, but that woman is terrifying."

"Mrs. Hart?" she says. "She makes apple pie for goodness' sake. She's like five feet tall. How can she possibly terrify you, someone who is essentially an American Jedi?"

"Has she ever chased you around the kitchen with a barbecue fork because you broke her T.V.?"

Olivia gasps. "She did not do that."

I hold up my hands. "Swear to God."

"I'll have to ask her the next time I see her because I just can't picture that."

"You'd be surprised."

She narrows her eyes at me as if she's still not fully convinced. "Can you grab some more paper towels for me? They're just up there in the cabinet." She indicates the one above her head and holds up her dirty hands.

I stretch over her and my chest brushes against her

back. She turns to me and our eyes lock. I find myself leaning toward her when Jack bursts in through the back door again. We spring apart like a couple of guilty teenagers.

It's going to be a long night.

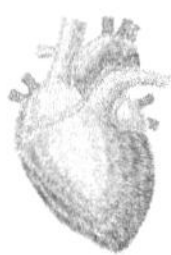

Her laugh sounds, and even across the distance that separates us, I can feel it in my stomach like a sucker-punch. My gaze lifts from the bottle of beer I had grabbed from the cooler and I find her in the center of the group, her eyes shining and cheeks pink with laughter. I pop the top and chug—both to ease the heat building in my chest and to stop any inclinations I may have about finding out if she still tastes as good as she looks. *Bad idea.*

The first swallow is smooth, but does little to erase the imprint of her smile. I lean against the deck as I watch the crowd gathered by the gently lapping water. Their voices and the soft crackle of the bonfire creates a soundtrack I commit to memory. Friends, simplicity, home. The simple shit normal people take for granted.

Those are the things I miss the most.

When the constant attacks seem endless, when I haven't showered or slept in days, it's nights like these I remember. That I want to come back to, even though I never seem to be a part of them. I'm more of an outsider looking in. But unless there's a gun in my hand or bullets flying by, I can never quite relax enough to enjoy them.

The irony isn't lost on me.

I'll admit, I'm not one to wax poetic about women—in the past, they'd been nothing more than a distraction between assignments—but there had always been something special about Olivia.

Special in an untouchable kind of way.

Her brother Jack nudges me with his shoulder and leans against the deck railing next to me. "Gonna nurse that beer all night, Monica?"

I tear my eyes away from my unabashed appraisal of his sister. "What's Livvie doing here? Isn't she supposed to be at school?"

"She finished, man. Starts teaching in August."

Nodding, I turn my attention back to her. To the summer sundress that's just a little too low-cut, a little too tight, and a whole helluva lotta tempting. From what I've heard from Jack, when his parents adopted her, she gave up the rebellious ways that bounced her from home to home, and tried to tame her wild side. But the little spitfire inside of her often makes an appearance when she's either pissed off or three sheets to the wind. I have little will to resist the way her eyes snap or the sexy as hell way she cocks her hip when she's throwing sass. She bites off a comment to her brother and I stifle a groan.

As I think about how much I'm gonna miss her, the

firelight catches the red-gold of her hair and turns it into a halo of flames. I can't help but wonder how it would look spread across my bed with her generous curves steeped in shadows. Her brother chatters on about my upcoming deployment, but I tune him out when Olivia shucks her cardigan and even more of her gorgeous milky skin comes into view.

Silence falls, and I see Jack watching me from the corner of my eye. "I'm sorry, man. What'd you say?"

Jack shakes his head, a knowing look in his eye. "I'm telling you from experience, dude. Love her to death, but you're about to leave. Not a good idea to go there."

"I wasn't planning on it."

"Good." He stares at me intently for a moment before turning away. "She's got a good thing going at that fancy art school. Got her life together. The both of you have shit timing, I swear."

"I'm not the only one." I nod toward Sofie. If Olivia and I had shit timing, Jack and Sofie have it ten times worse. Even now, they could barely stand to talk to each other. They only gave each other cow eyes when they were certain the other wasn't looking. Otherwise they spent every interaction sparring.

"When do you leave, exactly?"

I clear my throat and shake my head a little to dispel the image. "Ah, next Monday."

"Well, I'm glad you could make it out here before you had to ship out."

"Thanks for inviting me."

Jack slaps me on the shoulder as he heads toward the group. "Keep eyeing my sister like that and I'm going to start regretting it."

"Fuck you," I reply.

After dumping my now empty beer in the trash, I grab another and reluctantly follow Jack down to the beach. Night has fallen completely, and the only light comes from the small flickering bonfire and the few rooms still lit up. Memories of hundreds of similar nights gone by wash over me.

Our history is made up of a series of nights like this, and there is a gnawing feeling in my gut that this is going to be the last one. She isn't a starry-eyed teen anymore, and I'm not some pissant private. Soon, a man would see what I am seeing and take it. And I would have to resist the urge to break his fucking jaw as I could only watch the distance between us become greater.

I chug the beer to soothe the sudden burn in my throat. Pre-deployment leave always makes me nostalgic.

A few more days and I can put Olivia behind me. For another year, at least.

I just have to get through tonight.

Sand shifts beneath my feet as I sit on one of the creaky

old lawn chairs we'd drug to form a circle around the fire pit. I nod to Jack and our mutual friend Logan Blackwell. The three of us had gone to boot camp together. Jack and I joined because we couldn't imagine doing anything else, Logan because of the extended family he had to support. Though we had different jobs, we always seemed to find our way back to hang out on our time off. And it was always nice to touch base with my guys when we had the chance.

Logan had recently separated from the Marines. In addition to serving as my going-away party, we'd also gathered to take his mind off his troubled marriage. On the positive side, he had only just started working as a cop. At least he had that to look forward to.

Yet another reason why it wouldn't be smart for me to get involved with Olivia. Not that I expected her to cheat or give up on me, but who was I kidding? Most women could barely handle normal separation, let alone that of the military life. Our dangerous lifestyle had a notorious burnout rate—both for the men and their families.

I drown that sorrow with a healthy tug on my rapidly emptying bottle. If I kept up this pace, it would be one of those times where I wound up on the beach the next morning without my clothes...or my dignity, if the guys had anything to do with it.

My mind begins to wander to the possibility of Livvie joining me, and it doesn't take long for that fantasy to spiral abso-fucking-lutely out of control. Images form of her slick skin against mine, her eyes dark with need. I clear my throat, shifting in my suddenly uncomfortable seat, and refocus my attention to the conversation between the others, steadfastly ignoring the intense look Jack is shooting my way.

Livvie sips delicately from her cup, likewise ignoring her best friend Sofie.

"C'mon, Liv. This is a once-in-a-lifetime opportunity! If there were any reason to give it a rest and live a little, this is it. It's not every day the stars align and our favorite band, since we were tweens, is playing a reunion show an hour away."

Livvie shrugs, smiling guiltily. "I don't know. You know school starts in a few weeks, and I have so much to do with the classroom and lesson plans. I just don't want to screw it up my first day and be caught unprepared."

"If I can handle my crazy-ass roommates 24/7, you can manage one day off from your group of artsy types. Besides, we haven't gone out in forever. Where did my crazy sidekick go?"

Jack scoffs and rolls his eyes. "Give it a rest, Sofie."

Sofie cuts a glare toward Jack. "No one asked you."

"What are you even doing here, anyway? I thought you were living it up at UNF with all the other brainiacs." He takes a heavy swig from his drink. "You wanted to go so bad, maybe you just should have stayed there."

Sofie stands and swaggers to Jack's side as he watches

with hooded eyes. Olivia gasps beside me as Sofie upends her drink over Jack's head.

"Thought you could use something to cool off your hot head," Sofie quips.

Jack lunges to follow as Sofie prances away, but changes his mind, slumping back into his seat instead. "You gotta stop inviting that fucking girl," he says.

"She's my best friend, you asshole. The least you could do is keep from insulting her. This is the first time she's been able to visit since she started grad school. You keep this shit up and I'll never get to see her at all."

Olivia tails after Sofie, leaving me, Jack and Logan staring sullenly at the fire. We're a sad sight, that's for sure. *Women.*

I smirk. "Don't go there, Jack. Not a good idea."

He scowls at hearing his own advice to me from a few moments ago, using the tail of his shirt to mop the beer dripping from his hair. "Fucking women. Not worth the fucking trouble."

"That's the damn truth," Logan slurs. "Fucking women. You think you can trust them. Think they're good, honest people. So you marry them. Put them up in a nice house, let them leech off of your benefits and fucking awesome medical insurance. Then, the next thing you know, you go overseas to defend your country and come home to find that they've maxed out your credit cards and have been letting a fucking *Jodi* sleep in your goddamn bed since the day you shipped out." He gestures with his drink, beer sloshing over the lip.

Jack raises his bottle. "Here, here."

"So glad you're done with her," I tell him. "You feel like shit now, but it's a good thing."

"Now you just need to get in the gym with me, let my dad's guys shape you up," Jack says. "They'll have you so black and blue and exhausted that you'll be like, Denise who?"

"Hell, yes," Logan hollers.

"Maybe you should slow down a little, man."

Logan answers with a burp and chugs the rest of his drink. I shake my head at him.

Jack turns his attention to me as Logan lumbers off to get another drink or take a piss off the dock. "Next time you're home, you better come see us at the gym. Bust out some of your spec ops moves."

I shrug. "I would hate to put all your boys to shame there, Jack."

Jack arches an eyebrow in my direction. "You're on. You and me, to the mat. Next time you have leave, if you don't show up, we'll know who the real badass is."

"It'll still be me, bitch, but I'll take your cute little challenge." I sip my beer. "How's the small business life treating you, by the way?"

"Not bad, man, not bad. We've hit a rough patch since dad turned it over to me, but we'll bounce back. Is your ole' man still busting your ass about taking over the auto shop?"

"He brings it up at least twice every time we talk. I had to leave earlier because I didn't want to get the third degree."

"Are you gonna take him up on the offer?"

When I joined the Marines, I fully intended that it would be for life. But after eight years, a lot of things have changed. *I've* changed. I thought the degree in business was a smart move *just in case*. I never expected that I would actually be in the situation to use it.

"Don't know. I'm due to reup after the next assignment, but I don't know if that's gonna happen. Don't you dare say a word to him."

Jack lifts his beer. "Sure, man. I hear you. When Dad had his stroke last year I knew it was time. I wasn't ever going to be a lifer, though. Running the gym was always my endgame. You just have to figure out what your endgame is gonna be." He glances at Sofie who is holding onto a laughing Olivia. "Then again, sometimes that endgame changes, so who the hell knows?"

Logan starts ambling up the dock, swaying considerably, so Jack abandons his beer and the seat to make sure our friend doesn't drown his sorrows—and himself—in the lake.

"You're being quiet." Olivia snags Jack's empty chair next to me. Her sweet vanilla scent carries on the soft breeze as she leans toward me, her dress dipping scandalously low in the front. I force myself to look her in the face when I respond.

"Got a lot on my mind," I say, glancing back toward Jack to make sure he isn't lurking nearby.

She nods, licking her lips. "Well, we're gonna miss you around here."

My gaze travels over her again. "I'm not here enough for you to miss me."

"Then maybe we should remedy that."

We share a heated look. "Not so sure that would be a good idea, Liv. Your boyfriend might not like you spending time with someone else."

Olivia quirks an eyebrow. "What boyfriend?"

"Hey, Ben," Jack calls. "Need you to take the big guy home. I think he's had enough."

"I swear to God, I'd like to beat his ex-wife. Poor guy," Sofie mutters as she joins us.

"I'll go with." Livvie stands and wipes her hands on her dress. "You've been drinking, and besides, weren't we just saying that we haven't had near enough time to catch up?"

"Hell," I tell her, unable to stop myself, "we may need all night to do that."

She smiles, and the wicked curve of her lips makes my mouth go dry. "I've always wanted to give your big truck a try. If you'll let me drive, that is."

Heat unfurls in my stomach, which has nothing to do with the beer. "You got it, Spitfire," I say tossing my empty beer bottle in the trashcan.

She looks back over her shoulder. "Do you think it's safe to leave the two of them here alone?"

I jerk my chin toward Jack and Sofie. "They're big kids. They should be able to play nice."

Besides, she should be more worried about herself.

I follow her back to the house, trying to look anywhere but the shapely lines of her hips and waist as she climbs the steps in front of me.

Livvie opens the sliding glass door and we step into the house. She closes it behind me, shutting out the laughter and conversation from those outside. My truck is parked next to the back porch. I toss her the keys, and she catches them with a wide grin. My heart damn near jumps out of my chest when she slithers into the driver's seat. And not because I'm nervous about letting her behind the wheel of my baby.

I climb into the passenger's seat reluctantly. Her face is entirely too eager, and she laughs at my expression when she cranks the engine.

"Oh, come on, Ben. I promise I'll be gentle." She winks.

My throat goes dry. "For some reason, I don't quite believe you."

She frowns at me. "What's not to believe? I'm a good driver."

"That's just the problem," I tell her. "It's always the good ones you have to watch out for."

Logan ambles his way to the truck and manages to haul his bulk into the back seat.

"You all right back there?"

A groan answers and I snicker when I see him sprawled out, his head leaned against the window.

She eases out of the driveway and carefully maneuvers around the other parked cars. "Who said I was good?"

I catch my bottom lip beneath my teeth in order to swallow the urge to test her rebellious nature. Her cheeks pink when she catches my intent stare. I gesture with my fingers. "My lips are sealed."

I change the subject until we reach Logan's house a ways across town—for her own sake, really. My restraint can only last so long.

Logan lives in a little apartment complex, a far cry from the two-story brick house he and his wife bought after they married. I wrestle him to the front door and take a risky dip inside his pants pocket for his house keys.

We manage to stumble into his living room and I shoulder him onto the couch, where he falls face-first into the cushions mumbling something about wanting Captain Crunch. I ignore him and stick to making sure he won't suffocate and head out, locking the front door behind me.

I step outside to get a little air and hopefully a good dose of reality. I feel like I'm on a ledge and the only thing keeping me from falling over the edge is my own good sense—and I'm running terribly low on that.

Olivia eyes me from where she stands by the truck. She sends me a hesitant smile. "Do you mind if we go for a drive? Sofie just texted me. She's going home. Jack's probably grabbing a shower. I'm not ready to go home to an empty house and it's my last Friday before school starts."

From the sly look she gives me as she climbs back into the cab of the truck, I know she's interested in more than just a drive.

I know I shouldn't go there. Jack would have my ass, or other more sensitive parts of my anatomy, to say the least. Regardless, I find myself reaching for the door handle, my jeans now uncomfortably tight. A song comes on the radio, and from the corner of my eye, I can see her singing along with the music, though I can't hear her over the rush of blood in my ears.

We reach a stoplight, just as the song ends. We both lock eyes and I watch her throat bob as she swallows. I don't know if it's the fact that I'm leaving soon, or just something that's been building since the day we met, but when it comes to Olivia, my self-control has reached a breaking point.

I watch her shift in the seat, smooth thighs sliding on the summer-slick leather, and I wonder how different she'll be when I get back. Will she still bite her lip when she gets nervous? Will she still look at me with that expectant gleam in her eye, like she's waiting for me to make a move?

Or will she move on without me?

The thought makes my heart race and my blood heats.

Fuck it.

CHAPTER TWO

BEN

I REACH an arm around her and press a kiss to her lips. I inhale her sound of surprise, holding it deep inside my chest, tucked under my goddamned heart where I keep all the memories of her that I know I'll never be able to forget.

Absence may make the heart grow fonder, but it doesn't make the leaving any easier.

"Ben?" her voice catches when I run the tip of my tongue over her collarbone. "W-what are you doing?"

"Pull over somewhere, Liv."

"Are you sure?" She bites her lip and blinks at me.

I cup her cheek, turning her to face me. "I'm done playing fucking games. I want you," I tell her and watch as she smiles, ducking her head. I rub a finger over her lower lip. "I want to kiss you without having to worry about someone walking in. I want to do a whole helluva lot more, but right now I can settle for at least that."

She doesn't answer, and for a moment I think she's rejected me. The possibility leaves a bad taste in my mouth. She pulls away from me and straightens up in the seat, her hands coming up around the steering wheel. She drives a short distance, her eyes scanning the road, for what I don't know. I'm just about to apologize when she pulls off the road into a break of trees. I watch as she puts the truck in park and takes a deep breath.

"Liv?"

"Do you know what it was like for me when I first moved in with the Walkers?" she asks out of nowhere.

I let out a slow breath. "Jack told me some," I admit. When her head turns sharply, I hurry to add, "Not much. Just that you had a hard time adjusting."

She nods. "I did. The foster home I was in was pretty bad. I—I had nightmares about it for a long time..."

I pull her close to me and tuck her head beneath my chin. "I'm sorry, Liv."

"No, it's okay. Anyway, my point is that when I finally stopped waiting for them to get tired of me, I met you. You swaggered, seriously, it was a swagger, into their living room and told Jack that I was hot."

I bark out a laugh. "Uh...I did not." *I totally did.*

She pulls back only to knock me in the shoulder. "Yeah, you did. I was thirteen. That's not something impressionable young girls forget. I'm pretty sure you just said it to piss Jack off, but I think I fell a little bit in love with you all the same. When I met your parents, and saw that the whole idea of a normal family wasn't a dream, I realized that maybe wishes did come true."

I rubbed at the spot where she hit my shoulder absent-mindedly. "Kinda makes me sound like a jerk. I don't even remember saying that."

"Well you were a bit of an ass at the time," she laughs. "But I had the biggest crush on you for years."

"Okay, I lied. I definitely remember saying that you were hot. And it wasn't only because I wanted to piss off Jack, though that was a bonus. I was expecting a kid, you know? Lanky, braces, freckles...and I don't know if anyone has told you, but you were—are—fucking gorgeous."

She looks up at me, her face serious. At first I think she's pissed off for pretty much hitting on her when she was thirteen. Granted the four year age difference doesn't mean shit now, but I didn't want to freak her out, either. Not when I was this close to finally getting my hands on her.

"Then why didn't you say anything to me? Even after you kissed me at the fair."

"And have your brother murder me? When you were sixteen, he used to threaten every guy that even thought of coming near you. Plus, I was leaving for boot camp. I didn't want to lead you on."

"What about now? You're leaving now, aren't you?" she asks, looking down at her hands.

I put a finger under her chin and lift her gaze back up to mine. "I'm not afraid of your brother, Liv. We're all adults and I'm tired of seeing you and pretending that there isn't anything between us."

I use the hand on her chin to bring her lips to mine. I throw out an arm and in a moment, I have her in the passenger seat with me, her body just where I want it beneath mine. The scent of leather and earth mixes with her perfume. She drags a hand down my chest so slowly I ache with the need to have her touch me without any barrier.

"Livvie," I murmur against the press of her lips. "Baby, are you sure?"

She nods and her eyes catch mine as she sucks my lower lip into her mouth and bites gently. Sliding her palm underneath my shirt, my entire body stills at the simple touch of her skin against mine. I press my forehead into the curve of her shoulder where the scent of her is especially strong. I taste it with my tongue, and little nibbles with my teeth, until both of her hands are grasping at the muscles on my back. Needy. Wanting me. Finally.

"The things I want to do to you," I growl.

"Do them," she whispers.

Her hips arch, pressing against my erection, and I can't resist grinding forward just to watch the glow of pleasure ripple over her face. It goes slack, her mouth falls open and she moistens her lip with the dart of her pink tongue. She mewls in the back of her throat, and I seize the sound with my lips. The skin on her arms is hot to the touch, probably from too much sun, so instead of gripping her hard like I want to—like my body needs to—I force myself to be gentle and brush the backs of my knuckles down the outside of her arm.

I try to move back and put some breathing room between us, but she winds her legs around my hips to hold me close. My muscles clench and unclench in an effort to maintain my composure.

I groan as she moves against me. "What are you doing here? With me?"

She deserves more. She deserves better. And I want to be the man to give it to her.

Her gaze meets mine. "Because I want you. I've wanted you for a long time. No one makes me feel the way you do. I saw you today, and I couldn't let you leave again without seeing if you're still as good of a kisser as you were at nineteen." Her arms tighten around me until I can feel the thunder of her heart against my own. "Be with me for a while, Ben. Please."

I decide to give in, just once, just a little. Just one time. To have a memory that will last through the blood and loss. Loneliness and regret. One perfect night to help me make it through the next year of empty ones.

"I can give you one night, Oliva." I pull back enough so that she can see my face. "One fucking great night, but that's it. I'm not the kind of guy who can give you the white picket fence, but I can promise you that it's a night you'll never forget."

"As if I could ever forget you," she whispers, just before my mouth closes over hers.

She gives in with a sound of pleasure that goes straight to my dick. Fuck if it isn't already better than I remember. She plasters herself against me as my tongue strokes hers into submission. I shift backward until she's sitting on my lap with her arms wrapped around my neck.

It starts to rain, the sound of the raindrops hitting the top of the truck become the peaceful soundtrack to our stolen moments together. A sound that blocks out everything else. For a moment in time, nothing can touch what we have. For a moment, we're locked inside a perfect bubble where nothing matters but the feel of her pressed against me.

Everything I don't have the balls to say is translated into this moment. I want to tell her how much being away from her is going to kill me. God, I'm going to miss her. My girl. A fierce possessiveness burns through my chest and I growl into her mouth, one arm wrapping around her little waist to press her even more firmly down on my lap. She breaks apart with a gasp and her hips jerk instinctively against me.

"I've wanted to do this for a long time," I tell her.

"How long?" Her voice is barely a whisper.

"So long that your brother would kill me if he ever found out."

She shakes her head. "What does that mean?"

"It means if he knew the things I've thought about you, he'd find a way to get me permanently stationed overseas."

Olivia gives me a satisfied little smile, her hands braced on my shoulders. "What have you been thinking about me?"

I grin. "Why don't I show you?"

I use the arm wrapped around her waist and the hand on the curve of her ass to slowly guide her against the thick bulge of my erection as I renew the kiss. Her fingers dig into my shoulders, and she slows the kiss until it's nothing but our lips barely touching and our breath mingling between us. She glides one hand to cup the back of my head and the other holds my cheek.

Her hips begin to move of their own accord, tentatively at first then with a steady, jerking rhythm that elicits the most erotic of moans from deep in her throat. I have to close my eyes against the need to take her. Her flimsy summer dress and bathing suit are little protection against me and even though the layers of clothes separate us, I can feel every single movement as if we're skin to skin.

"That's it, baby." I whisper against her throat, "God, you sound so fucking good."

"You sure you don't want to go back to my place first? Somewhere with a bed?"

I scoot down in the seat to give her a better angle and press more firmly against the center of her. She moves her face to the crook of my neck, lips flirting with the shell of my ear. Her desperate little pants are definitely going to star in my fantasies in lonely months to come.

"No," I tell her, "I don't think I can wait. Later."

"But—"

I silence her with a kiss. As the movement of her hips intensifies, I slip a hand between us, teasing her until the cab of my truck is filled with her breathless sighs. Her grip around me tightens until I'm caged in her arms. I can feel her heartbeat through her chest and each heave of her entire body as it's racked with her cries.

She stiffens, stops breathing, and a low moan reverberates throughout the steamed-up cab of the truck. My own body tenses completely with the need to follow her over the edge. The temptation has never been so goddamn all-encompassing.

The remainder of her orgasm makes her shiver against me, and I grit my teeth against the riot of sensation. I feel her smile against my neck, as she smothers a laugh and stretches.

When she pulls back, her eyes are sleepy, half-lidded and lit with satisfaction. My hands trail up from the soft skin of her lower back to cradle her head so I can soak every moment of this in. Like a kid on Christmas morning, I never want it to end. Too soon, she stirs against me and groans, breaking the cocoon of silence that had surrounded us.

Carefully, I move to place her a safe distance away from me...like all the way across the state.

But she doesn't let me. Instead, she wraps her arms more tightly around my neck.

I move to pull back and look at her questioningly, to no avail. "Livvie?"

Her hands plot a dangerous course down my chest, her fingers snagging against the material of my T-shirt until she reaches the taut skin of my abdomen. She tangles with my belt buckle, and the sound fills my ears as if it were amplified a thousand times.

I'm torn between need and duty. Responsibility and recklessness.

Then she kisses me. One soft brush of her lips, feather-light against mine, and I fall straight into madness after her.

I cover here again, gripping her hair with both hands, as if I need to keep a steady hold on her or else she'll somehow escape me. Urgency tastes like firelight and the cherry-scented lip balm she favors. Somehow, while lost in the simple pleasure of her lips on mine, she manages to push my pants down enough to grip my hard length in her torturous hands.

The contact sends a shockwave throughout my entire body, and through my heavy-lidded eyes I see her smile in triumph. Dear God, if I thought she had me wrapped around her finger before, I was wrong. Dead wrong. She could demand anything of me in this moment, and I'm not sure I could deny her.

Then she slips off of the seat, down to the floorboard and slides the wet heat of her mouth over my cock. My eyes shutter closed and all I can do is fist my hands in her hair and surrender to the sensation. The slick, wet sounds of her tongue gliding up and down my length drive me fucking crazy. I finally regain the ability to open my eyes and feast upon the sight of her on her knees, thighs spread to kneel before me, her dress essentially a foregone conclusion, hiked up around her waist like an invitation.

I loosen one hand from my grip on her hair and grab the hem of her dress, pulling it farther down until the hastily tied knots around her neck give, pooling the dress around her knees. The expanse of her milky white skin is now only covered by a few scraps of material that match the pink blush covering her cheeks.

The thought of her breasts tipped in the same color

consumes my thoughts. I need to see if they're a match for my fantasies. I barter with myself, as though I'll stop after I get just one more taste. When, in truth, I know there's no stopping me tonight.

My hands reach for the strings of her bikini top with a mind of their own. Two tugs and her top gives way, the cool air bringing a chill to her flushed skin.

I press against her shoulders and she sits up. The playful gleam in her eyes has been replaced by a burning need that matches my own. I kick off my pants the rest of the way, and she's straddling my legs before I've even managed to shrug out of my tee.

She traps me that way, with my arms tangled in the material of my shirt and still positioned over my head. Her mouth finds mine and everything about her is emphasized in sharp relief at the darkness. Her sweet scent surrounds me, drives me crazy. Nimble fingers grip my length, and I arch and buck against her.

"Fuck, baby, you're killing me," I murmur hoarsely.

She releases my arms and I attack. My fingers are no longer teasing or tempting as they strip her of her bikini bottoms, but insistent. The moment she's completely bare to me, she slicks herself over the length of my cock like she can't resist the simple friction of skin against skin.

"Ben," she manages to choke out. "I can't—"

I capture her lips. "I can. Just hold on to me."

She sobs with pleasure as I guide myself to her entrance, her fingers digging into the muscles of my shoulders. Lowering herself down an inch, two, she groans softly, sweetly. I arch my neck, nearly delirious with the rightness of it.

This, is all I can think. *Everything about this and only this.*

I grip her hips and pull her the rest of the way down until we are thigh to thigh and I can't get enough. She pauses for a beat, maybe two, before she begins to move over me, seeking her own pleasure. I nip at her neck, repeating the simple movements I know make her crazy, arching my hips in time to tease her clit, nibbling her ear.

"Is that how you want it, Liv?" I ask. She mumbles something unintelligible in response. "Are you gonna come? I want to feel you come for me."

I don't even have to do anything other than urge her hips to keep our passionate rhythm and whisper all the filthy things I want to do to her before she tightens over me again—a tangle of want—and explodes.

I only manage to keep the sweet, steady pace long enough to work her through her orgasm before I follow right behind, lips pressed to her neck, clutching her around the waist like my life depends on it.

And my last thoughts as I follow her toward ecstasy are of how I want her to remember this moment as much as I know I will. I want to burn the memory of this night into her very core. I want her dreams to be of me, of this. I want the ghost of my touch to haunt her every day until I come back.

CHAPTER THREE

OLIVIA

Sweat slicks our skin together, but I can't seem to find the energy to move. I'm drunk on the scent of him. Of us. Aftershocks dance along my spine causing me to shiver against him. We fell into Ben's hotel room at some point, several hours ago, in a tangle of arms and tongues and moans. Our relentless exploration of each other frenzied with hurry like we cannot get enough, while lazy and reverent at the same time, like we never want it to end.

His hands tighten against me and he groans. "Don't move for a second."

I look down at him. "Why? Got a cramp?"

"No, you feel so good and considering that I'm going

to be surrounded by a bunch of dudes for the next year, I want to remember this feeling."

My mouth drops open and I slap his shoulder. "You are such an ass."

He smiles and I feel his cock harden inside of me. My eyes widen in response, and I let out a soft groan. "I fuckin' love it when you get feisty. Must be the red hair."

He moves below me and all of the sensitive nerve endings he'd stoked to life send ripples of pleasure throughout me. "It's not the hair, it's because you can be a jackass and unlike the other bimbos in your life, I'm not afraid to tell you."

"No," he says, "I don't think that's it. You just like arguing."

He angles his hips and hits a spot that has lights playing behind my closed lids. As the muscles in my stomach tighten, I try to focus. "I do not."

"Don't worry, Spitfire. I like it when you argue with me. You turn pink in some of my favorite places. If you come for me again, I'll show you where they are."

"I do not!" I try to protest but it's pretty useless because I can't stop smiling.

"Mmm-hmm." He slips a hand between us and my head drops back. "We can move over by the mirror, I'll set you up in front of it and make you watch while I show you. How does that sound?"

My body thinks that sounds like the best idea ever and within seconds, I come with a muffled scream.

"I think you like arguing with me, too," he whispers in my ear.

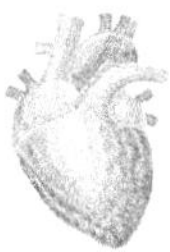

It's morning and I've been up for hours trying to turn back the clock. I got little to no sleep and I have the resulting aches and pains from a night of furious marathon sex to prove it. I stretch and feel the reassuring hardness of him at my back. The arm wrapped around my waist tightens and pulls me even closer to his warmth as he wakes.

My stomach clenches in delicious anticipation. Although I've done some crazy things in my past, I can't even begin to explain how I wound up in bed with my brother's best friend.

The jacket he used as a makeshift sheet comes loose as he tugs. It caresses the length of my body, and I feel it as potently as I did when he first touched me. I lie on my side, turned away from him, but I sense his gaze following the movement of the jacket as it reveals the side of my breasts, the dip of my waist and the flare of my hips. The scent of leather heightens my awareness until I'm nearly trembling in anticipation.

He pauses, studying me for a moment, and my breath catches in my throat. Then I hear the rip of a condom wrapper. After our impetuous sex in his truck, he made a point to wear a condom for each subsequent bout between the sheets. He pulls my body flush against his, and the heat of it feels like a brand. I can't help the moan that escapes my lips, even if I tried. His left hand snakes under me to turn my head to his kiss, while his right cocks my thigh over his leg.

I can feel the roughness of his fingers as they whisper up and down the length of my leg. They dip around my hip to the source of my wetness, and a mewl catches in my throat.

"Morning," he murmurs from behind me.

His fingers enter me in a prolonged stoke. "Good morning," I whisper brokenly.

"I can practically hear your brain working over there and it's too damn early for that."

The palm of his hand presses right where I need him as his fingers speed up. "I'm just wondering where I can hide you, so you don't have to go. I have a closet at home I think you'll fit in, maybe," I manage to say around a gasp.

He shifts his weight on top of me and I frown, having lost his fingers. "Hey, now," he says. "We're not gonna think about all that, remember?"

The rush of emotion startles me and I cover my face

with my hands. "I'm sorry, I'm sorry. Just give me a second and I'll be fine."

Ben kisses my fingers. "You don't have to apologize. I would miss me, too."

My responding laugh is watery. I wipe my eyes and peer back up at him. His dirty blonde hair is ringed with the buttery early morning light. I take a mental picture of the moment and pull his lips back down to mine.

His mouth doesn't leave mine as he slides inside. His thrusts this time are achingly slow and instead of being about quenching a thirst, this time feels like something else...something more. The solemn feeling that gripped my heart as soon as I woke up merges with tenderness, and I drape my arms around his shoulders in an effort to keep him as close to me as possible.

His thrusts deepen along with his kiss in a moment that feels endless. His hands worship my body with gentle caresses and the sounds that he makes in the back of his throat send ripples down my spine.

No matter how many times he tells me that all he can give me is sex—to satisfy a need—his actions say something completely different.

They say he doesn't want to leave me either.

I reach the realization just as I climax, breaking the kiss with shuddering breaths. His crystal-blue eyes meet mine and he grips my shoulders as his thrusts become more urgent. He lifts my legs over his arms and attains an angle that takes me from the peak and flings me even higher. As I clutch his shoulders he buries his face in my neck and we fly over the edge together.

"Oh fuck, Liv," he grunts out as he slams into me one last time. His back, damp with sweat, trembles beneath my touch.

His face stays tucked in the spot on my neck as we both come down, our heavy breaths beginning to relax. He's there so long I almost think he's fallen asleep.

"I'm just going to stay here," he says. "Hope I'm not too heavy."

"Not at all. You're pretty much a cuddly teddy bear."

"Great," he mumbles. "I'm sure the guys would get a kick out of that."

I smile. "What are they like?"

"Assholes, every single one of them. And they're all ugly as shit."

Laughter bubbles in my throat. "Do they have such nice things to say about you, too?"

I hear his sexy throaty chuckle. "I'm sure whatever shit they say about me is much worse." He untangles himself from me and leaves to dispose of the condom.

When he climbs back into bed he positions me so that I'm draped over his chest with my head tucked under his chin.

Eager to learn more about him, about the life that

takes him away so much, I continue, "Are they good guys?"

His hand trails idly up and down the arm thrown over his stomach. "Some of the best. I'd die for them in a heartbeat."

My voice catches in my throat and I try to erase that thought from my mind. "How long will you be gone?"

"About nine months."

God, that feels like such a long time. "That's not too bad." I try to sum up some courage to ask my next question. "Will I hear from you?" I hope that didn't sound as pitiful as it did to my own ears.

He squeezes me a little tighter. "I'm gonna be honest, it may be a while before you do. The place we're going isn't what you'd call developed, so there may be some kind of rough internet connection, but there may not be." I feel him drop a kiss to my forehead. "I'll do what I can though. That's not a line or a shitty excuse. It's just the way the job goes..." He trails off, and for a moment, I think he isn't going to say anything further, but then he continues, "It's also why I tried to stay away from you for so long."

"I understand." It's devastating, but I do get it. It is worth it to have a part of him that I'll always be able to keep. No matter how long he's away.

"You sure? I don't want to hurt you, Liv. That's the last thing I want."

I turn so that I'm facing him. "Trust me, I do." I reach up to kiss him. "I don't want you to worry about me while you're gone. The most important thing is that you stay safe."

His eyes turn serious as I look down at him. "I'm gonna miss you."

My heart squeezes painfully in my chest. "You haven't been here long enough to miss me."

A ghost of a smile crosses his handsome face. "Last night changed that."

I open my mouth to reply, but I'm interrupted by the sound of my cell phone going off on the nightstand beside me. I check and find a text from Jack asking if I knew where Ben went last night.

"What time is it?" Ben asks.

"Little after seven."

"I promised Mom I'd have breakfast at my grandparents' house."

I'm grateful that my face is once again hidden in his throat because the news that our time is coming to an end makes me more upset than I'd like to admit. "Yeah," I clear my throat, "I should be getting home before Jack sends out a search party."

Ben kisses my forehead again before slipping out of bed. I take a moment to admire his beautiful male form as he walks to the bathroom. While he's gone, I dress in my clothes from the night before, wincing as my sore muscles make themselves known.

I throw my hair up into a ponytail and smile in the mirror as Ben wraps his arms around me from behind.

"I'll take you home when you're ready."

I force a smile on my face. "I'm ready." Maybe if I fake it long enough, it'll start feeling like the truth.

Ben places a hand at the small of my back as he leads me back to his truck. The sight of it throws me back to the night before and my face heats. He opens the door for me and I get in. I watch as he rounds the truck, his T-shirt and jeans do amazing things for the lines of his body. I can't believe it took us this long to make it into bed together. If I'd known it was going to be so good, I would have found a way to get him there sooner.

"You need to stop anywhere before I drop you off?" he asks.

I swallow thickly. "No, I'm good, thanks."

As we get closer to my house, the sense of dread grows like a rock in my stomach. This was why I never wanted to act upon the attraction between us. What if things get weird between us? Then again, who am I kidding? Sex always complicates things.

I'm mentally kicking myself when I feel a warm touch on my hand. I look down and find Ben twining his fingers with my own. He brings our hands to his lips and kisses my fingers, and I swear, my heart skips a beat.

"Whatever is going on inside that head of yours… whatever excuses you're trying to come up with to explain away what you're feeling, you need to shut that shit down now. If I had more time to show you what I'm feeling, I would, but I don't and that's on me." He pulls the truck in my driveway, shuts off the engine and turns to me. "I need you to trust that it meant something to me. That you mean something to me."

I move closer, grinning at him like an idiot. "You mean something to me, too."

He full-on smiles at this, his eyes running across my face, almost as if he's trying to commit it to memory. "First chance I get when I get back, I'll find you." He looks out the windshield for a moment before returning his gaze to mine. "I shouldn't tell you to wait for me, Liv, but I'm a selfish bastard so I hope you will."

The next nine months are going to be hell on earth, but what I have to deal with is nothing compared to the dangers he's going to face. I don't know how he does it, and goes back again and again. Just watching him leave and knowing he may not return causes tears to spring to my eyes. I fight to keep my voice from cracking. "You remember what I said, Benjamin Hart. You stay safe. Or else."

"I will, I promise." He spares me a quick kiss. "C'mon, I'll walk you to your door."

Each step down the walkway to my small house makes

the yawning chasm inside my chest crack open a little more. How am I supposed to say goodbye when we've barely said hello?

We reach my front door and turn to each other. I can only stare dumbly at the concrete.

Ben pulls on my hand until I'm in his arms. I inhale the scent of his cologne and detergent, steeling my overwrought emotions. I don't want to make this harder on him than it already is.

When I'm reasonably sure I can control myself, I take a step back. My five foot five height puts me about eye level with his chest, where remnants of my mascara have dirtied his shirt.

"I messed up your shirt," I mumble, fingering the stain.

He smiles and cups my cheek with one hand. "It's fine. Now kiss me and say goodbye."

His lips press against mine for a moment, but those few seconds say more than any words ever could. I can feel the way his fingers grip my cheek more tightly, the way his body strains against mine, and the way his breath catches in his chest. He breaks our connection, resting his forehead against mine, his eyes closed.

"Now say goodbye," he whispers.

I manage to choke out, "Goodbye, Ben."

CHAPTER FOUR

OLIVIA

THE CUTE LITTLE café was about the only interesting place to eat in Nassau, the small town in Florida where I've lived all of my life. When I moved back after college to teach art at the school I graduated from, I made it my Saturday ritual to come here to unwind after a long week. I'd get a scone and a cappuccino and people watch. Marin County may not be big, but what we lack in acreage, we more than make up for in pure character.

Today's special is a decadent looking confection that boasts a triple dose of chocolate. Any other day I would have wolfed it down in two bites, but my stomach just isn't agreeing with me. The past eight weeks I've barely managed to eat anything, it seems. I take a sip of the water

I'd tacked onto my order and hope that the sour stomach will pass. I consider texting Sofie and asking her to pick up some antacids on her way to the café, but after a glance at the time I realize she's probably almost here already.

My fingers shake as I play with the brightly colored napkins. Around me people are chatting and laughing like they don't have a care in the world. A mom and her daughter giggling at the counter over a shared milkshake catches my eye and I glance quickly away under the guise of taking another sip of water.

Sofie enters the café in a flurry of muttered Italian and toting her customary laptop. She never goes anywhere without it, I swear. The sight makes me smile, even though I'm near tears. Or laughter. I can't really be sure these days.

"I swear to God, I'm glad I left this place when I could," she says, slapping her bag down on the table with a *thwack*.

"What? You don't enjoy our little Podunk town?"

"Pah!" she signals a waitress and brushes the long brown tresses out of her face. "The simple fact that it contains your brother is enough to keep me in the city."

"Please tell me the two of you aren't fighting again?"

"When did we stop?" she waves a hand. "That's not why we're here. You said you had some news?"

I clear my throat. "Let's get you some food first. I

would recommend the scone, but I haven't tried it yet. It looks good today, though."

Sofie nods at the waitress. "I'll have a scone and a coffee, black."

I make a face at her and she grins. The knots in my stomach loosen a little. This is just what I needed. "Thank you for coming. I know it's a bit of a drive. Not to mention, you swore you'd never come back after the last time, though you never really told me why."

"I refuse to let anything keep me from my best friend during a time of need. You said it was an emergency?"

My eyes water and I take a tissue and blot them. "I'm sorry, I promised myself I wouldn't cry, but it's not like I can control it anymore."

Sofie scoots her chair next to me and places a reassuring hand on my shoulder. "Come, mama, it can't be that bad. We've been through much worse together and we'll get through this, too. Is it Ben? Did that asshole ignore your calls again? I swear men are all shits. If you want, we can be lesbian lovers."

I laugh through my tears. "You're so crazy. And I told you he's in the middle of nowhere. It's not like he can just pick up the phone and chat for a while."

"You're always making excuses for that man, but I'm telling you, they're all pigs. Which brings me around to my next point. Lesbian lovers, yes?"

The waitress arrives with Sofie's order with raised

eyebrows. Sofie accepts and gives her a dazzling smile. Progressive though Nassau may try to be, I wasn't sure if they were completely ready for Sofie when she was born. When we became friends, the town council had to have had a meeting to plan against our tactics.

"I don't know," I say around the lump in my throat. "I may get fat."

"Fat, psssh. I like a woman with curves."

"Like really fat."

"Well, at least it's not like you're pregnant."

Sofie laughs and takes a bite of her scone. She glances at me and her eyes widen in surprise when she realizes I'm not laughing with her. I watch her throat bob in an effort to swallow. She takes a big sip of her coffee to choke it down and winces.

"You're not pregnant, are you?" When I don't answer she practically shouts, "Good God, doesn't that man know the meaning of a condom?"

I slap her on her arm. "I'd appreciate if you didn't announce it to the world. I haven't even told Dad and Jack yet and you know Jack is going to flip his shit. Ben's his best friend!"

Sofie groans. "Jack routinely flips his shit—don't worry about him. And your dad loves you. Besides, wasn't he just moaning about grandkids the other day? They'll be fine. I'm worried about you, though. A kid?"

I give a watery smile. "Yeah. I had the same thought

when I realized it. What am I going to do, Sof? I barely had a family until the Walkers. What do I know about being a mother? My own mom abandoned me when I was five years old! What if that's genetic?"

It is said in jest, but once the words are out of my mouth, I realize that I'm not really joking.

Sofie shoves my shoulder, muttering Italian profanities her mother would blush to hear. "If you decide to be a mother, you'll be the best one I've ever known. Who else will teach them the proper way to do a Jello shot?

"That's not funny." I glare at her. "I'm being serious."

She turns to me and I realize her eyes are as wet as mine. "I know you'll be a good mom. And I know you're scared, but you have a lot of people that love you. Your dad, me..." She makes a face and says, "Jack."

"I'm so not ready for this, though. I planned for kids in the distant future." The *very* distant future. One that included a tenured position as an art professor and a house that wasn't falling apart around my ears. "What about Ben?"

"What about him?"

I sigh and nibble on my scone. "After ten years, we finally get together and the first time we have sex—"

"Not the only time, if I remember correctly." Sofie grins.

I ignore her. "The first time we have sex, I get pregnant."

"Must have been pretty potent," she quips.

"I don't even know if I'll be able to get ahold of him until he gets back. What am I supposed to do? Welcome him with an armful of baby and say, 'Welcome back. By the way, you're a dad?'" I groan. "This is such a mess."

"Ben isn't a bad guy. Sure, it's not the best timing—"

"Uh, yeah."

"But," she continues, "we'll just have to make the best of it. If Ben gives you shit, you'll just have to take me up on my lesbian lover offer."

We share a laugh and finish off our scones and coffee. As we're leaving the café I turn to her and say, "I think I'm going to try to find my bio family."

Her eyes widen and she pulls me off the sidewalk to a bench. "I thought you didn't want anything to do with them. From what you told me they sounded horrible. Why would you want to find them?"

I shrug as I watch the cars zooming by on the highway in front of us. "I think it's time. I think I've always known I would go looking for them eventually. I kind of want to know where I'm from if I'm going to know where I'm going. Logan said he'd help me out."

The look on her face tells me she doesn't quite understand, but she gives me a hug anyway and I realize how lucky I am to have such a great friend.

I can only hope my dad will take the news as well as she did.

I don't even want to think about how Jack is going to react.

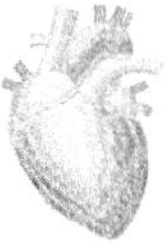

I bought the small two story bungalow when I thought I'd have years to fix it up just the way I wanted it. As I stand in the living room surrounded by evidence of a small demolition a.k.a renovation, I wonder how a baby will ever fit into this mess. I see nails on the floor and chemicals that can burn your nose right off. Can you even bring a baby into a recently painted room? Surely the smell was toxic to their little lungs. I think of my art room and the paints I have there. My stomach clenches. Moms-to-be should know these things. Moms-to-be should know *a lot* of things.

Moms-to-be should, at the very least, have dads-to-be by their side as they wait to break the news to their family.

Or at least be on the same continent.

The kitchen timer dings and shakes me from my thoughts. I check on the pot roast I'd thrown together in the slow-cooker and wince when my stomach roils unpleasantly. Morning sickness—not a fan. Pot roast is my dad's favorite meal, though, and I made it a point to make it occasionally since my mom died a year ago from cancer.

I couldn't quite get it as good as hers, but it always puts my dad in a good mood.

I know he's going to be supportive about the pregnancy; he always has been for anything I do. But I don't know how he's going to take the news of my wanting to find my biological family. He's been a little touchy about the subject since Mom passed.

The knock at the door sends my stomach into my throat. I take a sip of water and walk to the door, my heartbeat thudding in my ears. I paste a smile on my face and open the door, but my smile falters when I see my dad on the stoop with a woman by his side.

There's a beat of awkwardness and I shake it off. "Dad!" I give him a one-armed hug. "Thank you so much for coming."

"Livvie-Lou, you look beautiful, as usual." He smiles and turns to the woman. "This is Melissa. She's just been dying to meet you."

As Melissa and I exchange pleasantries and I invite them in to the dining room, I try to cover up my shock. Not that Melissa isn't a good-looking woman, in fact, she seems almost familiar. She looks to be mid-fifties with coarse black hair and friendly brown eyes. I just can't get around the fact that my father must be dating again.

I guess we both have big news to share tonight.

Dad and Melissa settle at the dining room table and I thank my lucky stars I at least got the dining room renovations done. I serve bowls of steaming hot pot roast complete with potatoes, baby carrots and a side roll.

"Anything to drink?" I ask them, shifting nervously from foot to foot.

"Water's fine for me," Melissa says with a kind smile.

"Come sit down, girl. You look famished." Dad takes a big bite of the pot roast and groans. "Delicious, as always."

I do as he asks, but I can't stomach a bite and instead sift through the pot roast as they eat and make small talk. I learn that Melissa is a secretary at the Marin County School Board, which is probably why she looks familiar. She has an easy smile and my dad clearly adores her, so I choose to be happy for them.

"How did you two meet?" I ask. I manage to nibble on my roll, which is just about the only thing I can stomach these days.

"Melissa bought the cabin next to mine a few weeks ago."

"He came over to help fix my front stoop when the boards started rotting out."

They share a smile.

As we clean up the dinner dishes I pull my dad aside. He smiles, his weather-worn cheeks dimpling and the corners of his eyes wrinkling. "What's going on, Livvie-Lou? You've been twitchy as a lighting bug all night. I hope you didn't mind that I brought Melissa over."

I shake my head. "No, no of course not. I'm glad

you've started seeing someone. Mom wouldn't have wanted you to be lonely."

Melissa excuses herself under the guise of freshening up and I send her a grateful smile. Dad guides me to the porch swing he'd installed for me a few months earlier.

"Tell me what's wrong," he says, his voice firm and implacable. He throws a reassuring arm around my shoulders and pulls me close to his side.

I sigh, content. After I was adopted it took me a long time to warm up to my new family, my new house...my new life. Dad would always take me on the front porch and talk to me—about nothing really. Life, the stars, the bats that swoop down catching bugs. After a while, I started talking back. Some of my favorite memories take place at night on a porch swing.

"I don't exactly know how to tell you," I start.

He doesn't push or prod, just rubs my arm and gently rocks the swing with one booted foot.

"I'm going to have a baby," I blurt. "You're going to be a grandpa."

His arm stills and tightens on my shoulder for one significant pause before the swing rocks unsteadily as his feet thump to a stop. He throws his burly arms around my neck and squeezes the breath out of me.

His breath catches in his throat and I hear the soft rumble of his voice in my ear. "That's good news, honey. That's good news."

Tears spring to my eyes. "Are you sure?"

"Yes, I'm sure. If adopting you taught us anything it's that children are always a blessing." He pulls back and cups my chin in one hand. "When your mother learned she couldn't have any more children she was heartbroken. The day you came into our lives proved to her—and to me—that even when it seems like there isn't any hope, there will always be something to prove you wrong. So yes, it's good news. Do I get to know the lucky dad, too? Or should I pretend I haven't been seeing Ben dancing around you since you were a girl?"

I laugh and squeeze Dad tight, my nose filling with the scent of grease, sweat, dirt and cologne. A scent I will always associate with happy childhood memories. "Yes, Ben's the father. I haven't had the chance to tell him yet, so don't go spilling the beans to the Harts until I can."

He gestures over his mouth. "My lips are sealed."

"Now the part you'll probably be upset about is that I'll be looking into finding my birth parents."

Dad's hold on me loosens and he releases a long breath. "I knew this day was coming," he says. "I'm not going to say I'm happy about it, because I'm not, but I will say I understand."

"Thank you, Dad, I appreciate it. Is there anything you can tell me that will help? Was there anything you were told when you adopted me."

He shakes his head. "The only thing we were told is

that your biological parents were short on money. It was a rough time and they couldn't take care of you the way you needed. I don't wish hard times on anyone. After all, it brought you to us."

"I just want you to know that I've always considered you and Jack and Mom to be my real family. And you'll be this baby's family. They'll never mean as much as you do to me, but it's just something I need to do."

"Don't sweat it, girl. Your mom and I never wanted to hide your past from you. I'll look through my office at home and get you the adoption papers. I'm not sure how much it will help, but—"

"Was this the swing you were talking about, Henry?" Melissa takes a few steps on the porch and stops. "I'm sorry, I didn't mean to intrude."

I smile. "No problem. Yes, he put it up for my birthday. Why don't you two sit for a spell and I'll refresh our drinks?"

I leave them on the porch and retreat to the kitchen. One Walker male down, one to go. My stomach churns just thinking about telling Jack.

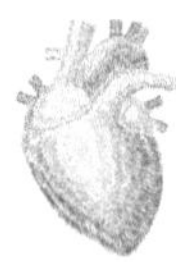

The gym where Jack trains and teaches on his off-time now that he's separated from the military used to be the place I went to for answers, guidance. A retreat. As funny as it sounds, it's one of the places where I feel truly at home. For the first time in my life, I dread walking into the familiar warehouse-turned-rec center aptly named, "The Pit."

I doubt I will find much comfort today.

My father owned the gym for twenty-five years before he passed management on to Jack. If I'm lucky, today is one of the days Dad shirked his responsibilities to go fishing. As it is a Saturday, I'm counting on the call of beer, bait, and bass to be too strong for him to resist. There isn't a man I know who can say no to that. He's supportive of the pregnancy, but telling Jack is something I feel I need to do alone.

I don't see his truck, but I do see Jack's. I look in the rearview mirror as I pull into the parking lot. I am as white as a sheet. Is this what I have to look forward to? Seven more months of ghost-face and nausea. The joys of motherhood. My stomach is pitching like it has a serious case of the butterflies. I can't tell if it's from nerves or the leftovers from today's morning sickness. Probably a healthy combination of both.

It is a dreary September day. The kind that makes everything gray and gloomy. The sky is blotted with dark clouds, and it's been raining off and on for hours. The lack of sunshine is like a void, sucking all the color from the landscape. Even the bright lights and sign on the gym's face are dull.

Water from puddles in the cracked pavement soaks through my flip-flops and jeans, chilling me to the bone. Shivers rack my body as I push through the double doors. I rub my hands over my slightly rounded belly in an attempt to calm myself. Familiar scents and sounds wrap around me like a comforting blanket. I'd spent all of my teen years trailing after Jack and my father, participating in all the classes they didn't explicitly forbid me from taking, training with champion fighters, sleeping on the worn couch in the office. I'm almost surprised by the sense of ease that washes over me. I should have known that if there would be one place in the world where I feel at home, centered, it would be here.

Jack is hanging on the ropes, watching as two men circle each other in the ring. One is a regular, a trainer. The other I don't recognize from the back. I remember Jack and Dad mentioning a new trainee. Marines, both current and former, from the surrounding counties often came here to train. My dad had been a coach the few years he'd been in the service. When he retired to run the gym, his students followed and they'd been here ever since.

The bell dings as the door closes behind me. Jack looks up, surprise crossing his face followed by an easy smile. The smile doesn't last long when he takes in my appearance. He motions to the trainer to continue, then hops from the ring and strides to my side.

"Livvie. You look like shit." He wraps an arm around

my shoulder and steers me toward the office.

"Thanks." I clear my throat. "Is Dad around?"

Jack holds the door open for me. "No. Why? Do you need to talk to him? He'll probably be on the water, even though it looks like it'll be raining buckets all day."

I set my purse on the floor beside the couch and shake my head. "No. I came here to talk to you, actually."

He settles into the chair behind the desk and guzzles from a bottle of water. His hair is wet with the sheen of sweat. He is a miniature version of Dad. The same strong jaw, powerful but sleek build and discerning brown eyes. "Well, I'm here. Talk to me. Does it have anything to do with why you look like death?"

I laugh, but it's hollow-sounding to my ears. "I don't know where to start."

His eyes narrow. "Spit it out. What the fuck is wrong? Are you hurt or something?"

"No, no." I take a deep breath. "I'm pregnant."

The news rocks him back in his chair like a powerful blow to the solar plexus. "You're pregnant?"

"Yes."

He shakes his head as though the information doesn't quite fit. "Are you sure?"

"Yes, I'm sure." I roll my eyes.

"How can you be pregnant?" His voice is disbelieving. What am I, a sexless creature with no reproductive organs?

"The usual way, Jack."

"Smartass." He rubs a hand over his jaw. "I didn't know you were serious with anyone."

I study the blotter on the desk because I can't bear delivering the news to his face. "I'm not."

"So, who's the father?" He's near-shouting now, and I glance at the door to make sure it's closed all the way. The last thing I need is for a roomful of Jack and Ben's old buddies to know I'm pregnant with Ben's kid. That's a conversation I know I'll have to have with him... eventually.

My cheeks burn. "Not that it's any of your business, but we got together at Ben's going-away party a few months ago. I don't think you can classify our relationship as dating. Currently."

"I really don't want to know this."

"I really don't want to tell you."

"What's his name? Jesus Christ, it's not that Chad idiot who's been drooling after you, is it?"

"Well, see, here's the thing—"

"Jesus Christ, Livvie, spit it out."

"Don't," I warn. Then I do spit it out before I lose what little courage I've built up. "It's Ben, Jack."

He doesn't even blink. In fact, if I didn't know him better, I'd say he didn't even look surprised. My face scrunches in confusion and Jack finally says, "Shit."

He stands and starts pacing back and forth. "How long have you known? Does Ben know?"

"I'm around ten weeks along. The first trimester. And no, Ben doesn't know yet. I've tried emailing him, but he hasn't responded back yet. He told me that he'd probably be out of touch for a while. I guess he'll get back to me when he can and I'll let him know then." I pick a paperclip up off his desk and start making it my mission to take it apart. Anything to keep me from having to look at my brother any longer while we discuss the logistics of me telling his best friend that I am knocked up with his kid. "God, that'll be a fun conversation."

"I'd definitely like to see that go down." Jack plops back down in his chair. "I've always known there was something between the two of you. On Ben's side, at least. But there's no way in hell I expected you to come in here and say this. Shock the hell out of me, why don't you?"

"You?" I sputtered.

He purses his lips. "Not that I want to be having this conversation with you, but you two are old enough to have had the safe-sex talk."

I groan and cover my ears. "*Anyway.*"

Jack eyes my belly. "I thought you were gaining some weight. I was about to tell you to start with some more cardio."

I growl at him and aim for his head with my paperclip-sword, though it sails past him when he ducks. "Asshole."

"Is there anything you need? Do you want me to be there when you tell Dad?"

I shuffle out of my lightweight jacket, suddenly feeling hot and cold with dread. Again. "I've actually already told him. I was more worried about you, to tell you the truth."

"There's nothing to worry about, baby sister. I'm just glad it's you and not me." He studies my face again. "Are you sure? Could the doctors have fucked up?"

It's at that moment when I promptly motion him with my finger to hold on a moment, while I proceed to throw up in his trash can.

CHAPTER FIVE

OLIVIA

THE DRIVE to the doctor's office takes a small eternity, even though it's usually possible to get anywhere in Nassau within ten minutes. Both Jack and Dad had offered to come with me. Even Sofie wanted to take off work and drive down. I told them all the same thing I'd repeated since I told them I was pregnant: I could do it myself. None of them believed me. Dad even threatened to show up anyway. "Tough shit," he told me. I managed to convince him not to follow through, as long as I called him right afterwards with the news about the gender.

I smooth the skirt of my maternity dress with clammy fingers. My knees tremble as I open the door to the cool interior. The person behind me pushes it open more fully and I turn to thank them, until I see Jack's familiar face.

My jaw drops. "What are you doing here?"

I throw my hands around his neck and he responds in my ear, "You should know better by now than to think I would let you do this alone."

Tears threaten, but I urge them away with a few deep breaths. "Thanks, Jack."

"Anytime," comes the rumble from his chest. He sets me back with his hands on my arms and nods. "Let's do this."

I check-in with the nurse at the front desk and head over to the waiting area where Jack sits in a too-small chair with a pinched look on his face. His obvious discomfort makes me smile and I forget the anxiety that had begun to build on the drive over.

"What exactly are we doing today? There isn't—" he clears his throat. "You aren't going to be getting naked or anything, are you?"

I laugh. "They're just going to do an ultrasound, make sure the baby is still developing as he or she should."

"He," Jack says. "It's definitely a *he*. There's no way Ben's sperm made a girl. That boy is jacked on testosterone. You should come see him next time he's at the gym. He's a fucking powerhouse."

I elbow him in the ribs when a mother shoots him a stern look. "Watch your mouth," I whisper-scold , "The last thing I need is for the kid to come out cussing like you guys.”

Jack just grins and I know that’s exactly what is probably going to happen.

The tech calls us back and either my nerves or the baby make my stomach flutter. I’m going to ignore the nerves and focus on the baby. Either way, I can’t wait to find out what I’m—what we’re—having.

The exam room is separated into two different areas with a green paper curtain dividing them. The tech indicates the farthest table and I hop up, my clammy hands resting on my lap in front of my little stomach.

“Why don’t you lay back?” the tech suggests with a small smile. “Then we’ll take a looksee.”

Jack takes the chair by the table and places my hand in his.

I pull up my top and settle back. The tech squirts the gel on my stomach and I flinch a little at the cold.

“Sorry about that,” she says.

A blurry image appears on the screen and I squint to discern some type of body shape, but I don’t recognize anything at all.

“What the hell is that?” Jack says, leaning over me for a better view at the monitor.

I sigh and resist the urge to tell him to shut up. Thankfully the tech laughs him off and wiggles the gelled wand on my stomach. “Ah,” she says. “There we go.”

The picture coalesces and I recognize the roundness of a little belly and what looks like and arm...or maybe it's a leg. Either way, my eyes grow wet and I press a hand to my lips.

I've always treasured the Walkers. To me, they are my family, no matter what. But the moment I see my own flesh and blood, I realize that there has always been a part of me looking for that connection; something I know is wholly mine. It floors me to find it in such a small person. I'm speechless as the tech points out each body part and prints off the photos. I don't even notice when she stops speaking or when she leaves the room.

Jack, who remained quiet the whole time, finally pipes up. "I don't know why you're over there crying. It looked like an alien to me. Are you sure you weren't abducted?"

I don't even smack him this time.

When the tech returns, it takes me a moment to sense the seriousness of her demeanor. But the downward pull to her lips is unmistakable. My elation starts to melt away and I feel my heart start beating more quickly in my chest.

"What's wrong?" I ask.

"I don't want to worry you, Mrs. Walker, but there were some areas that I felt Dr. Hamilton needed to take a look at. Just a precaution," she explains as though to stem my growing worry.

I appreciate the sentiment, but it doesn't ease my fear.

Jack squeezes my hand. I return it, probably cutting off his circulation in the process.

Doctor Hamilton, a stout older man with grey hair and a matching a no-nonsense mustache appears with his white lab coat billowing behind him.

"Mrs. Walker," he says.

"Ms.," I correct, my voice faint.

"Ms. Nothing to worry about, but let's just take a look and see what we're dealing with."

He settles down in the chair with the tech hovering behind him. Everything in my vision narrows to the little monitor that I'd been watching so reverently only moments early. Now, a feeling of doom settles in my stomach and it makes me want to snatch the wand away from the doctor and throw the monitor out of the nearest window.

I try to discern the abnormality they're looking for, but every body part looks perfect to me. As the doctor shifts the wand I see two arms, two legs. The outlines of fingers and the shape of the baby's head. It's so beautiful and perfect that it makes me want to cry.

Then the doctor pauses and says, "There seems to be an abnormality in the development of your baby's heart. I want to order a fetal echocardiogram, just to be sure."

My own heart skips a beat. "Abnormality? What's wrong?"

"I can't say for certain without more tests to confirm,

but I'm concerned about the size the left side of your baby's heart. At this stage it would be larger than it is which leads me to believe he may have hypoplastic left heart syndrome, which simply means the left side of the heart is underdeveloped. It's a serious condition so I'm going to have you schedule an echocardiogram before you leave. We have an excellent cardiology and neonatal unit here at the hospital."

I can barely speak but I force the words out. "Is—is it fatal? Is my baby going to die?"

"With early detection and care, there is a good chance of survival. If the echo confirms HLHS, he'll need several surgeries after birth to redirect the blood flow of the heart. I don't want you to worry about this until we do the echo and confirm. In the interim, I recommend that you take good care of yourself. Make sure you get enough rest and stay healthy. I know this isn't easy news to face, but you are in excellent care."

After a few more words and recommendations from the doctor, Jack and I are left alone. I immediately crumple into a heap of tears on the exam room table.

This is supposed to be one of the happiest moments of my life and it's probably horrible that I spend it mourning the baby I am still carrying. As tears wet the shoulder of Jack's shirt, I cry for the healthy, happy baby I'd dreamt of for the past four months. I wish for a magical clock to turn back time to the night I told my dad

I was pregnant and that joy that I felt when he was so excited to learn he was going to be a grandpa.

Jack holds me through it all. He hears the deepest, darkest of my fears and allays them with quiet murmurs and a strong hand rubbing my back. He exchanges dark words with a nurse who asks when we're going to leave the room for the next appointment.

I don't know how much time passes before I'm able to staunch the flow of grief. By the end of it, my eyes feel swollen shut and my nose won't stop running. Jack offers a handful of tissues and I take them gratefully.

"You know I love you, right?" Jack says, his hand cupping my raw face. "No matter what happens, we're here for you. We're a team."

I sniffle into the tissues. "I love you, too, Jack. I'm so glad you came."

He grins, but I can see the redness in his eyes, the evidence of his own tears. "Of course you are."

The nurse knocks impatiently on the door and I turn to look. "We better get out of here before they call the cops or something," I tell him.

"Take all the time you need, Liv. I'll take care of them if I need to."

"No, it's okay. I need to go tell Dad. Do you think you can call and have him meet us at my house?"

He kisses my brow. "Anything for you, sis." He turns to head out while I collect my things and to wipe the gel from my stomach, but he stops by the door, turns and says with a grin, "You notice that the doctor said 'he,' right? You're having a baby boy."

So like Jack to play games and make jokes, even during a serious moment, and then wiping away all the pain by reminding me of the joyous parts.

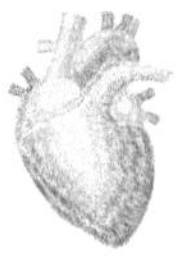

"When is the next whatchamacallit?" Dad says a few hours later.

"Echocardiogram," I supply, having researched the hell out of it when I got home. "And it's in three weeks. Apparently Child's has a neonatal unit and one of the best cardiology departments in the state. From what I understand, they'll use the echo to get a better look at the heart and see what we're dealing with."

Dad palms my head and face plants me in his chest. "Whatever the results, you know Jack-boy and I will take care of you."

"I know," I say, my voice thick with emotion.

"I'm sorry, baby girl."

"Me, too."

"What happens after the echo?" he asks.

I sit up and wipe my puffy face with the back of my hand. "There's nothing really they can do until the baby is born. Most of the fetal procedures right now are experimental and I don't like the thought of them doing an experimental surgery. After he's born there will be a series of surgeries to redirect the blood-flow from the smaller left section of his heart to his lungs."

"He's a Walker," Dad says. "He's a fighter. He'll make it through all the damn surgeries."

"That reminds me..." Jack plops down on the chair across from where Dad and I are sitting on the couch. He has a beer in hand and a bowl full of chips and dip in the other. "Since you found out it's going to be a boy, have you thought of any names. Personally I think Jack's a winner, but that's just me."

"Over my dead body," Dad retorts. "She promised your mother when she was fifteen that she would name any son she had after me. Henry Arthur Walker. He'll be the best looking kid in the state of Florida. I guarantee it."

I shake my head at the both of them. "There's no way in hell I'm naming him Arthur, Dad. And I only promised her that because she said she would get me a convertible for my sixteenth birthday. Considering I got a ten-year-old sedan, I believe that promise is null and void."

"The hell it is," Dad sputters. "I won't have any grandson of mine named some frou-frou name."

"It won't be a frou-frou name, Dad."

"Damn right it won't."

"Because she's going to name him Jack."

I sigh. "I'm not naming him Jack *or* Arthur, so get it out of your heads right now."

"Then what are you going to name him?"

I blush furiously and stare at my toes.

"Oh God," Jack scoffs, giving me a disgusted look. "You're going to name him after Ben aren't you?"

When I don't respond, both my dad and Jack groan.

"I can't believe you'd name him after that dick face and not your own brother!"

"Hey!" I say. "He's your friend!"

"Which gives me the right to tell you he's a dick face and that Ben is a shitty name."

"It is not. Stop being an ass."

"Hmmm," Dad says. "Benjamin. Benny. I like that."

"I was thinking something like Benjamin Cole. Maybe call him Cole?"

Dad smiles at me and throws an arm around my shoulders. "Benjamin Cole it is. God help us all if your mother kicks all of our asses when we join her in heaven."

After they leave, the lighthearted feeling goes with them. The darkness and uncertainty presses around me like a thick noxious cloud. Doubt and fear crowd the bed as I lay my head down to sleep. I wrap myself in second guesses and what ifs.

What I didn't tell my Dad was that there is a one in five chance the baby won't survive the first procedure. That there's a chance the three surgeries won't make a difference and he'll still require a heart transplant before his fifth birthday. After the transplant, he'll still have to be on preventative medicine to make sure that his little body doesn't reject the new heart.

The first procedure will have to be done before he's two weeks old. *Two weeks* and he'll have to have heart surgery. How am I going to deal with that? How does any mother deal with that?

Hot tears seep from my eyes and soak my pillow. I grab my phone and the glow lights up my bedroom. I tap out a desperate email to Ben, hoping for some kind of connection. Any kind of connection that will pull me from the hole I'm sinking into.

I hit send, but I fall asleep while waiting for the reply I'm afraid will never come.

CHAPTER SIX

BEN

THE FRIGID COLD seeps through the material of my gear, no matter how many layers I wrap myself in. I fumble in my pocket for the only thing that's kept me sane the last four months. The photo is beyond crumpled now, with a smattering of age lines snaking over its surface. Despite the tattered quality, it doesn't diminish the immediate calming effect its subject has on me.

My gloved finger traces over the miniature of Olivia's smile and it warms me from the inside out. *Soon*. Only five more months and then a year at my last duty station and I'll be back home. This time for good. And this time I won't be leaving until Olivia is a permanent fixture in my bed. And in my life.

I fold the picture along the deep grooves and tuck it safely away, both literally and figuratively.

I readjust my legs and hope that my socks weren't completely soaked through from the ruck across the stream. The last thing I need is a case of foot funk to accompany the raging headache from the two days without sleep and the frozen ass thing I've got going on. The only food I've got left in my pack is an MRE, one that I've been putting off eating because I'd almost rather die than eat the beans and 4 Dicks of Death. They've long since stopped looking like beef links and smell like someone's junk that hasn't had a shower in weeks. Maybe years. I inhale them, chewing quickly so it spends the least amount of time near my taste buds. It doesn't help. They really do taste like death. And janky dicks.

The wind howls in the distance and I hope we aren't assaulted by yet another dust storm. The beard I've grown and the cloth across my face protects me somewhat, but that shit gets into *everything*.

"Hey, No-Heart!" comes a call from a ditch on the other side of the hillside where we're camped out for the foreseeable future.

"The fuck you want?" I answer through a smile.

Scott Greene was attached to our unit with the local group of Marines. And his name suited him in every way because he's fresh out of boot camp. It always surprises me to see kids barely out of high school out here. I'd saved his ass on more than one occasion yet the younger guys had taken to calling me No-Heart because of my so-called "ruthless nature."

"Got anything left in that MRE?" Greene asks.

I smile and wave a packet at him. "Sure do. I got some crackers if you want 'em."

The other guys start smirking and laughing, but Greene is too busy belly-crawling up the hill. "Fuck, I'm hungry. Toss 'em up, would ya?"

"Sure," I tell him and pretend to toss the packet before stopping. "But, you can only have them under one condition."

One of the guys next to me starts laughing and Greene starts to look unsure. "What is it?"

"I dare you to eat them without drinking from your canteen."

He smiles. "You're so fucking stupid. Toss 'em up."

The guys next to me are out and out laughing now, but Greene has gained back his confidence. He opens the packet and takes out the two freeze-dried crackers. Laughter rises in my chest, but I manage to keep it contained.

"Remember," I tell him, "no water."

"Yeah, yeah."

He takes one of the crackers and stuffs it in his mouth so sure that he's got this. It only takes a few seconds for his face to register that those fucking things are basically like eating dust. He tries to play it off and chews, his jaw working furiously against a mouthful of cracker. My stomach is aching with the effort not to lose my shit. When he manages to down that bite, he looks at the cracker and takes another, smaller, bite. When that one proves to be even more difficult than the first, he spits it out.

"You're a fucking dick," he says to me.

"Hey, you should know better by now."

He downs a few gulps from his canteen. "What the fuck is in that shit?"

"I'm pretty hurt that you don't like my cooking, Greene. I thought we were friends."

He starts to reply, but his answer is cut off by the short, staccato bursts of gunfire coming from the squat little houses across from the ditches we'd carved into the hillside. Houses that had been empty when we scouted the location hours earlier. Scott dives back down to his ditch. Our gunner, Jim, takes aim as spotters cover the area. Unfortunately, until we actually spot someone with a gun aiming at us, the ROE, or rules of engagement, don't allow us to return fire. The higher ups are more concerned about earning their chest candy than actually winning the war. No matter how much they try to change things, each of my deployments have been like Groundhog Day—the same thing on repeat.

It is complete bullshit and costs precious lives, but hey, at least we're being politically correct.

I pop a piece of gum in my mouth to keep my face from going numb with cold. My fingers are clumsy and feel twice their normal size, but I manage to pull up the screens to check our locations. As the Joint Terminal Attack Controller, or JTAC, on shift I am in control of air firepower in the field for precision air strikes. The lives of our enemies and the lives of my fellow Marines are in the palm of my hands.

No matter how bitter I'd become about my role in this war, no matter how useless I sometimes felt in the big picture, it paid to remember that there were people that depended on me. People who had families that needed them to return safely. In the end, I have a job to do and I've trained for a lifetime to do it right.

"Greene, you alright?"

"No the fuck I'm not. Still choking on that shit."

I smile, rubbing my eyes as I settle back down to wait the next move. Should all hell break loose there are a couple of A-10s around for the next few hours that I can divert in our direction for cover. The A-10 (aka the Warthog) is my favorite aircraft; the only one built specifically to carry the 30mm Avenger Gatling Gun. There aren't any fast movers in the vicinity, so the A-10 is the only thing covering our asses.

Our objective is to obtain intel from the next village,

but in order to do so we have to make our way down an alley lined with abandoned homes. Essentially a death trap if we get pinned on either side.

Surprisingly, whoever is keeping watch in the house stays quiet for the rest of the afternoon. I come back a few hours later after some much needed shut-eye and about a gallon of coffee.

Command sends a group of our guys into the city to engage with snipers over top and me in the wings in case shit goes down. The moment they enter the far end of the alley, however, all hell breaks loose and fire starts coming in from a dozen different directions.

I call in air support, double and triple checking my maps and calculations. The telltale sound of the A-10 drones in the background and despite all my training, my stomach drops at the devastation it's about to wreak.

I don't focus on the loss of life or the casualties. I do my job.

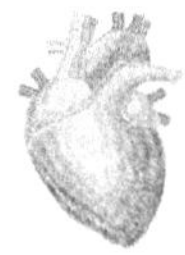

Later that night as I rest on my cot, still fully clothed all the way down to my boots, the ramifications of what I've done weigh heavy on my mind. When I joined the military, it was about being a part of something bigger than me. Fighting for my country. Doing the right thing.

As I fall into a fitful sleep, I can only wonder if I still am.

I wake to chaos. My teammates are arguing loudly outside of the tent. I jump from the cot and head outside to find dozens of wounded and as many dead being loaded into the massive Chinook a field away. I can hear the buzz of several helos in the distance.

"What happened?" I ask my team leader.

"Ambushed. I need every man we've got. We're going back out."

I ready my gear and watch from a distance as the Chinook lifts and flies away. I follow the team to the trucks and we head out.

We don't make it a mile outside the gate before the first truck in the line explodes in a belch of fire and black smoke. My ears pop from what must be a concussive rocket, which are a bitch to be around as they hit, explode, implode and then explode all the fuck over again. The truck is blown off the road and onto the shoulder, flipping twice before landing belly up. My ears pop from the resulting change in pressure.

Those of us in the following vehicles bail out, guns at the ready and eyes on the horizon. A group of us makes it to the heaping mass of metal and flames. I can hear the high-pitched screams from the men inside and my adrenaline shoots off the charts. I go to the other side, where the frame hasn't collapsed and see Greene pinned with one leg under a thick piece of metal.

One of the other guys covers my back as I drop to my haunches to leverage the weight off of his pinned limb. The blast or the pain has knocked him unconscious—which is no doubt a good thing, considering the shape of his limb. I block that out and manage to get some breathing room.

"Hey, grab him," I tell the guy behind me as I reach with my free hand to unbuckle the lap belt. The guy reaches up and manages to catch Greene as he falls. Even though he's passed out his body jerks and his face contorts in pain.

I experience a rush of relief, my body going hot and cold with it, as we pull him free of the truck. I back up, lifting his limp body in my arms. The other guy brings his weapon up for cover, but it doesn't matter.

The second RPG hits the convoy, but this time, it doesn't just flip over one of the trucks. It explodes with deadly force. I'm thrown back against the first downed truck, my head striking against the metal. I manage to hold onto Greene by sheer will alone and we both crumple.

I glance up, my vision going dark, and the last image I see is a fiery inferno where my team used to be. There is barely anything left of the men I've spent the last few years with. What I can see, I wish I hadn't.

As I lose consciousness myself, my last thought is that I don't hear the other men inside the truck screaming anymore.

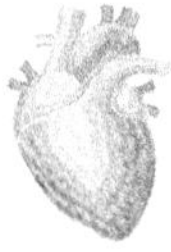

I hear the faint echo of a scream and my entire body jerks on the bed. The T.V. show I'd been attempting to watch mocks me from across the room. I glare at it ineffectively. Even though I can only hear a ghost of the sound, the sound of screams still sends a chill right through me. They remind me too much of the nightmares I can't shake. I look around for a remote and then remember the room I'm in doesn't even have one so I can't chuck it at the screen.

I press the button for the nurse and throw myself back on the bed, grunting as the pain in my head makes itself known. Not that it's dwindled any in the two days since I regained consciousness in a German hospital.

It's not even the constant ringing or the never-ending headache that pisses me off. It's the realization that this is one time they won't be able to patch me up and send me back—if there is even anything to send me back to. My entire team is gone. Just...gone. And for what, I wonder.

I hear a hollow knock coming from the door and I sit up, scrubbing a hand over my face. "Yeah?"

A nurse peeks her head in the door and says something that I don't quite catch. I try to focus on her mouth to figure out her words, but fuck, I haven't learned to read lips yet and she's talking to me while she's looking backwards at someone in the hallway.

"What?" I ask, probably too loud, but I don't care. The new ones sometimes forget they have to talk to my good side.

The nurse moves to my left side and says, "Sorry, sweetie. I asked what you needed."

"Can you turn down the volume?" I nod at the T.V.

Her response is a little muffled, like she's speaking through cotton. "Sure thing. Let me know if you—" and then she turns again, forgetting that the single-sided deafness I now have as a result of the blast makes it harder for me to hear when people are facing away from me.

I fucking give up.

"...said she was your mother. Did you want us to get her on the phone for you?"

I sigh. "I'm sorry, I didn't catch that. What did you say?"

She gives me a pitying smile that I want to rip off her face. "A woman by the name of Sheila Hart called, said she was your mother. Did you want us to get her back on the phone for you?"

The sound of her name causes my hands to tremble underneath the stiff white bedsheets. I clench them against my legs and ignore the pulsing behind my eyes. "No, that's okay. I've already spoken to her," I lie. "Thanks."

She takes a couple steps toward the door and then hesitates. "Are you sure there isn't someone I can call for you? We have computers where you can video chat with your family or maybe a friend. I know they've got you on a flight home soon, but I figured I'd check."

"I think I'm going to try and get some sleep."

The nurse smiles again, checks the machines for what-the-fuck-ever and leaves. Finally.

I should have known better than to try and sleep in a hospital because it feels like no time at all has passed when another knock comes at my door and the doctor steps in.

"How are we doing today?" he asks as he looks at his clipboard.

"Fine," I answer. "What's the verdict?"

"I'm afraid the single-sided deafness is permanent. When you get back stateside the doctors there will fit you with an appropriate hearing device. Depending on the one you choose an outpatient surgery may be required. Keep in mind there are several options. Like I said, the doctor will go over them with you."

It takes a few minutes for me to compose my response. My thoughts aren't as ordered and clear as they used to be. "And the memory loss? The seizures?"

"Most cases of mild TBI persist for a year or more.

Each case is unique, like each person. They can persist for a time and heal or they may go on longer."

Even though I already knew the answer, to hear it confirmed is still devastating. It could be worse, I admit, much worse. A thousand different kinds of hell worse. I almost wish it was. I wish I'd died with them. Gone down in the blaze of glory that I'm owed for my sacrifice.

Instead, I'm sitting on a hospital bed. Alive. Down half a sense and can't trust my own goddamned brain.

The doctor explains the symptoms of a mild traumatic brain injury but all I hear is that I shouldn't be alive. I shouldn't be this lucky. I don't deserve it. I don't deserve it half as much as some of the men that died that day, or the innocent men and women that have been slaughtered for a war they can't control.

He finishes and I mumble some kind of response that enables him to leave. The next round of nurses come in for the evening shift and with them the medication for pain, both physical...and emotional.

I check my phone again, only to realize that I'd checked it minutes before. Along with the hearing loss, the traumatic brain injury guarantees that I'd never return to Afghanistan again. I'd never see the conclusion of the war I fought so hard to win. I'd spend the next year med-boarding out of the Marines and riding a desk at my new duty station.

That reality is a hard one to swallow. Even though

I'd been considering leaving the Marines after my time was up, I hate having it taken away from me against my will.

To pass the time, I check my email and surf the Internet. My heart damn near stops in my chest when I see a new email from Olivia in my notifications. I glance at the photo of her I have on my side table and hesitate, one finger hovering over the little envelope.

I take a deep breath and click.

Dear Ben, it starts.

I was thinking about you today and I thought I'd give emailing you another try. It's okay if you don't respond. I just miss talking to you. There are so many things I wish I could say. I was hoping we could meet when you get back. Maybe grab a cup of coffee? I could really use one of your smiles right now.

Missing you, Olivia.

I click back and see dozens of previous emails she'd sent over the months I'd been deployed. My hand aches to move the mouse and devour her words. I nearly do it, but I'm distracted by the ringing in my ears—tinnitus, the doctors call it. It's another one of the things I'll have to deal with for the rest of my life.

I thought I was broken before? That is nothing compared to the desolation I feel now. Now I'm a warrior put to pasture and forced to rejoin the world with death and destruction on my conscience.

My lips firm into a line and I select all emails—from Olivia, from family members, guys attached to my unit—and I bulk delete them.

That was my old life. Who knows what the hell my future will hold for me, but the least I can do is save Olivia from the shell of a man I've become.

CHAPTER SEVEN

OLIVIA

THE DATE to the echocardiogram rolls around, no matter how much I try to distract myself with work and finishing up the renovations on my house. Despite how much they wanted to come, Dad has a fishing trip that he's been planning for months and that I refused to let him bail on. Jack has some kind of promotional thing at the gym that he couldn't get anyone to cover for him. I promise them I'll call them with the results and ensure them that Sofie volunteered to come.

The hospital is a modern-looking building, all smooth white stucco and glass. The cardiology unit, especially, is clean and high-tech. I appreciate all the gadgets that we pass and my reverence for doctors and all their hard work grows a million-fold.

"You sure you don't want me to go in the room with you?" Sofie asks.

I shake my head. "Yeah, I'm sure. They said this exam could take a while and I'll just be laying there. Feel free to take a nap or something." I laugh, but the sound is breathless and lacks conviction.

"I'll be here if you need me." She pulls me into a quick, hard hug.

There is a repeat of the gel and the wand. I try to pay attention to the screen and the tech, but in truth, my mind is racing too fast for me to notice anything other than the long time it takes for the exam. The tech lets me clean up and I go back to the waiting room to sit with Sofie until the cardiologist calls me to discuss the results.

Sofie holds my hand, but doesn't try to start a conversation or give me meaningless assurances. Her simple touch keeps me from coming unglued as the minutes tick by.

When the receptionist calls my name, I jump and Sofie tightens her grip on my hand. We rise and follow the nurse back to another exam room for another lengthy wait. I can't decide if it took so long because they're being thorough or if they have bad news and just want to put off delivering it. By the time the doctor arrives I'm nearly overcome with shivers.

"Ms. Walker, I'm Dr. Foley." She's a woman in her late forties with red-blonde hair pulled back into a bun. She has kind, watery blue eyes and a brightly colored, heart-bedecked stethoscope. I like her immediately and take back every negative thought I had while we were waiting.

I offer her a faint hello. Sofie stays quiet, but smiles, lips betraying her outer shields with a tremble.

I watch as Dr. Foley's lips move, but after the words, "Your son has HLHS," I stop listening.

Sofie makes sure to take note of all the important information and literature. She tells them that I'll be coming back if I have any questions. But for the most part I think she just wants to get me out of there before I lose it.

But I don't. I think I've cried all the tears I have in me. On the drive home from the hospital, I can do nothing but sit and stare blankly out the window with my hand on my stomach where I can feel him moving.

"Can you drop me at the gym?" I ask Sofie when we make it back to Nassau. "I promised him I would come by afterwards to let him know the news."

"Absolutely, anything you need."

I know the situation must be dire if Sofie is willing to go within speaking distance of Jack.

She stops at the entrance, puts the car in park and turns to me. "Are you going to be okay?"

"I'll be fine. *We'll* be fine."

"Are you going to try to get ahold of Ben again?"

I stare at her in surprise. In the shock of the doctor's news, I hadn't even thought about it. After the last non-answered email, I hadn't tried to reach out again. At least by the time Cole was due, he'd be home. Maybe then I'd be able to get ahold of him.

"I sent him a million emails. I haven't heard back, so I think I'll just wait to hear from him and talk to him then. Right now I just want to make sure to keep us both as healthy as possible."

She gives me a hug and I heave my exhausted body out of the car. It's nearing the busiest time of the day for the gym, but it's practically empty. I look around and find Jack in the office cursing at paperwork.

"How'd the promo thing go?" I ask.

Jack rubs a hand through his messy hair. The fact that it's sticking up in all directions pretty much answers my question, but he says, "Miserably. Barely anyone showed up. But you don't worry about that. Tell me the news."

My lip trembles and my look must tell him all he needs to know. He rises from the desk to envelop me in a hug. "I'm sorry, Livvie."

"Has Dad gotten back from his trip yet?"

"No, but he said he'd come straight here after."

I plop wearily onto his couch. "Do you mind if I crash here until he gets here? I'm kind of wiped after today."

"Of course."

A few hours later I hear Jack get up from the desk chair with a loud squeak. I come awake with a groan. For a moment, I don't even recognize where I am. Then I hear the dull thuds and grunts from the gym and catch the scent of sweat and leather. I relax into the couch, lulled by the familiar setting.

My dad is due back any minute according to the time on my phone. As much as I would like to bury the news I have to deliver, I know Dad will be the guiding light I need to get through the next few months.

I wipe the sleep from my eyes and get to my feet. I'm inhaling a bottled water I found in the mini-fridge to combat the sour taste in my mouth when the office door opens behind me.

Jack has soaked through his shirt since I saw him earlier. His normally tanned skin has an abnormal gray pallor. All my life, I've known when bad things are going to happen. The sensation is akin to falling. At first, there is confusion as the world shifts under my feet. Then denial, because how could this be happening to me, anyway? Then resolute grief because no matter how much I try, there's not a damn thing I can do to change my circumstances.

Even knowing this and having been through it several times in my short life, I still go through each stage.

Confusion.

"Jack?"

I watch his Adam's apple bob as he hesitates in the doorway. He takes a stuttering step forward then stops to run a hand through his hair. "Sit down, Liv."

My hand automatically presses against my stomach. "Jack?" I repeat a few octaves higher. "What's going on?"

Denial.

I follow his glance to the gym, and I see the faint figures of men in uniform talking to a huge guy in sweats that I recognize as Logan. They must be cops he works with. My stomach drops, and I shift my attention back to Jack.

He takes a few cautious steps toward me, but I hold my hand up and shake my head. "Just tell me."

Images start to flit through my mind. Ben. The pregnancy test. My father's face the first time I met him, a few weeks after I'd turned thirteen.

I register Jack closing the door to the office. "It's Dad," he says.

And for the second time in my life, I find myself feeling utterly alone in the world.

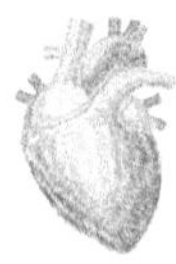

Four Months Later

Benjamin Cole Walker is born after ten harrowing hours of labor with the help of a specialized team of OB/GYNs and Dr. Foley, who waits on standby to give Cole his first evaluation. They place him on my chest for the briefest of moments and we lock eyes; mesmerizing crystal-blues identical to his dad's. Everything inside me seizes, and for a few perfect seconds, I don't worry about the uncertainty with Ben or the upcoming surgeries Cole will have to endure or the difficulties he'll face in his life. Instead, I experience the most profound and all-encompassing wave of love and awe, that I'm still stunned when the nurses come to take him for stabilization. Thankfully the hospital has one right next door so that when I'm able, I can watch him through the window.

Jack narrates what the nurses are doing as he watches through the glass. "They're hooking him up to an IV now. Prostaglandin, I think."

I recalled that as the medicine that will help keep him stable and improve blood flow until his first surgery which will take place in two days.

"Now they're attaching him to a bunch of crap for his vitals. He looks good, sis."

I smile wearily from my place on the bed. Once they get his vitals stable they are going to have to move him down the hall to the Cardiac Intensive Care Unit to prep for the first of the three surgeries. I didn't like being separated from him so soon, but I'd been preparing for months for these procedures. I had to be strong for him.

After Cole's diagnosis, I made monthly trips to the Fetal Cardiac Program for observation with Dr. Foley to keep an eye on his development. We prepared and discussed for his birth more than I thought possible. Dr. Foley turned out to be a Godsend. She answered all (million) of my questions and took all of my frantic calls, no matter how off the wall.

Dr. Foley and the team at the FCP explained that after a series of surgeries, one performed after birth, one around six months and the other around eighteen months, Cole's heart would essentially function as a one-sided pump instead of two. The first year was going to be rough, but he was in excellent hands and I was determined to give him the kind of family I never had.

I learned early on how important it is to take each day at a time and to stay positive. After Dad's sudden heart attack, I went through a dark place, one that I didn't think I would survive, but I did because I knew Cole needed me. He reminded me a lot of myself after I was put in foster care. Only I would never give up on him. He would always have me.

Jack turns from the window and says, "I hate to tell you this, but that baby looks just like Ben."

I groan. "I do all the work and the kid doesn't even look like me? How is that fair?"

"At least Ben isn't totally unfortunate looking, I guess. You could have really been screwed."

Coming down from the adrenaline of giving birth, I burst into tears and I'm not entirely sure why.

Jack smiles and says, "Dad used to tell me Mom did the same thing after I was born because she was so happy. Then again, he said she only did it because she was terrified I would turn out just like him."

I hiccup through my tears. "She did not!"

Jack simply shakes his head and plops into a chair next to me. "She did," he said as he taps the window and waves at the probably sleeping baby. My heart clutches at the sight. "She knew it was a lost cause. No matter how hard she tried, I still turned out just like him." We both fall into a contemplative silence and I shed a couple tears for a completely different reason. I so wanted him to be here to meet my son and it's killing me that he isn't. I'm trying to be positive though, for my son and for Jack, who has been having an especially hard time with Dad's death over the last few months. Jack hears my sniffling and turns back to me. "You did good, girl."

I give him a watery smile. "He's beautiful, isn't he?"

"Olivia." Jack's face was pinched. "Boys aren't beautiful. He's ruggedly handsome. Or he's a strapping lad."

"Lad?" I ask with a quirked brow.

Jake merely smiles at me. "He's perfect."

I tug Jack's arm down to the bed so that he's sitting

next to me. I can't help but feel like the Walkers were chosen for me. That Jack was the brother I was meant to have. "Thanks for being with me today, Jackie."

"Nowhere I'd rather be, sis. Though, you *could* have gone easy on my hand. I never should have let you train with us. I think you broke it." He flexes the hand in question.

"I highly doubt that."

We share a laugh and as it trails off, I watch Jack's face turn serious.

"You still haven't heard from him?" he asks in a low voice.

I suck in a deep breath and paste on a happy face. "No, but Logan said the mail where he's at is spotty at best. I sent him a few emails with updates and one of the ultrasounds, but I don't think he got them. I would have heard back by now."

"I know you don't like to talk about it, but I'm your big brother. I just didn't want you to be alone today. Or for the surgery. It's going to be a rough year and I just want to make sure you're both taken care of."

"I'm not alone. You were with me. You'll be here for everything. I couldn't have asked for anyone better."

"I know they're sending him to a pretty hellacious place and he'll get in touch with you when he can. Just let me know when he does."

"Of course, Jack. If I ever do. If I don't, that's fine, too."

For a while after Ben went out on his deployment, I'd waited with bated breath. Each time the phone rang or the mail ran, I expected for it to be him. It never was. Losing my mom, and then Ben, and then my dad... it has just been too much. I can't stand the thought of losing anyone else in my life. So I've come to the conclusion that if he shows and wants to be involved, great. If not, then we'll be fine without him.

Jack studies me for a few minutes, but the bone-deep exhaustion has left me too weary for any kind of discussion. Jack and I take turns watching Cole so I can grab a couple hours of much-needed sleep. He only wakes me when there are updates and whenever he's snuck more food into the room. It occurs to me that Cole and I are very lucky, the luckiest, to have him in our lives. And we don't need anyone else, I decide.

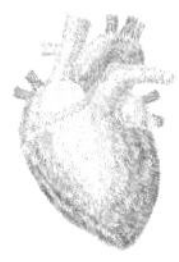

"Are you sure you don't need anything? Did you get enough diapers from your shower thing?" Jack looks around the living room like he'd find an errant pack of them hiding in a planter or something.

"Yes, I have plenty. If we run out, I can always call you to run to the store for me."

Jack brightens. "I can do that now. Where do I go?"

I laugh. "Jack. We're fine, I promise. You've covered everything and Melissa made enough frozen meals for us to last through the next year. Now, go; you've done enough. More than enough."

I walk him to the door but stop when he pauses in the doorway.

He opens his mouth to say something then pauses. "Are you sure you're going to be okay alone?"

"Absolutely, Jack. I know I wasn't prepared for the whole mom gig initially, but I've spent more than enough time in the hospital learning how to take care of him. I made the nurses teach me everything at least twice. I could give him his medicine and check monitors in my sleep. We're going to be just fine."

Jack wraps his arms around me, and I tuck my head under his chin. At six foot two, he towers over my small frame, but I always fit, like we're two pieces from different puzzles that somehow work.

"You're my little sister. It's my duty to make sure you're okay."

I squeeze him extra tight. "And you've always done a great job. Now, get. You can come see us this weekend. For now, I need to get used to this all by myself for a little while."

He gives me one last hug, then leaves. I wave at his retreating figure before shutting the door behind him. Cole begins to fuss where he is stirring in his bassinet.

We stayed in the hospital for a few months after the first surgery to recover and learn the ropes. The fact that he made it through the first stage is a positive sign. Thankfully, Cole took to a bottle and the breast milk and the special formula he has to take. I was relieved to see that he was gaining weight regularly. We're one of the lucky ones. There were no complications from the first surgery. He suffered from no infections and has started healing nicely. For the next few months I've been instructed to watch who he interacts with to stave off any contact with anyone who could give him any sort of illness.

After we were released from the hospital, Jack insisted we stay for a couple of weeks at his place so he could help out. Even though I'd loved spending time with him, I'm grateful to be back in my own space without the constant in and out of the nurses—or the hovering of an over-protective Walker male. Nine weeks after Cole's birth and we were finally home.

I settle into the rocking chair Melissa gave me as a shower gift to feed Cole. Dad and Jack both stepped up to help me finish the renovations on the house, though after Dad's heart attack, it was just Jack. All of the rooms have a fresh coat of paint, most of the faulty wiring has been updated or replaced and my kitchen is rocking new appliances.

There was enough money left from Dad's life insurance that I can care for Cole for the next few months without worrying. Once he's healed and stable I'll worry about going back to work. Until then I plan to spend each and every day of it soaking up the moments with my son. I've already scoped out daycares in advance, as he'll need round-the-clock care and supervision. I dread the moment I'd have to leave him.

The phone rings and shakes me from my thoughts. I glance down to see Cole still passed out in my lap and I smile as I answer the phone.

"Hello?"

"Hey, good lookin'," Sofie says. "How's my main man?"

"Sleeping. We were just taking a nap. What's up?"

"So your no-good brother mentioned something to me that I thought you should know. And before you ask, no I'm not going to tell you why I was forced to talk to the devil and yes, I would have rather eaten meatloaf made of glass."

"Couldn't have been anything too earth shattering because he dropped us off not too long ago. Surely he couldn't have ruined your day in such a short time."

"God love you, Olivia, but you have blinders on when it comes to that man."

"Speak for yourself. Jack's been nothing but supportive since Cole was diagnosed. I couldn't have done this without him."

I hear Sofie's sniff of derision over the line. "*Anyway.* Don't you want to know what he said?"

I sigh. "What did he say?"

"Only that a certain baby daddy is coming home next week before he goes to his last duty station."

CHAPTER EIGHT

OLIVIA

I finish washing the dishes, my fingers turned to raisins, and shut off the water. I take a moment to rest, just to shut off my mind, and lean a hip against the counter. My head pounds in a vicious rhythm, but I set that aside.

We survived our first at-home scare. I am both terrified of the future and so very thankful for the present.

A few days ago, I picked Cole up from his nap and noticed that his skin, especially his lips, had turned a faint blue. When I pressed a hand to his little chest, he was breathing rapidly. I immediately dialed 9-1-1 and we were rushed to the hospital for evaluation.

Thankfully, the doctors were able to get him stabilized

again, and after a short stay, we were allowed to go home. There would be more scares and more hospital stays. We would just have to take each day as they came. This time we were lucky.

Thinking back, I count my blessings I got to him in time. Still, I lost precious moments fumbling with my touchscreen to get the right numbers. Moments where I knew if I failed, he would lose his life and it would be my fault.

It felt like it took an eternity for the paramedics, policemen, and even a fire-response team to arrive, all sirens screaming bloody murder, in my driveway. In reality, it was probably a few minutes at most, considering how small Nassau is.

The sound of the sirens didn't even disturb Cole from his slumber and his little chest kept pumping away. He slept when they pulled him from his bed and throughout the ride to the hospital. For a moment, I was certain he'd never wake up. Then, after his examination, he opened his eyes and blinked owlishly at the doctor, confused. He twisted his head from side to side and kicked his feet. Then, he started to cry. There had never been a more glorious sound.

I try to draw on that feeling of happiness now, when the house is asleep, everything is dark, and I am so alone. When I feel trapped by circumstance and hopeless. I walk through all of the rooms, turning off lights as I go. I let out Hank, our Boston Terrier, for one last bathroom break.

Quietly, so as not to wake Cole from his deep sleep, I gather his limp body in my arms pad up the stairs and down the hallway to his nursery. I carefully lay him in his crib and pull a light blanket over his legs to ward off the chill.

I pull his door to and pause for a moment in the hallway, trying to discern if the soft noise I hear is a figment of my imagination or just my dog, Hank, trying to make his arthritic way up the stairs for the night.

I listen for the sound again, but instead of calling out for Hank, like I would any other night, something stops me. Then I hear it again: the telltale creak of a shutter easing open. The one next to the back door in desperate need of replacing.

My heart thuds in slow, determined beats that feel as though it is trying to jump out of my chest. I freeze at the top of the stairs, unsure of what to do. A split-second of panic turns my veins to ice.

The stairwell is set at two angles, so I wouldn't be able to see anyone coming up until they were nearly on top of me. This is fortunate for me, though, as the person downstairs won't be able to see me, either.

I hope Hank is somewhere in hiding. That he somehow knew to get away from this person instead of displaying false bravado. He is getting on in years and sometimes has trouble getting up the stairs at night. I fervently regret not bringing him up with us.

I retrace my steps to the crib and carefully lift Cole to me as I inch into a sitting position. He nuzzles my neck at the movement, but otherwise remains asleep. I feel his steady heartbeat against my chest and I send up a short, fervent prayer that we get through this unharmed.

My bedroom door is still open and I know my cell phone sits dutifully on the nightstand, plugged into its charger. A floorboard creaks downstairs, much closer-sounding than before. The sound spurs me into move-ment. As quietly as I can, I tiptoe back down the hallway to my bedroom. If nothing else, it's the last room on the floor. Whoever is downstairs will have to check all of the other rooms before reaching mine.

If we're lucky, I can get to my phone, notify the police, and hide until they arrive.

The alternative is too terrifying to contemplate.

I make it to the bedroom door where I ease it closed, hoping the hinges don't betray me with a squeak. Fortu-nately, it closes with only a small click to signify the move-ment. I throw the lock and the hook-style chain then hurry to my bedside to grab my phone.

Cole begins to murmur in his dreams as my fumbling fingers navigate the touchscreen. I have to try three times before I'm able to dial the numbers, my fingers too slippery with sweat.

"9-1-1, what is your address and emergency?" The voice sounds dangerously loud in my ear.

"4837 Mill Road. This is Livvie Walker. There is someone in my house. They're coming up the stairs. I'm in my upstairs bedroom with my baby and the door is locked. Please, send someone to help. Hurry!" My voice breaks and I drop the phone, careful not to end the call just in case. It's the *just in case* that makes my heart race.

This can't be happening.

I slowly inch toward the walk-in closet that leads directly into the bathroom. From there, I can go directly into the hallway once the burglar goes into my room. It's dangerous, but I don't want to be cornered with no options, especially with Cole in my arms, relying on me. I tiptoe into the closet. Through the wall of my closet, I hear the subtle squeak of shifting weight as they make their way down the hall. If I hadn't been paying attention, I never would have known until it was too late—that's how quiet they are. I hear the door to my spare room click open and there is a momentary pause in their progression down the hallways as they investigate.

My knees go weak as I realize my room is next. Cole shifts in my arms and I jiggle him up and down to soothe him back to sleep. The absolute last thing I need is for him to wake; his screams would draw them right to us. I steel my knees against the panic that wants to overwhelm me.

I consider using the separate exit to the bathroom, then going out to the hall, but doing so would trap the burglar behind me and expose our position. I have no guns in my home—I had always considered Nassau to be a safe place before now. A foolish miscalculation on my part, one my father had always lamented. A tear streaks down my face at the thought, wrought of fear and sadness and desperation.

I hear the handle of my door jiggle. Only once at first, but then more forcefully. I duck between some of my dresses, hoping for a modicum of camouflage in case the burglar comes bursting in.

Just as I'm wishing Ben were here, the door to my room explodes open in a wave of splintered wood. I stifle my scream of surprise. Footsteps inch into my bedroom and with each thump, my heart beats louder and my breath grows increasingly ragged. The steps stop just outside the closet and I hold my breath, keeping Cole wrapped in my embrace. Before they can take the final step into the doorway, the room becomes bathed in flashing red and blue lights. It takes a moment for my ears to register the scream of the siren over my beating heart.

This time, Cole is startled from sleep by the sirens. As hurried footsteps recede back down the stairs, he begins to wail. The sound is a welcome one as it signifies that we're both still alive. I'm lightheaded with sweet relief.

A few minutes later, a knock sounds at the front door. I manage to soothe Cole back to sleep with a pacifier and set him in the bassinet on my way down the stairs, taking care not to step on the splinters of wood from my mangled door.

I find Hank scratching at the mudroom door, thankfully unharmed. He'd been locked in our fenced backyard and immediately started barking at the pounding at the door. I grab a long coat from the coat stand and shrug into it. It does little to cover my legs, but the small, filmy nightgown wasn't something I'd like to greet the police in. I feel bare and vulnerable enough as it is.

I pull open the door and stare in open-mouthed shock when I'm greeted by Logan on the other side. "What are you doing here?" I blurt.

He peers past me into the room. "Is the intruder still in the house?"

"No, they left through the back as soon as they heard the sirens. They busted open my bedroom door, though. It's upstairs."

"I'd like to take a look, if that's okay."

"Sure, whatever you need." I have a feeling it's going to be a long night. "Thank God you got here in time. Can I get you something? Water? Coffee?" I know I'm rambling, but I can't seem to stop.

He jerks his chin, which I take to mean yes. "I'll just be a few minutes. My partner is checking the perimeter for any signs of forced entry, but we didn't see anyone lurking. They're probably gone by now."

"Thanks, Logan."

The simple process of making coffee distracts me from my scattered thoughts. Measure grounds. Fill the water dispenser. Flip the switch. Grab a few coffee mugs. I stare out the kitchen window and see nothing, but that doesn't erase the unease that skitters along my shoulders.

Steps thud above me as Logan makes his way back down the stairs. He appears in the kitchen doorway as he buckles his radio back onto his belt. I hand him a cup of coffee, pleased that I judged him for a no-frills man when he makes a sound of pleasure at the first taste.

He steps inside the kitchen and leans against the butcher block island. "Few questions for you, Livvie, then I'll get out of your hair."

I sip my coffee. "It's no trouble. Please."

"Tell me what happened tonight, up until I got here."

Deep breath. "We got back from errands around seven o'clock. I always keep the doors locked, and windows, too. Habit. My father used to insist on it. We got to bed around nine. We hadn't been there long when I realized our dog, Hank, hadn't made it upstairs. He's old, so sometimes I have to help him up. I was going to get him when I noticed all the lights downstairs were off, and I always leave at least one on. I'm prone to clumsiness. Then I heard a noise downstairs. The sound of the shutter opening. I called 9-1-1," I continue on, telling him the rest of what happened until they arrived and scared off my unwelcome visitor.

"It looks like they forced one of the windows open, tore the screen off and broke off a section, then unlocked it. You'll need to get that repaired as soon as you can. We're going to turn in the report, dust for prints near the window and on the bedroom door handle. We'll run it through the system, but that can take some time and if they aren't in the system, we won't have much to go on."

"I understand." It scared the shit out of me, but I knew there was only so much they could do. Never mind the new paint the outside of the house needed. A new security system was going up first thing. It had been on my home improvement to-do list before Cole was born, but I had always felt safe in our neighborhood.

"We can have a patrol car come around every couple hours, just to make sure," Logan says. "Do you want me to call Jack to come stay with you?"

My shoulders round and I huddle around my coffee cup. The last thing I need is for Jack to become even more overprotective. "That's okay. I appreciate it, but we'll be fine. I probably won't be getting any sleep tonight anyway, and all he'll want to do is nag. You'll let me know if you find anything?"

"You'll be the first person I call." He puts his finished cup in the sink then turns to me, placing a hand on my cheek. I lean in to it, grateful for the moment of support. "You sure you're going to be okay?"

I nod, but in truth, I feel far from okay. I've just learned how to deal with it on my own.

A knock at the door sends Hank into another wheezing fit. I excuse myself to answer it while Logan rinses the dishes in the sink—a decidedly homey task considering the horror of the night. My heart returns to a relatively normal rhythm and I take a deep, calming breath before opening the door, hoping it's Logan's partner and not Jack, who always seems to know when something has gone wrong.

I'm looking down to grab a hold of Hank, who's winding excitedly around my legs. Once I have him secure in my arms, I notice that my visitor isn't wearing the usual police-issue black shoes, like Logan is. They're black, but they're a very specific type of combat boot that I've only seen grace one pair of legs before. I glance up, and instead of finding that other officer, what I'm met with is a pair of familiar crystal-blue eyes instead.

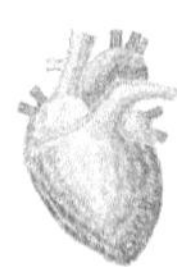

"Why are there cops at your house at two in the morning?" Ben asks without preamble. As though he hadn't spent a good part of the past year incommunicado. As though I don't have a life-changing baby upstairs.

I struggle to gather my wits over the blood rushing through my ears. A million thoughts race through my mind, none of which are the answer to his question. "Break-in," I manage to say.

He tilts his head toward me, a furrow between his brows. I notice something wrapped around his ear, but I'm distracted when his curious expression hardens. I'm reminded of the fact that he must have just returned from his deployment. I can tell from the deep lines around his eyes and mouth that weren't there the last time I saw him that he hasn't slept. I resist the urge to trace them with my fingers.

"What are you doing here, Ben?" I ask faintly.

"I was driving by and saw the lights. I wanted to make sure you were okay." His eyes roam over my body, no doubt taking in my state of undress and calculating the possibility of injury. "Are you okay?"

I nod faintly, my ears perking up at the sound of a cry in the distance. My heart stutters in my chest. *I'm not ready for this.* I thought the few months after Cole's birth would have given me time to prepare for this very conversation. But it hasn't. Especially not after my father's death,

Cole's diagnosis, and tonight's fresh trauma. *How much can one person handle before they break?*

"Olivia," he says sharply when I don't respond.

I refocus and clear my throat. "I'm fine. Logan got here just in time."

Speaking of, I feel his presence at my back. I turn to let them both say their hellos, but a frigid tension lingers. They both eye each other, and I hurry to explain. "Thankfully, I was able to call the police while I could. Logan and his partner were able to scare whoever it was off before any harm was done. Well, aside from my door. And my window."

Ben nods at Logan in a gesture of gratitude, I surmise. A loud squawk comes from the baby monitor I'd placed on the kitchen counter. I wince at the sound, but use the interruption to flee the situation.

"Excuse me," I tell them, face burning and shame roiling in my chest. So I do the thing I hate most: I run. Their murmured conversation follows me up the stairs, but my mind is racing too much for me to concentrate.

Instead, I tiptoe over the mess left in my room and lift my baby's small body against my own. Cole provides a welcome reprieve. Even through the chaos, there is something about holding him that calms me. Since my father died, it's felt like it's been just us against the world. I sit in the rocking chair and begin to try to rock him back to sleep.

A few minutes later—not nearly enough time to calm my thundering pulse—I hear footsteps approaching. My skin ripples with awareness as Ben appears in the remains of my broken doorway. I watch as he surveys the damage, his expression unreadable. His eyes follow the path of destruction to where I sit near my bedroom window.

Though he doesn't show anything outwardly, I can feel the shock reverberate across the room as he takes in the sight of the bundle in my arms. There are so many things I want to say to him, but I haven't the slightest idea where to begin. For months, I'd planned for this very conversation, but now that the time has come, the words seem to have evaporated into thin air.

He clears his throat, looking between Cole and me. "Logan says they're going to do ride-bys every couple hours to make sure you're safe," he says hoarsely.

My brow furrows, because of all the things I'd imagined he would say to me, that hadn't been anywhere on the list. "I-I—" I lick my lips and try again. Ben angles his left side toward me, tilting his head again. I manage to regain my thoughts after a moment's pause. "Yeah, he told me. I'm going to have a security system installed first thing."

He watches my lips intently. "Good," he says vaguely. "He said you didn't want to bother Jack, but it would probably be best if you had someone stay the night. At least until you have the system put in. Call him," he urges.

I feel my head bobble in a nod as my stomach plummets. Something is off about his expression. The tone in his voice. His eyes don't quite reach me. The entire situation makes me feel nauseated and unsure. Like the ground beneath my feet is moving and I can't quite catch my balance.

"Ben, I—"

"Is he yours?" Ben interrupts, his face suddenly harsh in the shadows.

The weight of his gaze on me makes my insides freeze up. "Yes, he's mine," I manage. "He—"

He looks away from me, shaking his head with a humorless chuckle. "Guess it didn't take too long for you to move on did it?" he spits, his voice raising a few octaves. "Logan was right."

I'm so stunned by his sudden change in personality that I am completely rendered speechless.

Logan appears in the doorway, his expression hard. "I heard loud voices. Is everything okay?" His eyes are pinned on Ben.

"Yeah," Ben says, "we're done here."

He turns to walk away and I automatically get to my feet, like there's an invisible thread connecting us and if he moves, I move, too. He stops me with one look and I'm finally able to see the device attached to his ear. It's a hearing aid. I stare at it uncomprehendingly for a few seconds.

"Ben?" I ask and I watch his eyes drop again to my lips. My stomach drops and my eyes widen when I finally understand. I want to go to him and I automatically take a step forward to do something, anything, but he steps back.

"Let's not do this, Liv. It was fun. I'm glad you're okay. That's it."

When I'm not able to find the words for a response, Ben shoots a nod at Logan and turns to walk away. He disappears down the stairs and I feel the thread connecting us snap.

PART TWO

CHAPTER NINE

SIX MONTHS LATER

BEN

"IT'S A BEAUTIFUL SPOT. Panoramic views of the lake —a private lake. It's a very close community. In fact, the residents are holding a potluck tomorrow night. If you're free, you should consider joining. I'm sure they'd love to have you."

My mind flashes to Livvie, but I push that aside.

"Boats are prohibited here," she continues, "so everything is in pristine condition. You're getting a prime piece of land at a bargain basement price." The real estate agent stands in the doorway, her smile just a little too eager and her eyes a little too bright.

I let her sell the whole pitch, but it doesn't matter.

I decided to buy the house six months ago when I learned it was on the market, before I'd even moved back to Nassau. I figured if it was still here when I got back from my last duty station that I'd buy it. Contacting the real estate agent was the first thing I did when I rolled back into town a few days ago as a civilian once again.

The rooms are empty and her voice carries as I walk down the worn halls. "The previous owner passed away—heart attack—not too long ago, and it's been sitting on the market ever since."

I move to the back hallway and out to the deck that looks down to the waterline. This puts the agent on my right side allowing me to tune her out. I already know everything about the place anyway, but I've got time to kill and she seemed so damn happy to sell me on it, that I didn't want to ruin her moment.

There's movement from the house next door and I wave to a petite woman who eyes me curiously. I feel the vibration of footsteps on the deck floor and turn to catch the end of the agent's speech.

"With your financing, Mr. Hart, this place could practically be yours tomorrow." She looks at me expectantly. "So what do you think?"

I think of the last time I felt relaxed. The last time I remember being happy. Both feelings are so foreign right now, that I'll do damn near anything to get them back.

Even buy a house that I know will stir up more shit than I'm ready to handle.

"I'll take it."

I look out the floor to ceiling windows and across the very familiar McCormick Lake. I couldn't let someone have a piece of Olivia's life. Her childhood home is one of the things she treasures above all else. If I'd fucked up my chance of being with her, I could at least keep this part of her to myself.

Then again, maybe I'm at a point where I'm ready to stir things up. I remember the last time I saw her, just home from deployment, driving by her house only to find cop cars out front. I was overcome with panic. When she opened the door, greeting me in a tiny nightgown, the first thing I wanted to do was crush her tight little body against mine. I was so relieved to see that she was all right. I had missed her so god damned much, despite all the shit I'd been through. But then my worry morphed into anger.

I had always been protective of Olivia, but this was a step further. I was overcome with an irrational level of anger over her not calling her brother to stay with her. At the fact that she was staying alone. At the fact that she didn't have a god damned alarm system. I knew I was acting crazy, but I was unable to reign my shit in. I knew my recent brain injury was at least in part to blame. The doctors had talked about the mood swings. The short-temperedness.

The short-term memory loss that could all result from the TBI. That's why I knew it wasn't the right time. That I had to get out of there as fast as possible before I fucked things up even further. I had gone up the stairs to say goodnight. But when I saw her cradling that baby, I snapped.

"As if I could ever forget you."

Her words to me from our fateful night in my truck echo in my head. So much for waiting. It was selfish of me to even suggest it at the time. I would be even more of a dick to be upset over the fact that she didn't when I ignored all her attempts at contact while I was gone. I shouldn't be surprised that she moved on, and I'm not. But I'm an asshole, so it doesn't change that fact that I'm pissed off about it.

Satisfaction spreads over me at the thought of just how pissed off *she's* going to be when she finds out about my new address.

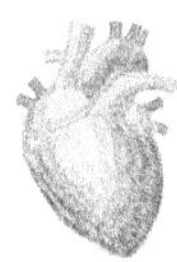

"Your mom is going to put me in an early grave, God love her." Dad closes the hood of the car we're doing a tune-up on and leans against it. "What's it to her if I get a motorcycle? I'm old, not dead."

I lean against the car and take a swig from the water bottle he holds up. "I completely agree with you, *old man.*

I've always said she's crazy, but no one seems to believe me."

"If she hadn't spent the last week yammering on about the number of deaths caused by motorcycles each year, I would kick your ass for talking about your mother like that."

"Just give her time. You know she likes to spout off when she's pissed about something. She'll cool off."

"Yeah. Yeah, you're probably right." He nudges my shoulder and ambles out of the shop.

I wipe my face with one of the greased up rags lying around and toss it back onto the countertop. There's only an hour or so before closing time and it's been slow as hell, so I rest against the counter, my head hanging on my hands. The headaches are less frequent these days, but if I push it, I get fatigued easily and dizzy. The seizures have slackened off too, and hell if I want a repeat of those.

A tap on my shoulder sends my responses into over-drive. I spin around, heart racing with a combination of fear and automatic shame.

The guy trying to get my attention throws up his hands, keys jangling, and says, "Whoa, there guy. Didn't mean to freak you out. I called your name a couple times and you didn't hear me." His eyes flicker to my hearing aid and back at me.

"It's fine. Can I help you?" I make sure to keep my good ear facing him.

"Yeah, uh, I need the oil changed in my SUV, if you can. Do you know about how long it will take?"

I rub a hand over my neck. "About a half hour. We've got a waiting room around front."

"Alright, thanks man."

He turns to leave and a woman steps into the garage doorway. I have to squint my eyes for a second because at first I think I'm seeing things. The bump on the head can cause visual disturbances, not that I've had the pleasure of those...yet. Blinking doesn't erase her presence, though. I knew it would only be a matter of time before we would run into each other. I just thought I'd have more time to get the fuck over her before I did.

"Hello, Olivia."

The guy stops and looks between the two of us with a stupid look on his face. "I gotta take a piss. I'll see you in the waiting room, yeah, babe?"

"I'll meet you there, Chad," she tells him.

I wonder if this chump is the kid's dad. Fuck if I can picture her with a dumb shit like this guy, but what the hell do I know?

Chad leaves and I turn back to find Livvie glaring at me.

"Please tell me that you didn't do what I think you did."

I grab the keys Chad left on the counter and head out

to pull the car up. Livvie follows close behind. "Hey," she says. "Hey!"

"What do you need, Liv?" I ask, pausing by the SUV.

"Tell me that you didn't put an offer in on my dad's house. Please, for the love of all that's holy, Benjamin Hart. Please tell me you didn't do that."

"How could you possibly know that already? It's barely even been eight hours."

She growls in frustration. "It's a small town, Ben. People talk. Now answer my goddamned question."

I stare at her, cheeks red with anger, her bright red hair shining in the sunlight. I look down to where she is holding a baby carrier-type contraption, a sleeping baby boy inside of it. "I'm sorry to hear about your dad, by the way. He was a good man." I look up at her to find that my words have caught her off guard. Her anger seems to lose steam for a second, just a second, before her emerald eyes narrow at me. "And as for the other thing, there was a house for sale. And I put an offer in on it. Simple as that, Olivia."

Her eyes spark with rage. "You can't do that. You just can't disappear and then reappear and buy someone's house!"

I slip into the car. "Someone's? It was no one's house. Pretty sure that's what the For Sale sign meant. So, sure I can. I'm going to be living here now. And you frankly don't have a say in what I do or do not buy. Happens to be a good investment. Unless you can beat my offer, I'll be the proud new owner of a house on McCormick Lake."

"Dammit, Ben." Her voice breaks, but I stand my ground. "You *know*—"

Chad pokes his head out the door. "Hey, babe, everything okay?"

She settles me with an icy glare. "Yes, everything's fine. *We're done here.*"

Olivia turns to storm off and I let her, watching her hurried steps as she stomps away from me. And for the first time in over a year, I smile. The action feels almost foreign to my face which has seen a gamut of emotions over the last year, happiness definitely not being one of them. She might be a mom now and she might be slumming it with some other chump, but my little spitfire hasn't changed one bit.

Something else makes me smile as well, and that is the knowledge that Olivia and I may be a lot of things, but we are so very far from being *done here.*

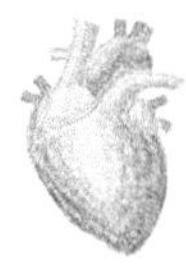

SEVEN YEARS EARLIER

"You're not wearing that," Jack says, his voice sharp.

I turn from my vantage point by the truck to see what's

holding us up. Jack is standing by his truck, arms crossed over his chest, glaring at Olivia and Sofie. Sofie is smiling widely at Olivia, who is scowling at Jack.

"C'mon man," I tell him. "The concert is going to start before you even get your ass in the truck."

Jack turns to me and throws an arm in the girls' direction. "Do you see this shit?"

Olivia blushes, but doesn't back down from my stare. She's dressed in booty shorts that truly deserve their name, as they leave very little to the imagination. The tank is skin tight and a deep purple that sets off her emerald green eyes, even from where I'm standing. She sure as hell hadn't looked like that before I went off to boot camp. But telling him that would mean that I wouldn't get to stare at her legs all night. Probably because he'd use his famous right hook to blacken both my eyes.

"She looks like she's going to be late," I tell him instead.

"I'm not changing, Jack. You can kiss my ass," Oliva spits out, eyes flashing and her hip cocked. With her red hair in thick curls that whip around her heart shaped face, she looks like a goddess about to wreak havoc on the world... or maybe just me.

"You're being a jerk," Sofie says, slinking to Jack and wrapping her hands around his waist. His attention immediately reverts to her own "assets." Forgotten, Olivia rolls her eyes and walks over to me. The smirk on my face freezes as I catch the scent of her perfume.

"Do you mind if I ride with you? They'll be all over each other and I love Sofie, but I don't need to know her that well."

I laugh. "Sure, hop in."

Sofie finally manages to get Jack distracted and in the truck. Thank God. The state carnival wasn't much to write home about; just a bunch of rides that had seen better days and junk food guaranteed to shave a couple years off of your life. This year, though, they'd managed to snag a band I'd been dying to see.

That is, if we didn't miss them.

"I can't wait until we get there. I've been craving a funnel cake," Olivia says, leaning a shoulder against the window. Her curves are illuminated in the light of oncoming traffic. I manage to keep my eyes on the road... barely.

"That shit is horrible for you, you know."

She lifts a creamy bare shoulder. "I don't even care. I'm headed straight there."

"After the concert," I say pointedly.

"Keep telling yourself that."

The ride to the fairgrounds is short, but the line to find a parking spot snakes through the Florida back roads until there's nothing in front of us but hundreds of twin red lights.

"Where are you headed to next?" Livvie asks.

"Hawaii."

Her mouth gapes open. "You lucky bastard!"

"I know. I'll think of you while I'm there."

She slaps my arm. "Just for that, I hope this line takes a loooooong time."

"You're an evil, hateful woman, Spitfire."

"Nope, just a hungry one."

I look at her and watch the play of carnival lights over her face. When I first met her, she'd been this knobby kneed ginger with an attitude. She sure as hell wasn't knobby kneed anymore and her hair was now a deep red, but I could tell she hadn't lost that attitude.

We sit in a silence for a while, listening to the soft music on the radio and the horns from passing cars. Her fingers tap out a beat on her exposed thigh and my eyes go right to them. My fingers twitch where they rest on the steering wheel as I wonder what the skin there feels like.

Livvie clears her throat and I meet her eyes. Busted.

I open my mouth to—what, I don't know—when someone starts banging on my window. Thank God. I turn and find Jack glaring at me, which effectively kills the growing hard-on I've got going on in my pants.

He motions with a hand and I roll down the window. "Line's not moving. Those dudes told us to pull over here and park."

Probably a good thing. Being in an enclosed space next to Livvie is proving to be more of a clusterfuck than I thought it would be.

We join the mass of people making their way toward the fairgrounds. I hear the squeal of an amplifier in the distance and stretch to see over the heads of those in front of me. A sharp elbow connects with my ribs and causes me to grunt.

"Chill out," Livvie says. "You're gonna make it."

"You'd be the same way if you'd been locked up with a bunch of other dudes for the past year, too."

The concert arena is jam packed by the time we make it there, full of rednecks and rodeo queens from the surrounding counties. Peanut shells litter the ground and beer flows freely from surrounding taps and concession stands. Jack automatically hovers over the girls. I stay close, though I keep a healthy distance between me and Livvie. There's no way I want a repeat of the awkward moment in the truck.

A sense of peace washes over me as the first opening band starts up. I manage to coerce a vendor out of a glass of beer. They saw my military haircut and nodded without a word. Buzzed, relaxed and having a damn good time, I weave through the crowd back to Jack and the girls.

I find Olivia, face flushed and damp with sweat. Without asking, she takes the beer from my hand and takes a deep swallow. Dumbfounded, I watch her throat bob. She wipes her mouth with the back of her hand and says, "Thanks. It's hot as hell out here."

Jack is luckily focused on keeping Sofie out of the hands

of the surrounding guys, so he doesn't see her hand the beer back to me. "You tryin' to get me killed?"

"Oh relax, Ben. One sip won't kill me. Besides, the band's about to start. I didn't want to lose my place trying to get a drink."

"Yeah, but—"

A shrill scream breaks through the night and is followed by a roar. The crowd surges forward, carrying us with it. I wrap Olivia in my arms to protect her from the sharp elbows and burly guys who've had way too much to drink. My arms and back get pummeled, but the crowd flows around us. We lose Jack and Sofie somewhere in the melee. By the time the riot is calmed by the patrolling cops, the headliner is halfway through the first set.

I don't know how it happens, but Olivia stays in my arms the whole time. I'd forgotten what it was like to be with a girl, not just a random girl who ends up in my barracks because I managed to sneak them back from the bar. But a girl I know, a girl I've grown up with and care about. She feels so damn good in my arms I don't ever want to let her go.

Her body is plastered to my front and she hasn't let go of my hands the entire time. A part of me knows that I should just walk away, should try to find the others and put some much-needed space between us, but I can't.

I don't want to.

When the last note of the final song rings out she turns

in my arms and looks up at me. I'm frozen to the spot, my hands resting on her hips, people pushing past where we're frozen in the crowd. Finally someone knocks into us and I wrap a protective arm around her shoulder and usher her out of the way.

We wind up at the base of the Ferris wheel, hidden in the shadows of two looming carnival games. The crowd spills on either side. Bright lights dance in the distance. For the first time in my life, I don't have a goddamned thing to say. Sensing my hesitation, she raises her hands to my shoulders, her fingers slide up my neck and she pulls my head down to hers.

I crowd her against the particle board siding of the stand, unable to keep from touching her. She tastes like beer and the sugar from the funnel cake she'd snagged. I lick it up, tracing her lips with my tongue. She nips my bottom lip and I can't help but grin against her mouth.

She arches her neck and I taste the skin at the curve of her shoulders. Her fingers flex against my chest and she trembles against me. Or maybe it's me. I feel like I'm a fucking virgin with her in my arms. I nip a line up her throat and my hand moves of its own accord to the exposed line of her stomach. Her skin is satin-soft and I feel her hum as my hand moves upwards. Hopefully she can't feel them shake.

She urges me closer and I use my free hand to hitch her up against the wall as my lips find hers again. We groan in unison as her legs wrap around my waist. I can feel her heat through our clothes. I've never been so hard in my life.

My hand inches up the bared expanse of her skin. I trace the line of her bra with a finger and she does a full body shiver. "Touch me," she says.

The sound of her throaty voice breaks through the haze of my arousal. Even though it hurts, literally hurts, I manage to put some distance between us.

She looks up at me, her lips puffy and red. "What's wrong?"

"We should—we should head back."

I take a step backwards, trying to regain control over myself.

What the fuck was I thinking?

Livvie grabs my arm. "No, not until you tell me what's wrong."

"You're not that girl, Livvie. I'm not about to fuck you against the wall." She blanches and I feel like an asshole. "I'm leaving again soon and you're better than that."

Her face falls, but she covers it up with a fake smile. "Right. I'm going to go...find Sofie."

I watch her walk away, cursing myself for making that move...and for not following through on it.

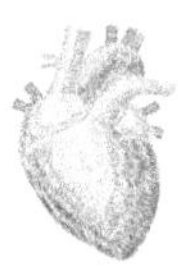

Maybe this is my second chance. As I watch them leave, I vow not to make the same mistake twice.

Later that afternoon, unable to stomach my parents' house for another second, I head to Jack's gym, almost hoping that he's there. We hadn't talked much since I got back, he's probably pissed at me for sleeping with his sister. If I were him, I'd want to kill me, too.

Unfortunately, he's not there when I shoulder my way through the front door. I pay for a day pass and a locker rental, hoping to pound out my frustration on the mats. The locker rooms are empty as I change into my gym clothes and turn off my hearing aide. It does come in handy when I want to check out of the world. The loss of sound helps center me...it isn't always like that, though. Sometimes the silence can be deafening.

The doctors had advised against too much strenuous activity. But fuck 'em. I needed this.

A couple of guys were sparring on the mats. I joined them to wait my turn. When it came, I was paired up with a big motherfucker. I bared my teeth at him as we started our round. He managed to work in a couple of powerful hits that jarred my ribs, but he stayed away from my face. I return with a right hook to his chin that pisses him off. It makes me smile and the weight in my stomach lessens.

Then he manages to land a glancing blow off of my ear and everything goes white. When I come to, I'm on the floor, looking up at the dirty ass ceiling and Jack's ugly face is hovering above me.

He's talking, but I can't hear him over the ringing in my ear and the pounding behind my eyes is only making it worse. I wave a hand at him and manage to get back up to my knees. Blood drips from my ear onto the mat and my fingers come away smeared with it. *Fucking great.*

I get to my feet easy enough, growling at anyone that comes to try and help. Jack watches with narrowed eyes, his thunderous expression tells me that the time has come for us to have it out.

I stumble from the ring and head to the showers. Deciding that I'm not ready to talk after all, I do what I have become expertly good at over the last six months, avoid someone who used to be close to me. Close like a brother. He can fucking follow me if he wants to have this conversation.

He looks at me as he talks and his expression says he would love nothing more than to beat my ass. I nearly smile at him because I could use a good dust up.

It's several hours later, that evening, when I answer the door with the twins screaming at the T.V. in the background. When I find Jack on the other side my back straightens.

My mom touches my shoulder to get my attention and I turn to see her at my elbow. "Jack!" she exclaims. "I haven't seen you in forever. Why don't you come in? I just made some tea."

Jack smiles at her. "Thanks, Mrs. Hart, but I don't have time to visit. I just needed to talk to Ben here for a minute."

"You tell that sister of yours she needs to come see me one of these days."

Like hell.

"Yes, ma'am."

I join Jack outside in case he does decide to kick my ass. I bet Livvie spilled that we slept together out of pure spite. I turn to tell him that I don't give a shit what he thinks, that we're not together, but he beats me to the punch.

"You about done avoiding me? I'm starting to feel like some needy chick around you."

I turn my attention out over the backyard and shrug. "Just had a lot of shit going on."

He makes some clicking noise with his mouth before saying, "Right. What was that shit this afternoon? Even I know you shouldn't be in the ring yet. What are you trying to do? Get yourself killed?"

I chuckle, though on the inside, the walls are starting

to close in. "I already have an all-up-in-my-business-mother inside for this shit, Jack. Is there some reason you're here?"

"Fine. I'll cut to the chase. For the record, Liv doesn't want me telling you a damn thing about this, but I'm sick of watching her try to do it on her own. I've given you time since you got back from Afghanistan and you've been fuckin' dragging your feet."

"Telling me what?"

He runs his hands through his hair and groans. "I know you think that Livvie slept with someone while you were deployed, but she didn't. Not that it would matter if she did, because she didn't promise you anything. Her baby is yours, man. You'd have to be a fucking idiot to think she'd be sleeping around."

My mouth opens and closes, my brain tripping over itself. "Why didn't she just tell me?"

Jack turns toward me, and with the look of rage he's throwing my way, I'm positive he's going to take a swing at me this time. "Because, you jackass, you come home and shit all over her, and then you've blown her off ever since." He breathes a heavy sigh and steps closer to me. "I know shit's been rough for you lately. I wanted to give you your space. But you're not the only one battling demons. She barely survived Dad's death or having a kid with a heart defect that almost killed him. She thought she could count on you. She held on to that shit. But she couldn't. Why *would* she tell you?"

The air seizes in my chest. I remember the emails that I'd deleted in the hospital. The one that said she needed to talk to me. I remember her stunned expression the night I showed up on her doorstep. I remember the small bundle she held in her arms.

And then I remember all the other people I'd failed.

Disgust rolls in my gut. "I didn't—"

Jack sneers. "No, I don't want to hear it. The person who deserves your apology is my sister. Like I said, I know you went through some shit and I get that, but that doesn't excuse you being a dick. Man up, Ben. Livvie will never admit it and she'll probably never talk to me again for doing this, but she needs you. And if you can't do that, she needs you to at least not be such a douche about it. I'm tired of seeing the two people I love the most in fucking shambles."

And with that, he walks away from me and heads back into the house, leaving my world turned on its axis. I'm overcome with every emotion at once: anger, elation, shock. Olivia and I made a life, and I didn't even know about it.

I've been stateside for six months now, without a clue that I have a son. I'd done my best to hide away from everyone in the months that I'd been back, only seeing my dad and family at the shop since I got back. I've barely been able to manage to keep going every day. To push myself out of bed every morning. To fight through the headaches, the nightmares, the struggles with my hearing loss. What could I possibly have to offer the life of another person? That of an infant, no less.

Olivia's pained expression the night at her house plays in my head. I could throttle her for not telling me. She'd failed me. But, if I'm being honest, I'd failed her too. The list of people I've failed only seems to continue to grow.

CHAPTER TEN

OLIVIA

CHAD TRENTON sure is nice to look at. Short blonde hair, endless blue eyes. He has the southern boy charm shtick down to a work of art. We hadn't been at the McCormick Lake potluck two minutes and we were already catching the attention of the people gathered on the beach.

He comes from a good family, doesn't have any plans of running off to kill himself, and he sure seems to enjoy my company. The no-strings simplicity of our dates is what drew me to him. His parents own most of the farming land in Nassau, so he won't be leaving the area any time soon. I'm comfortable with him. Even my son enjoys his presence. Then again, at seven months, Cole does little more than eat, play, and sleep. Even now, he's tucked away at Melissa's spare room next door, oblivious to the goings-on.

"Just remember I have to be out by eleven," I tell Chad.

A flash of irritation crosses his face, but he replaces it with a sugar-sweet smile. "Of course, sweetheart."

The night is cool, and I stop when we reach the beach to toe off my sandals. I hold them in one hand as we're absorbed by the crowd. As it is with near everyone in the surrounding areas, I've known Chad for years. He and Jack went to school together, though I didn't get to know him in truth until a few months ago. He is easygoing and handsome. I don't want or need to be blown away by lust or fall madly in love. A simple relationship of comfort is all I could handle, especially with Cole now in the picture.

Thankfully, Chad seems to understand that so far.

Music is pulsing from one of the cars someone parked on the grassy knoll which borders the beach to the lake. A smooth, male voice drifts from it as I relax into one of the white plastic lawn chairs and listen to the chatter around me. Chad leaves soon after I'm settled to flit around the crowd, social butterfly that he is. He has a boundless supply of energy and has never seemed content just to sit and watch with me. No, the moment we get wherever we're going, he's off to engage someone in a game of beer pong or daring someone to strip and jump in the lake.

I set the baby monitor I'd brought from home on the table next to me so I can hear any stir from Cole. Through it, his soft murmurs comfort me. It was a good idea after all to let Chad drag me out here. I haven't been out since before Cole was born, so it's nice to just relax with people who can actually talk back to me. I'd forgotten what adult conversations were like. Especially if they're not about work, hospital procedure, or babies.

A couple of the guys' dates gather around with the girls I'd invited from work and we make idle chit-chat about their drunken antics. Though they're younger and seem more interested in guzzling down beer after beer, I find myself laughing along with them as Chad convinces one of the new guys from the gym to jump naked off the docks into the frigid water.

At that moment, I feel the air change. It shifts over my skin, snapping and crackling until I shiver with awareness. My eyes flit over the bobbing heads of the other people and land on a shadowed figure by the car. George Straight croons about getting carried away, and my heart starts to beat faster. It's as though it somehow recognizes that its other half has returned. I curse it for its flighty affections. When will it ever learn? I should have realized by now that hearts are fragile things. They break easily.

I don't realize that I've stopped breathing—or that the figure is almost within touching distance—until Chad appears at my side, clapping an arm around my back and forcing air back into my lungs.

"Ben!" Chad's breath fans over me in a noxious cloud of sour beer. "I didn't know you had a place around here."

Stupid. I should have known he'd be here.

"Good to see you man," Chad continues, completely oblivious to the tense looks we're sharing and the fact that most of us have known each other for decades.

Ben nods, his eyes elsewhere, though I have a feeling he's catalogued everything about me in seconds. And damn if he doesn't look downright edible cleaned up in a pair of jeans and a tight T-shirt. The baseball cap throws a shadow over his eyes and the firelight flickers over his beard.

I refuse to let my fingers tug down the hem of my shirt to make sure the infinitesimal white lines that mar my stomach aren't visible. Doing so would only emphasize the new fullness of my breasts. As if on cue, I can feel them tighten and come to attention.

His face is all hard, uncompromising angles, almost too harsh to be attractive, but somehow it is. The light of the fire flickers in his crystal-blue eyes and it takes a moment for me to realize that he's ceased his perusal of the goings-on and is now staring right at me.

"Good to see you, too," Ben murmurs to Chad, his voice flowing over me like silk.

A shout distracts Chad from the conversation. "Let

me get you a beer, okay? Sweetheart, you want something?"

I shake my head but am unable to tear my eyes away. Chad departs, ever oblivious, and howls welcome him back into the fold of partygoers. The girls sense the tension, as well, and leave under the guise of refreshing their own cups. I shift my weight from one foot to the other, suddenly feeling like we're alone even though we're surrounded by people. And I can recall quite vividly what transpired between us the last time we were alone. In this very spot.

The memory breaks the current flowing between us. I dig in my purse for the water I'd stashed there and take deep, refreshing gulps. I fold into the chair again, determined to ignore his presence and get back to my good time.

I hear the scrape of a chair being dragged along the sand, causing my heart to beat ever faster in my chest. His spicy, clean scent surrounds me, and damn if it doesn't throw me back to tasting the spot on his neck where it's the strongest. I'm too far away from the fire to feel its warmth, but I do feel the heat emanating from the closeness of his body.

My words bubble up in my throat. "If you're here to rub the fact that you bought Dad's house in my face you can kiss my ass."

He sighs. "That's not why I'm here, Olivia."

I concentrate on my water bottle, not yet feeling strong enough to look in his direction. "Then why *are* you here? You made it damn clear that night that you didn't want anything to do with me. Nassau may be a small town, but it's easy enough to stay out of each other's way."

"I don't think that's going to be possible. Do you?"

I glance over at him. "You've managed to do it for the last year and a half. I don't see why anything has to change now." The arm of my chair jerks in his direction and I squawk in outrage. "What the hell are you doing?"

"Let me put this into plain words so that there aren't any further misunderstandings." He moves closer to me, his lips so close, I ache to feel them on mine, despite how furious he makes me. "I was an asshole to you that night and I'm sorry. I didn't buy your dad's house to piss you off, even though we both know I love it when you get pissed off. I bought it because I know how much it means to you."

My breath catches in my throat. "You did what?" My purse starts buzzing and I drag my gaze away from his to dive in it for my phone, noting Melissa's name across the screen. "I-I appreciate the apology. Don't take this the wrong way, but Melissa—she was Dad's girlfriend—is watching Cole and she just sent me an SOS. We do actually need to talk. Soon. But, right now I have to go."

I can feel his gaze on me as I pack up my bag and shoot

off a text to Chad letting him know where I'm going to be.

"Tomorrow," he says.

I blink up at him as we both stand. "Tomorrow?"

"Come to dinner with me."

"I don't know. I have a doctor's appointment with Cole tomorrow. He's usually cranky for a while afterwards. How about the day after?"

Before he can reply, my phone buzzes again. "Yes—yes okay. Um, I have to go." In my haste, I throw my things into my purse and head across the double driveways to Melissa's. I can feel Ben's intense stare following me the entire way.

Melissa's house, more a two-story cabin, is blessedly quiet save for Cole, who is squalling more insistently now. I hurry through the bare kitchen and living room to the stairs, waving at a beleaguered Melissa in her robe and slippers. She's been a godsend in the past few months. If it weren't for her, I would have never been able to handle all of the doctor's appointments and office visits for Cole.

Cole is wiggling in his little bodysuit, not quite a full tantrum but definitely working up to one. He sniffles and his head lolls as I pick him up from the portable crib I'd brought. I cradle him in my arms and make shushing sounds to soothe him. Cole contents himself in my embrace with a bottle. The process calms me as well, thankfully. I hadn't expected to see Ben again. Not until I found the right words to say.

"Oh, Cole," I whisper. "What am I going to do?"

He squints up at me and for a moment, I'm distracted from my troubles. He releases the bottle to smile, all gums, and I melt. I rock him from my perched spot on the bed until he stills again in my arms. I yawn, wondering how drunk Chad is and if I should just leave him here and make it an even earlier night than I had planned. Feeding always makes me sleepy and part of me wants to curl up here, succumb to my exhaustion, and forget the mess I've made of my life.

I nearly do just that when a sound coming from the landing of the stairs startles me awake. I glance blearily around and spot Ben leaning against the doorframe.

My belly clenches with nerves. I steel myself. The last thing I need is to feel vulnerable around him. His penetrating stare can read my every thought.

"Melissa let me in. You dropped your phone."

My cheeks burn in response. I feel trapped. I've gotten so used to thinking of Ben in the removed sense that I'm nearly dumbfounded by his sudden presence. "Thanks."

I settle Cole into his car seat where he snuggles contentedly, never stirring as I buckle him in. I quickly fold up the portable crib and stuff his blankets and diapers back into his diaper bag. My movements are stiff and jerky and my fingers shake when I attempt to do up the zipper to the bag.

I rise to leave, but Ben grabs my hand. The heat from his palm sears a path of recognition straight through me, and my heart thuds expectantly in my chest. I feel exposed by his touch and I move to pull from his hold, but his fingers tighten. I look at him in alarm. He stands and I automatically move back. Somehow, I know that being near him again, even as innocent as this, will be devastating.

Unfortunately, he follows, crowding me against the wall next to the bedroom door. I stare pointedly at the floor, unable to look at him when he's so close.

I hear the sound of someone stumbling up the stairs and the telltale rustle of Melissa's robe as she makes her way to the bathroom across the hall. For a moment, I hope she remembers I have Cole in here and thinks to check on me. Anything to break the spell Ben has me under. My voice—and willpower, for that matter—is nowhere to be found.

But she doesn't. Instead, she uses the bathroom and leaves me at Ben's mercy.

Being in such close proximity to him dredges up memories I would much rather leave buried. I feel the faintest touch of his lips against my bare shoulder and I tremble. His arms slip around my waist in gradual increments. He buries his face in my throat. Then his hands slide down the sides of my rib cage, slowly mapping the way to my hips. He gathers me in his strong arms and simply holds me there for a moment.

When he pulls back, my body follows his lead. I don't know who makes the first move, but somehow his lips are on me and his body is pressing mine against the bedroom wall. We kiss like the night we were alone in his truck. No holding back. No real life to intrude. It's even better than I remember it, and for a moment, I forget about the worrying and the stress. All I can think about is the stroke of his tongue against mine. The way the cage of his arms makes me feel safe and protected.

I close my eyes at the splendor of his embrace. Heat washes over me and loosens my stiff limbs. It would be so easy to forget the past and fall into bed with him again. So easy to give in.

The same thought seems to occur to Ben, because he releases me the slightest bit to look into my eyes. My gaze catches on the device on his ear and I lift a hand to touch him, but he shies away from me.

Ridiculously, stupidly hurt by the simple gesture that speaks volumes, I pull away. His arms fall loosely to his sides and his lips pull into a frown. I take a moment to calm my nerves against the feelings that have resurfaced. Once I feel reasonably calm, I return to Cole's side and collect his things.

"I'll see you the day after tomorrow, Ben." Then we

can finally put all of the unanswered questions to rest. He stares at me for a moment, and I almost think that he's about to reply, but he ends up nodding and giving me a weak smile instead.

I pick up Cole's carrier and resolve to have Jack pick up the playpen later. There's no way in hell I'll be coming back here again. I take determined steps to the doorway and pause, sending a dazed look back at him. When I turn around again, I find Chad standing in the doorway with a stunned, angry look on his face.

Just great. As if I needed another complication.

CHAPTER ELEVEN

OLIVIA

THE DOORBELL STARTLES ME, the baby, and one cantankerous old dog where we're resting—or at least trying to—on the couch.

Considering the three of us had been up since dawn with one unhappy teething monstrosity, it's no surprise when Hank nearly somersaults off the cushions, Cole rouses with a scream that could rival howler monkeys, and I pray for sweet relief. Normally, I'm blessed with a supernaturally well-behaved baby in spite of his illness. Believe you me, I count my blessings for that every day.

However, when Cole has a bad day, he has a *really bad day*.

When five a.m. rolled around and I still hadn't gotten

him to rest, I gave up and called in reinforcements. Thankfully Jack is able to have someone cover him at work. I don't like sending Cole to daycare when he's having an off day. The place he's at is great and I made sure they were all CPR certified before I ever let Cole start, but he won't be able to return until after he's cleared at his next checkup. His second surgery was a month ago and we've been having a time of it ever since.

A knock follows close behind the bell, and I tangle in my robe and roll unceremoniously from my perch on the couch to the floor, landing with a thump. I contemplate staying there for a while as I rub the grit from my eyes. Hank trots over to lick my face, and I stumble to my feet to answer the door.

I squint against the glare of the afternoon sun and find Melissa on my front stoop. Her familiar perfume wraps around me. I'd been trying to place the scent as long as I've known her, but to no avail. Her customary black hair has gone a little lighter at the roots and her button-up denim shirt is tucked into a pair of worn jeans.

I belt my robe over my yoga pants and T-shirt and offer a pained smile. "Hey, Melissa. I'd invite you in, but we're currently having a meltdown. Is everything okay?"

She smiles sympathetically. "I could ask you the same thing. I was in the area I just wanted to come by and check to make sure you and the little one are okay."

Melissa has no other family, and losing my dad hit her

quite hard. I thought it was sweet, considering they'd been dating less than a year. I love that my father had someone so caring after my mom died. He was never the type to be alone for long; he was a very social creature. Jack takes after him in that respect.

"Just a rough night of teething and the general discomfort after he gets discharged," I tell her. "Nothing some rest and a little pain reliever won't cure. Not to mention I think he knows he's due for another checkup at the cardiologist tomorrow. It's nice of you to come by and check on us, though."

"Poor thing." She pauses before gathering herself up and saying, "What I really wanted to talk to you about was...well, I couldn't help but overhearing your conversation with that young man last night. Ben, isn't it?"

I nod. "I'm so sorry if we bothered you. I hope he wasn't rude."

Melissa shakes her head with a laugh. "Oh no, honey. Nothing like that, I just wanted to give you some advice. I don't want to seem too forward as we haven't known each other that long."

"Please, I can't thank you enough for the days you've watched Cole for me. You're practically family to us now."

"That's sweet. Well, I just wanted to be nosey, really. That man last night? That was Cole's father wasn't it?"

"I—I...Yes, it was," I end on a whisper. "He's been

gone and I haven't found the right moment to explain things."

"You don't have to defend yourself to me. I've been in my fair share of complicated relationships. I just wanted to make sure that you'll let me know if you ever need anything. I'm always here for you. Talk, babysit. Whatever."

"Definitely. I really appreciate you stopping by to check on us."

"Anytime, honey. Give that baby a kiss for me."

As if on cue, Cole's wails reach a higher decibel and I wince. "I will. Thanks again."

Twenty minutes later, I rush out the door, already heinously late and feeling tremendously guilty. I can hear Cole's cries from outside as I unlock my car and load in my briefcase and paperwork.

Though the street is empty of traffic, a sense of unease skitters along my shoulders. Cole's screams follow me the entire way to work.

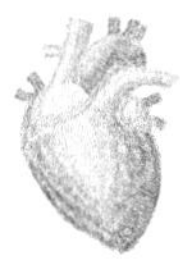

Most days, motherhood suits me surprisingly well. Especially considering I didn't have the slightest idea what I was doing. I took to it like it was second nature and so far, I haven't forgotten him in a marketplace or pulled my hair out in frustration. Though, I expect both are in my future.

Unfortunately, Cole must sense my growing distress because his mood is no better the next day. By the time we reach the doctor's office, I'm doubting my ability to handle this motherhood thing after all.

I didn't even change out of the yoga pants and T-shirt I wore to bed. Cole was little better in a stained shirt and pair of pants that were still twisted around his legs from the hasty diaper change before we left the house. I hadn't been able to skip another day from work, so we only had a narrow window between the end of my work day and the closing of the doctor's office.

Cole struggles against my hip. "Shhh, baby boy. We just have to see Dr. Foley for a few minutes and then we'll go back home."

I doubt he cares much, but it makes me feel better.

We stumble into the doctor's office a screaming, snotty mess. I am about ten seconds away from shedding all dignity and joining him in a rousing moment of self-pity. Heads swivel in our direction, a few mothers offer sympathetic smiles of solidarity, as the rest give me dirty looks. I ignore both, my cheeks burning, and march up to the receptionist desk. I don't recognize the new person there, but I sure hope they're having a better day than I am.

"Hi." I bounce Cole on my hip in an effort to soothe

him, to no avail. "We have an appointment for a checkup with Dr. Foley."

"Name, please?"

"Cole Walker."

The receptionist types into the computer while I try to distract Cole with the brightly colored flyers that paper the wall next to the window.

"The doctor will see you soon, if you'll just wait here." She smiles sympathetically and gestures toward the play area in the corner of the waiting room. "I'm sure Mr. Walker would love those."

I blow out a frustrated breath. Unable to handle his cries anymore, I hunker down in the play area with him and pick up one of the toys with blocks stacked on wires. Cole sits in my lap and runs the blocks back and forth across the wire. The motions keep his attention for a few minutes, and I use that time to calm myself down, as well. Subjecting him to a session of poking and prodding is only going to make his mood go back downhill again, so I take my moments of peace and quiet when I could get them.

"Ms. Walker?"

"Right here." I stand and walk to the window.

"Sorry for the wait. The doctor will see you in exam room three."

"Thank you so much."

She gestures behind her to the hallway that leads back to a row of rooms.

Twenty minutes later, we leave the doctor's office with screams echoing behind us. I take deep, cleansing breaths because seeing him hurting and unhappy has the same effect on me. I don't know how my parents ever raised Jack and me without going crazy. And they only had to deal with my teenage years. They made it look so effortless. I don't know how Ben's parents did it with four kids. One is definitely more than enough for me. Even though I know the risk of having a second baby with HLHS is very low, I can't help but feel a trill of fear at having another one.

A cool autumn breeze greets us and soothes my hot face. I absolutely hate my baby being in pain, and it only made it worse that there was only so much I could do to make him feel better. I hoped the preemptive medicine I'd given him for both the teething and the shots would kick in soon to take away some of the hurt.

I start to calculate how long that should be as I dig through my purse for the keys to my car. I hear the rev of an engine and squeal of tires, but don't pay it any mind as I find my keys wedged behind my wallet. I snag them and look up just in time to see an SUV roll to a stop in front of me at the doctor's entrance. At first, I don't think much of it. Someone is probably just dropping off an elderly patient or a new mom.

I brush off the thought and hitch Cole farther up on my hip. The parking lot was full to bursting this afternoon, so I had to park on the far side of the lot nearest to the busy side street. Cole's weight begins to pull at my side and a headache is making itself known behind my temples as I make my way across the lot. The only thing I want to do is curl up with a big cup of tea and maybe a nice bath and a book. I doubt I would get to do any of those things, but it is nice to think about.

The car starts behind me as I chatter to Cole about our plans for the rest of the day, which has become a habit of mine. His tears have abated, so I continue until we're halfway to where I parked. I hear the telltale crunch of gravel behind me and make a point to move out of the path of the oncoming car. I glance back to make sure there's plenty of room.

The car window rolls down, but it's in the direct path of sunlight and covered in shadows, so I don't get a good look at the driver. I see a nondescript arm leaning out of the open window and I don't make much of it. My brain must sense something off about the whole thing because I glance back again to see the hand is holding a gun.

And it's pointed straight at us.

A loud shot breaks the calm afternoon and I feel the bullet whiz past me and explode through the window of a nearby car. As glass rains down on us, everything in my brain slows to a single thought: *Don't hurt my baby.*

I shift Cole's body so I'm between him and the car, automatically dropping our bags in the lot so I can hold him more securely. I hear another shot sound off, and I can't help the feral scream that erupts from my chest. I dart between the nearest cars and crouch to the ground. I can hear the slow crawl of the attacker's vehicle behind me, so I scramble until we're on the sidewalk that leads back toward the office with a minivan separating us.

There are a dozen or more cars between us and safety, but I know our chances are better in there than out here with a gunman stalking us. I take a ragged breath and gather Cole more closely in my arms. I hear the squeal of brakes and the click of a car door behind me.

I use the advantage of surprise and stagger to my feet. I don't chance glancing behind me because it will only make me hesitate. Instead, I shoot toward safety, Cole's little body bobbing against mine as I sprint.

Another shot sounds behind me. I feel the heat of it graze my side, but I don't stop. The only thing that matters is getting Cole to safety. I don't even feel any pain. Sweat blurs my vision. Blood rushes in my ears, and I can't seem to catch my breath. The race to the door takes an eternity.

Footsteps pound the pavement behind me, and my heart lurches into my throat. Faces white with fear appear in the glass panels of the door.

"Open the door!" I scream, my voice breaking with the force of it.

Thankfully, they hear me and the door slams open so hard a pane of glass shatters around us. A few feet away and I think we're going to make it. It's going to be okay.

Then another shot comes, but this time it doesn't miss. I feel the bullet tear through my shoulder as though I'm watching it happen to someone else. The force of impact catapults me off of my feet.

I collapse half-in and half-out of the doorway, my head smacking against the unforgiving surface of the tile floor. I feel my body being dragged across the floor and then I lose consciousness, the sound of Cole's screams following me into the darkness.

CHAPTER TWELVE

BEN

My family has lived in the same house for forty years. I don't think anyone could pry my father away from his custom garage or my mom from her renovated kitchen even if they had a million dollars. No matter how much my siblings and I attempted to coerce them to host a huge yard sale for their collections and knick-knacks, they wouldn't budge. Now that I'm older, I thank them for it.

I find my two younger brothers, Mitchell and Garrett, wrestling over the gaming system in the living room. The now seventeen-year-old twins had been a surprise to our whole family after my parent's fifteenth anniversary. They both pause in their argument to toss off an acknowledgement my way.

My mother is in the kitchen, steam pouring from the oven and smelling a lot like heaven. She grins up at me over her boiling pots.

"Your father said you would blow off tonight, considerin'. But I knew it. I knew you wouldn't be so dumb. I should have known." She shakes her head at me and points a steaming wooden spoon in my direction. One I had been well acquainted with in my youth. "I don't even know what to say to you now, so you just sit there until I'm ready to deal with you."

I have no idea what the hell I've done this time, but around here? It could be anything. The twins were probably foisting the blame on me for something or another. My older sister Amanda could also be the culprit. As she had married a Marine—something I still get hell about on occasion—and moved away years ago, there wasn't anything I could have done to her.

Instead of worrying about it, I stuff my face with a piece of fried cornbread. I'd long since learned there was no use in arguing with a woman, especially if that woman was your mother.

The slide of our back door announces my father, and he steps in wearing his signature grease-spattered boots and simple T-shirt. His hair has thinned even more over the past year so only a single tuft is left at the top of his head.

"Benny boy!" he says in greeting.

My mom turns away from the stove to glare at him. "Don't you start 'Benny boy-ing' him, Lewis Hart."

Dad holds up his arms, a wide grin still pulling at his lips. He winks at me over Mom's turned back and heads to the sink to wash his hands of motor oil. Still clueless as to what has her mitts in a twist, I stuff my face with another piece of cornbread and grab a soda from the fridge to wash it down.

"Go wash your hands, too, Ben. Tell the twins to set the table. Dinner's ready."

I go to comply, but stop to press a kiss to her forehead first. I mumble, "Love you, Momma," into her hair before heading off.

Once I corral the twins into doing Mom's bidding, we sit down at the table and spoon up the food. I'm so lost in the comforting smell of a home-cooked meal that I dig in as soon as my plate is in front of me. I'm halfway through my second rib before I notice that no one else is eating.

I wipe my face with a napkin and direct my attention to my mom, who is giving me a death stare. "What?"

"Don't you 'what' me, Benjamin Thomas Hart."

I cringe at her use of my middle name. "Honestly, I don't know what I did this time, but if Mitch and Garrett are involved, it wasn't my fault."

The twins snicker and my dad cuffs Mitch on the shoulder so they both quiet down. My mom sniffs daintily and takes a sip of her soda. "It's been all over the news. Did you think we wouldn't notice? How could you keep something like this from us? I expect more from you, Benjamin."

"All over the news?" My stomach drops. Certainly a small town like ours wouldn't have picked up the coverage. The last thing I need is another story about the attack that killed my friends. I break out in a cold sweat. My easygoing, relaxed response to being back home disappears. "What are you talking about?"

Dad and the boys dig into their plates and studiously avoid my gaze. "Mom?"

"Come with me then if you want to continue this act. I'll show you."

Mom leads me from the dining room into the den where the TV is already on and at our local news station. I glance from it to her expectantly. When she doesn't say anything, I make an impatient gesture. "Well, are you going to show me?" I ask.

Before she can answer, a name on the screen catches my attention. If I thought being in hell for the past year was bad, I was sorely mistaken. My knees give and I slump onto the couch, my eyes glued to the reporters outside a nondescript office building. Behind the anchor and the crowd of people are an ambulance and a host of police officers.

Flashing on the screen is a picture of Olivia from high school. I remember the night it was taken. She'd just been accepted to Florida State University and her parents threw her a party to celebrate.

"Why would I hide that from you?" I ask, my voice hoarse. "Why is Olivia on the news?"

"Not that," my mom answers gently. She indicates the second picture on the screen. Olivia's son, Cole. And, according to Jack, *my son*.

I look at her quizzically.

My brain is still stuck on the image of Livvie's face on T.V. in relation to an accident. Adrenaline surges through me and I jerk to my feet.

"I have to get to the hospital. Jack. I have to call Jack. Why didn't you tell me when I got here?" My mind flashes back to the chaos after the first bomb. To the feeling of helplessness and sheer fear. Is she dead?

"Local law enforcement were called to the scene of the crime," the young female reporter says, "when nearby business owners reported shots fired. The events in question were confirmed by a second eye-witness report from a patient actually in the doctor's office at the time of the shooting. There are no fatalities at this point; however, a young woman was shot and has been taken by ambulance earlier this afternoon. Her young child, who was diagnosed with

hypoplastic left heart syndrome, a congenital heart defect, is undergoing evaluations by his cardiologist as a precaution. He will be released into the care of close family members."

My chest seizes as they flash the pictures on the screen again. As I leave my mother sputtering questions at my back, the only thing I can think of is the little boy's smile.

CHAPTER THIRTEEN

OLIVIA

I GROAN as I come awake, jerking to a sitting position. My head protests with a vicious throb. Instinctively, I reach to pull the covers off and get to my feet, but find I am too weak to move. I manage to open my eyes and find myself face-to-face with Jack. If his concentrated expression is anything to go by, I am in serious shit.

"Cole?" I ask immediately, because not a day has gone by since his birth that he isn't my first thought when I wake up in the morning. I remember the sound of gunshots and Cole's high-pitched wails in my ears and I ask more frantically, "Where is he?"

Jack shakes his head. "He's fine, he's fine. Ben has him walking the halls so you could rest. He wasn't hurt."

I try to sit up again, but a piercing ache in my arm nearly has me doubled over. "Shit," I gasp. "What happened? Why does Ben have Cole?"

"You were shot. Don't you remember?"

"I remember someone shooting at me, but I didn't see who it was. It all happened so fast. All I could think about was getting Cole safe." I raise a hand to my head. "I think I hit my head."

"You did. Real graceful-like, according to the nurses. You lost a lot of blood." Jack leans his head down over our clasped hands. "Scared the shit out of me, Livvie-girl. I can't believe I almost lost you."

"I'm sorry, Jack." Tears pool in my eyes, and I clear my throat.

"No, don't be. I'm just so fucking glad you're okay. All you need to focus on is resting, getting better. Logan is making sure they're interviewing everyone."

My brow creases. "Logan? Is he even allowed to do that? Wait, does he think it's related to the break-in?"

"He said we shouldn't rule it out. Besides, it can't just be a coincidence that your house gets broken into and then you get shot at. Fuck, Livvie. Someone wanted to kill you."

I shake my head and instantly regret it. "No, no, that can't be right. I'm no one. I've got nothing. Who in the hell would want to do that?"

"We don't know, but like I said, Logan's on it just to be sure."

A hard, heavy weight presses in on my chest. Tears cloud my vision. I can't catch my breath. I don't understand what Ben is doing at the hospital. The fact that he's wedging himself so firmly back into my life is almost too much to handle. I wipe my eyes as the tears fall and try to pull myself together. "I need to see Cole."

He kisses my brow then lays his forehead on mine for a few heavy moments. I am grateful. Grateful to the family that had given me up. Grateful for two generous, loving hearts. Grateful for the family I didn't deserve, but loved me anyway.

After he left, I broke down; I couldn't help it even if I tried. The fear and panic came flooding back and, coupled with the sense of relief that my baby was safe, it mixed and poured out of me in tears.

And the guilt. For every moment I wished I could go back to the single girl I'd once been. Even if they were only fleeting. What would I have done if he'd been hurt? I can't even fathom how I could repair that hole. It would have been my fault for not protecting him, not keeping him safe.

The thought crosses my mind that maybe he still isn't safe. What if Logan is right and I'm putting him in danger? How can one little person face so much adversity in a short time?

By the time Ben appears with Cole snoozing in his arms, I'm a wreck. My face feels raw with grief, and my eyes are so bleary I can't even see straight. The ache in my head has only intensified, leaving me feeling worse than I'm sure I look.

"Ben," I choke out. "I need to hold him."

His face is stony, resolute. I've never seen him so closed-off before—including our most recent interactions when I couldn't read him at all. He places Cole in my arms without a word and I'm thankful. I'm not sure if I have anything left after my crying jag to fight with.

Cole's face is slack with sleep, and I pull him as close to me as I can get him without aggravating the wound on my side and in my shoulder. Fresh tears spill, though even they have lost their strength.

I trace his lips with a finger, silently mapping the landscape of his face. The relief that he's here and safe in my arms is overwhelming. I don't know how long I sit there, but when I look up, Ben hasn't moved from his post beside my bed.

"Do you know if he's eaten?"

"I called Sofie. Luckily, she knew you were pumping milk for daycare and was able to get some and some of that special formula he needs from your house. It took a few tries, but yes, he did. He didn't like it much, but after a few hours, he seemed to get the hang of it."

I sigh, feeling one of the weights on my shoulders ease. "Thank you."

"No problem."

My head begins to throb more insistently, so I rest it on a pillow. I don't even know where to begin to process what happened.

I hear Ben moving around in the room, but I can't summon the energy to investigate. The bar lowers on the side of the bed and I feel weight shifting beside me. He settles next to me on his side, one arm carefully strewn across me so he doesn't hurt me or disturb the baby.

"What are you doing?"

Ben takes my free hand in his. My fingers automatically cradle his in my palm. "Give me this, please. I just need to be close to you both right now. Let me hold you."

I'm too tired to resist, and if I'm being honest with myself, I need him to hold me, too. The last thing I feel before I slide into the depths of sleep are his strong arms around my waist, holding me close to his side.

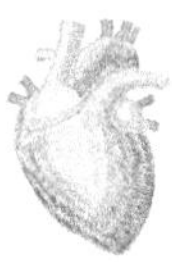

"Local art teacher Olivia Walker will be released from the hospital today in stable condition after a vicious attack Monday morning. The shooter, identified as an indi-

vidual wearing dark clothing and driving a white sports utility vehicle, remains at large. Her son, the other victim in the attack, did not sustain any wounds and remains in the care of his father, war veteran Benjamin Hart. Stay tuned to WTVB, your station for breaking news."

Ben pauses in the doorway, his eyes glued to the T.V. even though the anchor has moved on to another topic. I'm likewise frozen, my good arm hovering over my bag, clutching a handful of dirty laundry.

All of the things that we've put off while I was recovering hang between us. We lock eyes over the hospital bed and I fumble with the clothes I was attempting to sort neatly. Instead I dump them in a tangled mess and feign interest in my toiletries. The pain in my side is, thankfully, curtailed by a cocktail of drugs and luck, but that doesn't help, as the bathroom proves to be more of a trap than an escape.

"We need to talk," Ben says from the doorway, his arms crossed over his chest.

"I know." I don't turn to face him. I can't. Instead, I hobble to the sink to grab my toothbrush. Keeping my hands and mind busy is easier than facing him.

His footsteps sound behind me and I can feel his warmth against my back. I close my eyes, my entire body freezing at his touch. It was easier to be mad at him. I almost prefer it. Being mad at someone is a whole hell of a lot better than being raw and open to them. I open my eyes and find Ben watching me in the mirror. His hand covers mine on the sink.

"I'm sorry." He maneuvers my body gently so that I'm facing him. "I'm so damn sorry, Liv."

I fumble with the toothpaste. "Um, what do you mean?"

"For leaving you."

Unable to look him in the eye, I stare at the tile floor. "Don't be sorry for that. You didn't leave me. I don't blame you for any of it. I shouldn't have kept Cole from you for this long. When you came back, I fully intended on telling you before you left for your next assignment. I understand what it must have looked like, coming home to see me with a kid."

He wraps his arms around my waist. One hand on my thigh under the first bullet wound, careful not to touch me. The other splays across my back. I'd be lying if I said the heavy weight of his touch wasn't reassuring.

"That was all me," he says. "I don't want to get into what happened to me, but I was raw. It was a bad time and I overreacted. It scared me more than I want to admit to myself to come home and find that you'd almost been hurt. Now you *have* been hurt and I can't help but feel like it's because of me. I should have been there for you."

I feel like I'm in a dream because the words coming out of Ben's mouth are too good to be real. They are everything that I've dreamed of hearing from him, although I don't feel like I deserve them. And instead of happiness, I am overcome with guilt for keeping the truth from him for so long. "If anyone should be sorry in this situation it's me." My shoulders bow under the weight of shame. "I should have told you about Cole a long time ago."

His hands cup my chin and bring my eyes to his. "We've both made mistakes. When I saw the news, I thought you were dead. I thought I'd lost you. Him. Before I'd given either of you a chance. That's a weight I'll always have to bear. I don't want to make that same mistake again, Olivia."

A lone tear trails down my cheek. "I-I don't know what to say."

Ben wipes the line of salt away with his thumb. "There's nothing to say. Let's just focus on getting the both of you home and safe. We can worry about everything else later."

We both jerk away—with a hiss of pain on my part—when a knock comes at the door. I leave Ben in the bathroom as I hobble back into my hospital room. Sofie stands in the doorway, her rounded eyes locked on Ben in the doorway. She turns to me and mouths "Oh my God" although I ignore her.

"You didn't have to come down. I told you on the phone I was okay."

She waves a hand. "Since when do I listen to you? Besides, I had to make sure my best friend had a ride home."

"I got her, Sof," Ben says as he comes behind me.

Sofie purses her lips. "We'll see about that. Jack has Cole downstairs when you're ready."

"Thanks, Sof," I tell her. She nods, her eyes still assessing Ben. I give her a stern look and she shrugs her shoulders and leaves, mumbling something that sounds like *'Bout fucking time* on her way out the door.

Though the second I'm alone with Ben again, I wish she hadn't left. Now that the truth about Cole is out there, I don't quite know what to do with myself. Where do we go from here? Do we pick up where we left off? Do we raise our son as friends? My body says one thing, but my brain reminds me that I have a son now. A son with health issues who leaves very little time to deal with my tumultuous decade-long roller-coaster of a relationship with his equally complex father. I remind myself that I had been seeing Chad some lately, however, Chad is simple. And I know that Ben would be anything but simple.

"Um, I'm finished here. I've got some paperwork to do for release. Maybe if you wanted to come by sometime —not that you have to or anything, I just thought—"

"I've already talked about it with Jack. I'm going to take you guys home and check out your house. Logan's got a couple of his off duty guys coming by every couple hours just in case."

I blink rapidly at him. "You don't have to do that. Jack told me they were taking care of it. I'd hate to put Logan out, too. Plus, we had that security system installed after the break-in."

"It's already taken care of. You just focus on taking it easy. Do you have everything here?"

The past week has sapped me of absolutely all energy, so all I can do is nod. Once I settle in at home and can wrap my mind around what has happened, I'll deal with Ben.

I send him a tentative glance as we leave my hospital room. From the determined set about his eyes I have a feeling he isn't going to be so easily swayed.

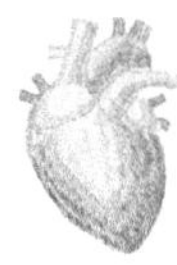

I nearly stumble over the pair of duffle bags heaped in front of my front door. Considering I'm recovering from a gunshot wound that almost killed me, it would have been sad if I returned the same day I was released from the hospital with new injuries.

"I'll get those." Ben moves around me, Cole in tow, and grabs up the bags, depositing them a safe distance away from the front door. Since my release from the hospital, those are the first words he's managed to speak to me that didn't have to do with my recovery.

I look at the bags, then at him, then back to the bags. "Uh, is there a reason why they're here? Those aren't mine."

"Nope, they're mine."

"Oh!" I say. "Did Jack leave them for you or something?"

"No, they're for while I'm staying here."

I blink, certain the blood loss affected my hearing. "Come again?"

"You didn't think I would let you stay here alone, did you?"

"*Let* me?" I echo. Apparently, I'm having a great deal of trouble with comprehension. Maybe that blow to the head did more damage than the doctors realized.

"Hold that thought," Ben says as he bounds up the stairs with a fussy baby.

While he's gone, I hobble into the living room and beeline straight for my couch. I'd requested my rattiest, comfiest yoga pants and my dad's old USMC shirt for my ride home with the sole intent of making a nest on the couch and never leaving. It is safer here, I reason. No one had shot at me here. Yet. At the very least, the new security system I had installed will give me a warning.

Sure, someone had broken into the sanctity of my home, but I still wasn't quite convinced that both incidents were related. It could just be the shittiest run of luck in this decade. Not that I wasn't taking either threat seriously. The first chance I have, I'll make it my personal mission to learn the ins and outs of the new security system. Again.

I also decide it's time for me to take Jack's offer to keep one of his guns on hand. My father had always been about gun safety, so when Jack and I were old enough we'd learned how to handle them properly. I have a healthy respect for weapons but up until now, I'd never seen the need to keep one in my own home.

The fact that I feel the need to arm myself frankly pisses me off. Even more so, the memory of Cole's frightened screams motivates me like no other.

I ease myself down, careful of the wound in the fleshy part of my waist. There hadn't been much internal damage, just an entrance and exit wound that hurt like a bitch. The bump on my head had gone down a great deal, thankfully. The skin there had already patched together for the most part, and I'm able to cover the unsightly bald spot with the rest of my hair. The gunshot wound to my shoulder was the worst, and the sling I had to wear was decidedly uncomfortable. I would be in for a few months of physical therapy to regain full movement in my arm.

Despite all of this, every time I look at Cole, I'm grateful it hadn't been worse.

Ben returns with a handful of stuff, which he sets on

the side table. He had barely said two words to me while I was recovering unless it was related to my care or to Cole. He only left my side to fetch me contraband food or sneak in the baby. He was worse than Jack and Sofie put together, and that's saying something.

"The ride must have put him to sleep. There was no waking him," Ben says offhandedly.

I'm unsure how to respond. This new Ben is completely foreign to me, even more so than usual. The elephant in the room has made any interaction with him decidedly uncomfortable.

"I doubt that'll last long."

Ben makes a noncommittal sound as he opens a pack of gauze.

I eye it suspiciously. "What are you doing?"

"You need to change that dressing. Lie on your side for me and take off your shirt."

Once upon a time, he said similar things to me. Soft whispers in my ear about how he wanted me to act for him. How much he liked the way I undressed for him. Things that not only lit my body on fire, but made his eyes go dark with need. Unfortunately, this is neither the time nor the place and those moments have long since passed, no matter how much my body protests to the contrary.

"I can do it, Ben. You don't need to stay. Really."

He doesn't respond, merely presses against my uninjured shoulder, so I ease down on the couch. He pulls my shirt up for me, careful not to touch the bandage.

I bite my lip and keep my eyes averted as he removes the old dressing. I'd made the mistake of looking while one of the nurses changed it before and, truth be told, I could do without seeing it again. I don't know how I'm going to manage when Ben leaves, but I'll figure something out. If the last year had taught me anything, it's that I'm stronger than I think.

He applies cream to the wound with the gentlest hands, and I use the distraction to study him. When he showed up at the party, I hadn't known what to expect. How could I? I still don't know what I'm going to do about him. After Dad died, I had hoped to keep things in their assigned boxes.

His brow furrows as he concentrates on applying the new bandage. His blonde hair has gotten longer at the top, but he still keeps it sheared short on the sides. To make matters worse, he'd grown out his beard. His strong jaw wears it well. And, from the kiss the other night, his beard is surprisingly soft. So much so that I had to resist the urge to cup his face in my hands and feel just how soft.

Ben pulls my shirt back down and stands. I cough to dispel the sudden tension that clogs the room and makes my skin run hot. He leaves the living room with my old dressing. Feeling vulnerable and oddly morose, I bundle up in an afghan and curl into a ball on my uninjured side.

I'm deep in thought when Ben comes back. He snags the remote from the TV stand and comes to the sofa. Lifting my torso, he slides in between me and the couch then rests my head on his lap.

"What do you wanna watch?"

"Erm, I thought we'd had the conversation about you not having to stay. Besides, I thought you were pissed at me. You have every right to be."

"We didn't have any conversation because you don't have any say-so in the matter. And yes, I am pissed. For the time being, I'm going to be here until I'm certain that you and *my son* are safe. That's the least you could do considering what you've put me through."

I feel the blood drain from my face. I try to sit up so I can express my objection, but his insistent hands keep me pinned to the couch. "Ben, I'm so grateful to you for stepping up with Cole, really. I'm really happy that you want to be in his life. But like I told you before all of this happened, I don't think we should—"

"This has nothing to do with our relationship," he interjects. "It has to do with the fact that you were attacked twice and almost killed. If you think I'm going to leave you alone after that, you're fucking crazy. Until this person is incapacitated, dead, or rotting behind bars, I'm going to be here. No one, *no one*, fucks with my family, and whether we are in a relationship or not, you're blood to me. *You're* my family now, and I will do everything in my power to keep you and my son safe. For the foreseeable future, that includes my staying here."

"But—"

"No," he says firmly. "This is nonnegotiable, Livvie. You do not realize how close I came to losing both of you. How lucky you are that the bullets only did minimal damage and the police came in time. I don't talk about it much, but I've seen people not be so lucky and..." he pauses, clears his throat. "Sorry... but I won't risk that with you. Or with Cole."

CHAPTER FOURTEEN

BEN

OLIVIA SPUTTERS, but I put a hand over her mouth. "There's really no use in arguing, baby. I'm not going anywhere."

Her face is abnormally gray and there are shadows underneath her eyes. My fingers twitch at the sight, though hell if I know what I can do to make it better. What I *do* know is that I won't be leaving her side, no matter how much she bitches about it.

She relaxes against my thigh and pulls my hand away. "I'm too tired to argue with you right now."

"Probably smart, because you won't win."

"Says the man picking on a woman when she's down,"

she retorts, curling into my legs. Every possessive male part of me wants to keep her there, where I know she's safe.

"Relax. I'll listen out for the little guy. You need a nap."

She shakes her head against me. "No, I can't. He needs a careful eye after surgery, especially cause of the past couple of days."

"I'm here, I'm going to be here. We both might as well get used to it."

Her lids flutter against her cheeks. "Are you sure you're going to be okay with him?"

"I'll be fine, Liv. I was only seventeen when the twins were born. I can diaper like a pro."

"He's not a normal baby, you have to be careful with him," she says in between yawns.

"He's a Hart, isn't he? I'm sure he's tougher than you think."

"If he seems like he's having trouble breathing or he—"

"Livvie, I'm trained in combat medicine. I can handle whatever happens. Now turn off that brain of yours and go to sleep so you can argue with me later."

She mumbles something in response and drifts off a few minutes later.

When she's nothing more than dead weight on top of me, I carefully shift out from underneath her and cover her with a blanket. I put the T.V. on a station that's guaranteed not to have any coverage about the shooting and make sure the volume is on low. I check on Cole and note he's still asleep. Even though I've got shit to do, I can't help but stare at him for a while as he sleeps.

My phone buzzes in my pocket and I step out of the room so I don't wake up the kid. I note Logan's name with a tense sort of anticipation. I almost hope he has a name for me. A thick, black rage has been building underneath my skin since I saw Olivia on the news. I just need one reason to let it loose.

"Better have news for me," I answer. Livvie's dog is whining at the back door when I make it back downstairs so I let him out.

"Depends on what you consider news."

"Don't fuck with me, man."

"What do you know about Olivia's boyfriend Chad?"

I think back to my limited set of interactions with the guy. "Seemed kind of pissed when he found me with my hands all over his date. Why?"

"A couple of people mentioned that he was spewing shit about Olivia this weekend. He has a vehicle that matches the description of the one at the scene. Just wanted to give you a heads up that we'll be bringing him in for questioning as a precaution."

"Appreciate it. He didn't strike me as the type for retaliation and I'd be shocked if he could tell one end of a gun from the other. I don't think he's your guy."

"I'll keep an eye out and let you know if anything comes from the interview."

"Thanks, man. You ever come up with anything from the break-in?"

"Went cold, not much to go on. Couple people saw a male, average height, average build in the neighborhood, but no one could I.D. the guy. We've got a couple prints, but nothing that matches anything in our database. You double check her security? The locks?"

"Yes, Dad. I'm staying for a while until this cools down. Make sure they're safe."

Logan lets out a low whistle. "I bet she loved that."

I chuckle, my eyes automatically going back to her slumbering form on the couch. "Nah, not too much."

"She ever hear anything about her family?"

"What do you mean?"

"She asked me a while back to look into her parents. Probably forgot with all that's been going on. Lemme know if she needs anything, okay?"

"Will do. Thanks for checking in. Let me know if that Chad guy has anything."

"Right. Later."

I spend the next half hour messing with her security system and checking on all the entrances and exits. I spot the grooves in the window where the bastard must have broken in as I'm looking around. I can't tell if the resulting burn in my stomach is anger or shame. I can't help but feel like I should have been here. *Strike one. I* shouldn't have turned her away after I got out of the Marines. *Strike two.* Hell if I'm going to let there be a strike three.

The monitor squawks so I jog upstairs feeling like I'm all thumbs. I hadn't been lying when I said I was used to kids. The twins practically made me their bitch when they were born, but this kid is different. This kid is mine.

Fuck if that isn't equal parts amazing and terrifying.

He stares up at me and reaches out his hands. I lift him up and cradle him awkwardly in my arms. The smell coming from his little butt ranks up there with the smell of uniforms and gear after a long stint in the field. I take him to the table in the corner and try to remember how the hell you change a diaper. If I could direct million-dollar aircraft, I can handle this.

His tiny pants tangle around his legs and it takes a good five minutes just to convince him that I'm not playing some sort of tug-of-war with him. By the time I actually get them off he's smiling at me, which I'll take as a success.

"You're making this difficult, you know. We could have been done by now. I bet you don't pull this kind of nonsense with your mom."

He answers by blowing spit bubbles.

"I see you've got her attitude. Which is a hell of a good thing. Just don't tell her I said so."

Butt clean and redressed, I lift Cole up and turn to find Olivia watching us.

She clears her throat. "Sorry, I didn't mean to spy on you guys. I called for you, but you must not have heard me."

I ignore that, not wanting to get into it. "You okay?"

"I'm fine. I told you I would be." She holds out her hands for the kid, but I angle him backwards.

"Doctor's orders. You need to be resting. No heavy lifting or strenuous activity," I tell her.

"Ben, c'mon. He's not that heavy. I would hardly characterize that as heavy lifting."

I frown at Cole. "I think we should be insulted." The kid actually mimics my frown and surprises a laugh out of me. "See?" I tell her.

"Ganging up on me already, I see."

She tries to hide it, but I can see the beads of sweat on her hairline and the pallor of her skin. I've known men twice her size that bitch about wounds a lot less severe. "Get used to it later. Right now you need to get your ass back down on the couch. I'll order something for dinner."

"You're still not staying here, Ben."

Cole laughs at her and I can't help my smile. I haven't felt this good in a long time. "We'll talk about it later."

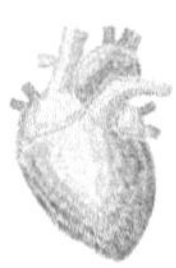

"Let me get those for you," I say, taking the empty paper plates from Olivia as she tries to get up from the couch. Cole holds out his arms to me from his spot on the floor. I manage to balance him and the plates. Out of the two of them, she'd given me more trouble than the kid.

I'd managed to keep her corralled through the afternoon with minimal fuss. The color had finally returned to her cheeks and she'd regained her spunk around the time I forced her to watch all four Lethal Weapon movies in a row.

"Please tell me there isn't another one. Seriously. I'd rather eat another runny hospital breakfast." She sits up on the couch and brushes the hair that's escaped the ponytail away from her face. Even in sweatpants and an old T-shirt, I still want her. In another time, in another place, I could have had her. I look away until the feeling passes. When I'm reasonably sure I can control myself from slipping behind her on the couch, I turn back.

Her face is tight with concern and I can tell by the way her eyes flick to my ear that she's studying my hearing aide. I sit back down on the chair and bounce Cole on my knee to keep my hands busy. Might as well go ahead and get it over with, much as I don't like talking about it she was bound to ask sooner or later.

"I'm sorry," she says, "I didn't mean to stare. I'd heard around that you'd been hurt."

"You don't have to apologize."

"No, I do. People used to see Cole sometimes, even people we knew, and would stare. You can't even tell anything is different about him. Not really. But most everyone around here knows me. They can't help it, really, but I get it. I get it and I should know better."

"You get used to it."

"I want to ask what happened, but I don't want to pry."

I swallow thickly. "Can't we go back to the surprise baby news? That was a much more interesting conversation." The pity in her eyes doesn't help. "Don't look at me like that. It's over. I'll never be able to hear out of my right ear, but the gadget helps. I'm alive."

Realization dawns on her face. "I'll try to be more aware when I talk."

"Don't. You don't have to treat me any differently."

"Is that why you got out?"

The credits from the last movie come to a stop and the DVD resets to the menu screen, but neither of us move to change it. The soundtrack fills the dim room with background noise and lulls the little guy into a stupor against my chest.

"I couldn't stay in, not with my injuries."

"Injuries?"

I tap my head with a finger. "TBI. Traumatic brain injury. But let's not talk about me. What about this guy?"

She smiles at him, her love for him brightens everything about her. Not something I ever thought I'd find attractive about a woman, but on her it's beautiful. "It's been rough, I'm not going to lie. But I didn't do it alone. Jack and Sofie were there for me every step of the way."

"I'm glad. I'm sorry that I wasn't there for you. I never really planned on having kids, but I want you to know that I'll do right by the both of you."

"I don't expect you to do anything other than get to know him. I would love for you to be a part of his life. But..." she trails off, her fingers picking at the blanket covering her legs.

"But, what?"

"I only want you to do that if you plan on being there, for everything. For always. I don't want him to lose as many people as I have. If I can protect him from even the smallest part of that pain, I will. I just don't want him to get hurt."

She doesn't say it, she doesn't really have to, but I can tell a part of her pain was caused by me.

"I promise you this, Liv. I will always be there for him. That's one thing that you won't ever have to worry about again."

"Thank you," she says, her voice thick with emotion. "And I know I said it before but I'm sorry for not trying harder to tell you. For being a coward, basically. There was so much going on after my dad's heart attack, then dealing with Cole's surgeries. To say I was overwhelmed is an understatement. That doesn't excuse it, but that's all I've got."

"Like I said, you don't have to apologize. How about we consider this a clean start? And don't consider this as anything other than a self-serving offer. I was a jerk to you."

"Deal."

Cole shifts against my chest. "When do they start talking?"

"He could start any time now. He's mostly an observer though, so I think it could be a while," Olivia says around a yawn. "I've been trying to get him to say Mom for weeks, but he hasn't."

"I'll have him calling me Dad in no time."

"Fat chance," she says, grinning at me.

"Time for bed. I'll put him down and then come help you up if you need it," I tell her when Cole starts to fuss.

She sighs. "Ben, seriously, you don't have to do all of this."

"Complain one more time."

"I'm just sayin'—"

"Yeah, yeah."

"Fine. If you want to be stubborn and unreasonable, you go right ahead. Sleep on the couch for all I care."

We head upstairs where she breaks off to her bedroom and I go to the kid's room. He murmurs as I lay him down in his crib, but settles back into sleep. I make sure the monitor by his bed is on and take the other set with me. I pull his door closed a ways and find Olivia in the master bath.

I'd dumped my shit in her closet so I go and retrieve my toothbrush and a change of clothes. She doesn't say anything when I come back in the bathroom shirtless, but I don't miss the way her eyes flicker over my bare chest. Shoulder to shoulder, we brush our teeth. All the while she's trying to ignore me in the mirror which makes me want to smile. I'm such a dick for enjoying her nearness so much.

She finishes and rinses, high-tailing it out of the bathroom like she couldn't wait to get out of there. I follow and plug my phone into the outlet beside her bed in case Logan has any updates for me. The more time that passes, the more I worry they'll never catch the asshole. I won't feel comfortable until they do.

"Do you want me to get some blankets for the couch?" Olivia asks after grabbing some clothes from her dresser. She hovers in the bathroom doorway, clutching them to her chest.

"Don't need 'em."

Her brows furrow. "Are you sure? It can be chilly sometimes."

"Not sleeping downstairs, Liv."

Her eyes flicker to the bed. "You don't mean you're going to sleep with me."

"I do and I am." I pull back the covers and slide in. The scent of her curls around me and I can feel every muscle relax and tighten at the same time. That scent has haunted my dreams for fucking months.

"Do you think that's a good idea?" she says timidly.

"I'm not gonna try anything. You're in too much pain for that right now." I let the implication that she may not be in so much pain later hang in the air.

"You would be fine on the couch."

"I'm going to be fine right here."

We have a little Mexican standoff as she glares at me from across the room. She huffs, spinning around to the bathroom. When she comes out in a pair of shorts that barely cover her ass and a skimpy tank top that leaves *not a whole helluva lot* to the imagination, I almost swallow my own tongue.

Maybe sleeping in the same bed wasn't such a good idea.

CHAPTER FIFTEEN

OLIVIA

Movement wakes me and I'm thankful that I'm in my own bed this time. My eyes adjust to the darkness and I see Ben beside me thrashing on the bed. His muscles are coiled beneath his skin, sweat sheens his forehead and his heart beats a visible pulse in his throat. As my nerves calm, my mind races to catch up. I don't know what to do. I've heard of PTSD and the resulting nightmares, but I can't remember if I'm supposed to touch him or wake him or what. A crying baby, I can handle, but I don't know what to do to help the man beside me. Ben comes awake with a jerk, his eyes finding mine in the darkness.

He doesn't say anything, he just pulls me down and fits himself against my back. Finally, I ask, "Are you okay?"

"Yeah, I'm good." He gasps for breath. "Just give me a few minutes."

I don't know what to say. I don't know if it's smart to have him hold me like this when everything is so messed up. The only thing I do know is that I want to take his mind off of whatever horrors he just relived.

"Does that happen often?"

"Nah, not really. Talking about it yesterday must have brought back the memories is all."

Sadness wells in my chest. Without thinking about it, my hand moves to cover his around my waist. "I'm sorry for bringing it up."

"Don't be." We're quiet for a few minutes and then he asks, "If I woke you up, I don't mind sleeping downstairs in case it happens again. It's pointless of me to be here if you aren't getting any sleep."

With the memory of his fear fresh on my mind, I say, "No, it's okay. I'm used to waking up every couple hours with Cole."

"Are you sure?" His hand flexes against the bared skin of my waist.

"Yes," I manage. "Yes, it's fine."

"Tell me something," he says.

"About what?"

He squeezes me tighter. "Anything to get my mind off it. Just talk to me."

I blurt the first thing that comes to mind. "Did you know I started looking into my birth parents?"

"Logan may have mentioned it."

I shake my head at him. "I swear you three are worse than a bunch of chicks. He learned they were very poor—to the point where child services was called several times. They'd filed bankruptcy a year or so before I was given up. The notes in the file said that my biological father got involved with drugs. There was some sort of incident—they didn't go into too much detail and I don't remember it. Anyway, that's what I've learned so far."

"Did your dad know?"

I nod, before remembering we're in the dark. "Yes, I told him at the same time I spilled about the pregnancy. He gave me what information he had, which was very little."

Short-lived relief fills me when I hear him chuckle, before he asks, "How did *that* go over?"

I think back to that conversation with my dad, how supportive he was, and have to work to speak past the lump forming in my throat. "He actually wasn't real surprised."

Ben is quiet for a moment, before I hear him clear his throat. "What made you want to look for them now, after all this time?"

"When I learned I was pregnant, it was just something I

felt like I had to know." My throat burns with emotion. "I can't help but wonder now that if I'd known my family, maybe I would have had some warning, or some way to prevent Cole's illness." I'd known Ben long enough to know his family didn't have the predisposition for heart conditions.

His hand moves to my hip and he pulls my body closer to him. "Stop. You don't have to be around that boy for five minutes to know how much he's loved. You're a great mom. You don't need to beat yourself up for things that are out of your control. But I know that's easier said than done, trust me."

I wonder what he has to beat himself up about. Does it have to do with his nightmares? His injuries? I ache to know what haunts him, but now probably isn't the best time to ask.

As he holds onto me in the darkness, I feel myself softening toward him. I should have known there was a reason why he kept himself away from me.

And now I'm determined to find out exactly what it is.

Unable to fall asleep for the fear that he'll have another nightmare, I listen to the sound of his breathing until the sun streams in through the windows. I scooch down the bed, trying not to wake him as I slither out of his hold. I nearly manage to make it free when his fingers tighten around me.

"Where are you goin'?"

"Check on Cole. Make breakfast." Escape the warm, fluttery feeling that's come back to life in my stomach after spending a night pressed up against him.

"He awake?"

I gulp. His voice is all morning-rough and gravelly. The cocoon of us under the sheets is too enticing. "No, but I still want to check on him, just in case."

"You can, but I want a minute with you first."

"Everything okay?"

His thumb begins a lazy pattern on my stomach. "Everything's fine. First time I've woken up actually feeling like I got some sleep."

"No more nightmares?" For some reason, I find myself holding my breath. It could be the fact that I want him to be okay. Or the slow heat that's begun to build in my stomach. Maybe a heady combination of both.

"Nah. Slept like a baby with you next to me."

His candid statement steals the breath from my lungs. "Good," I manage.

"Thank you," he says, his voice low.

"For what?"

"For chasing away my demons."

The hand on my stomach urges me to turn until I'm facing him. He looks so innocent with his face soft in half-sleep, his eyes a darker shade of blue in the morning. My fingers go to his chest and I note the new scars marring the skin there. I finger one of them, remembering how angry he was when he came home from his last deployment and the look on his face when he woke from his nightmare.

I open my mouth to ask about them, once and for all, but his hand slips from my hip to cup the weight of my ass and the words get stuck in my throat. The pain in my side and shoulder diminish underneath a rush of desire so potent that my entire body tenses.

"Ben?"

A small smile curves his lips. Lips that are inching their way closer and closer to *my* lips. And then his mouth brushes mine. There aren't words to describe how it feels to be able to touch him again, to kiss him, after all this time. Despite all that's changed between us, despite the months that have passed, I feel like a part of me has come home. For that reason, I melt against him, finally, and kiss him back.

He releases me for a moment to look into my eyes, our lips just barely touching. He presses a series of soft kisses to my jaw, my eyelids, then back to my lips. Then we're kissing slowly, deeply. One arm rests beneath my head, the other cupping my jaw as he claims me completely.

No matter how much I've tried to deny it, I've never been anything but his.

My fingers slide down from where they're clutching his shoulders to the muscles of his back. Oh God, and I swear there is nothing more perfect than the weight of him above me. I open one leg and encircle his hip, arching against him.

He breaks the kiss to inhale deeply. When he looks up his eyes are burning with desire. For me. I remember this feeling all too well. Our one night together was fuel for a year of fantasies and Ben far exceeds all of them in real life.

He starts to dive down for another kiss and we freeze at the sound of Cole's cry over the monitor.

My fingers dig into his back for a second, then I let loose, tapping him on the shoulder. "I, um, I should go get him."

Ben lifts up and I scoot out from under him, thankful for the cool air. I hear him plop on the bed and groan into a pillow behind me.

One day and I couldn't even keep my hands off of him. I press a hand to my hot face as I walk into Cole's room, body still thrumming from our kiss.

He is trouble. A big, hot, nearly-naked-in-my-bed pile of trouble.

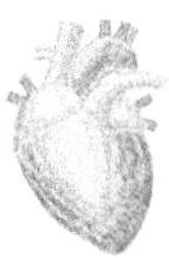

The baby squeals as Ben topples the tower they've been working to build. I smile from where I'm sitting on the patio. After this morning, I've strategically kept my distance. Much as I like kissing Ben, I'm not sure it's the best thing for either of us right now.

Ben looks up as Cole slings the blocks around on the blanket. "He was born on—"

"May 17th."

"Why Benjamin Cole?" Ben asks as he watches Cole's antics with a smile on his face.

I blush. I hadn't considered when I named him that I would have to explain the story. I clear my throat. "I wanted him to have a part of you—that's important to me. But I also wanted him to have his own name to go by, no offense."

"None taken," he murmurs as we reach the swings.

"Anyway, I know Marines are also called warriors. I may or may not have looked up all the boy names that mean warrior. Plus, Cole Walker sounds pretty badass, doesn't it?"

He chuckles. The sound is low and sends ripples through my stomach. "It does."

As Cole plays, Ben's smiles at me. "Thank you."

I glance up at him. "For what?"

He opens his mouth to answer, but Cole squeals in happiness and urges Ben to knock the tower down. Ben gives me a small smile and turns his attention to the baby, who is over the moon with all of the attention. As I take in the sight of them, I feel my heart squeeze.

"I'm sorry that you had to go through his surgeries alone," Ben says.

"Thanks. He came through them like a champ, though." Cole punctuates the statement with a squeal as the tower falls.

"I promise you won't have to go through anything alone again."

I turn sharply to study Ben's face to see if he realizes what he just said, how much it meant to me, but he's lifting Cole from the blanket and snuggling him to his chest.

I admire the picture they make for a moment before my phone starts ringing in my pocket. Because of Cole's condition he can't spend too much time doing strenuous activities, so I motion to Ben and we start heading back inside.

I answer the phone as Ben starts picking up the toys.

"Hello?"

"Hey, Olivia, it's Logan."

"Oh, hey. What's up?"

"We have some new developments. Can I meet you at your house?"

All happy feelings from the morning with Ben and Cole turn immediately to panic. "Sure," I reply around the lump in my throat. "We'll be here."

"Good. Give me about ten minutes. Is Ben there or should I give him a call?"

"No, he's here." Ben perks up and sends me a questioning look. When I'm unable to do little more than send him a frightened look, he carefully lifts Cole and comes to my side.

"Good. See you soon."

"Who was that?" Ben asks.

"Logan. He'll be here in a few minutes to discuss the case."

"Did he say what it was about?" Ben rests his spare hand on the small of my back as he guides me back inside.

"Just that there were new developments. He didn't go into much detail."

We wait in the living room for a few tense minutes watching as Cole entertains himself on the floor. When the bell rings, Ben is up in a flash. Murmured male voices come from the entryway and they appear in the living room. I pick Cole up so I have something to do with my hands as Logan takes a seat on the couch.

"Hey, Livvie," he says, running a hand over his nearly-bald head.

"Logan. Tell me you've got some good news."

"Of sorts. Do you know Chad Trenton?"

My lips pull into a frown. "Of course. We went out a couple of times until—" I break off and glance back at Ben. "Until a few days ago. Maybe a week? It was a little bit before the incident. I haven't seen him since."

"Is there any reason why he would want to hurt you?"

"Chad? I don't think so, I mean, he wasn't happy with me the last time I saw him because, well, I broke things off between us. But he's not the kind of guy that would hurt anyone."

"We'll take that into consideration, but he's one of a few suspects with a vehicle matching the description of the assailant's. We've brought him in for questioning just to be safe. Is there anyone else you can think of that may have a grudge against you?"

I shake my head. "No one at all. I've barely even left the house over the last couple of months."

"For what it's worth, I don't think he's our guy either, but we want to be sure. The other is an out of state vehicle. Some low-life named Mason Smith, lives in the next county over. He's a local thug. Drug dealer. Has a group of women that he pimps out on occasion."

"I guess it's too much to hope that you're bringing him in for questioning, too."

"He wasn't at his residence when they went by, but we've got men out looking for him. In the meantime, just keep aware. Set your alarms and check your locks, just in case. There is something about this that isn't sitting right with me."

"Of course. I appreciate the update. I know you're doing all you can."

Ben walks Logan out. When he returns, I send him a relieved smile, "I'm so glad we finally have some leads. I've heard of Mason before. He lives on the other side of town. I highly doubt Chad could have anything to do with this. He's not the brightest crayon in the box, but he couldn't hurt a fly."

He watches as I flit around the living room, tidying up things that don't really require tidying. "You can't be so sure of that."

"Mason is a drug dealer. If anyone has anything to do with this, I'd bet it would be him. Besides, Chad and I were really just beginning to see each other. Even after he saw us the other night, he wasn't that upset. Even when I broke things off."

Ben blocks the kitchen doorway with an arm as I try to squeeze through with a handful of dirty dishes. "You're delusional if you think he wasn't pissed off when he found me with my hands all over you."

"Your hands weren't all over me," I scoff.

"Baby, my hands were full of tits and ass. Any man who walks in on that, especially with a woman like you, they're going to be pissed off."

I look at him sharply. "A woman like me?"

"Yeah, a woman like you."

"What does that even mean?"

"It means if I were in his shoes, I would have been pissed off, too."

"So you're saying that you would have gunned me down in a parking lot if you saw me with another man?"

"I'm saying any man can snap, given the right circumstances. Losing you," he says, staring deep into my eyes, "that would definitely throw any man over the edge."

I don't even know how to respond so I duck under his arm and distract my racing heart with rinsing out the dishes. Desperate to change the subject, I blurt, "I bet you're relieved that you don't have to keep staying over here, huh?"

Ben follows me in the kitchen, leaning against the island behind me. "What do you mean?"

"Well, the police have some leads now. All they need to do is bring the guys in for questioning, then this will all be over. Do you want me to help you pack?"

"What the hell are you talking about?"

Ben turns me around to face him. I keep my gaze steady on his neck. "I'm just saying that now that they're making some headway on the case, you can relax a little bit. Get back to your own life."

"I don't fucking think so."

"You...don't fucking think so...what?"

"You're delusional. We just had the conversation about keeping you safe until this man is behind bars. That doesn't change because there have been a few developments."

"Ben, this is getting ridiculous. I'm fine. We're going to be fine. You don't have to stay here. If you're worried about me keeping the baby from you, you don't have to be. You're welcome to see him anytime you want. We can go see a custody lawyer and get started on that if it makes you feel any better."

Ben leans his weight on the kitchen counter and crosses his arms across his muscular chest. "It's not about the baby, Olivia. It's about you and me."

I flush and move to leave, but he cages me against the counter. "You mentioned that before but...things are just too complicated right now. I have to focus on Cole. I think it's probably best that there isn't a 'you and me.'" I can't entertain the thought of Ben and I again, even though my body is screaming otherwise. I would only lose him again. Like I lost my father and—

"Let me take you upstairs and I'll remind you of all the reasons why there should be," comes Ben's voice, low in my ear.

And that's exactly why I can't go there again. With one sentence, he solidifies my conviction and pours a bucket of ice cold water over my traitorous body which was once again heating up at Ben's sinful words and close proximity. There's no doubt in my mind that I can take Ben up on his offer right now and he would more than deliver on his promise. Attraction, sex...they've never been an issue between Ben and I. But I need more than that now. Cole needs more than that. And we can't have both.

"I'm not the kind of guy who can give you the white picket fence, but I can promise you that it's a night you'll

never forget." Ben's truth, which he gave me himself. He gave me the best part of himself that night. And it would have to be enough.

"I don't think so. I'm going to go upstairs and take a shower. You're more than welcome to stay for dinner." I move to leave, but he doesn't budge. "I'm serious, Ben."

"So am I."

"Are you listening to a word I'm saying?" I exclaim.

"Not really. Especially not when all that's coming out of your mouth is bullshit."

"When did you get so stubborn?"

"I've always been stubborn. You just always used to agree with me, so it was okay."

I square my shoulders, placing my hands on my hips, and give him my best no-bullshit glare. "Well, this is one thing that we aren't going to agree on, no matter how stubborn you are."

He moves in closer, going in for the one spot that he knows from experience always makes me weak. He presses his lips to my ear and whispers, "You sure about that, Spitfire?"

CHAPTER SIXTEEN

BEN

Livvie looks at me with wild eyes. I recognize the primitive fight or flight response. The way she wants to protect herself from me, keep the soft, vulnerable part of her hidden. The part of her that I like so much. Her gaze flickers around me searching for a way out.

"I'm not going anywhere, Liv. Get used to it."

I step back a bit and let her slide by. She sends me panicked glances as she disappears around the corner. Cole bangs on the little playpen for attention. I pick him up, careful to do so by holding his butt and neck the way Livvie taught me in order to not agitate his still-healing wound from his second surgery. He isn't quite sure of me yet, no matter how much fun we had this morning with the blocks. To stave off the tantrum I can feel coming, I give the kid a handful of snacks I find in the cupboard, which seems to satisfy him for the moment.

After pouring myself a cup of coffee—it seemed a better option than the six-pack I normally down each day—I sit at the island with the little guy and check my email. There are a couple of messages from people I knew in the Corps, the regular spam and adverts. Nothing from the one person I've been reaching out to for months now, to no avail.

I zone out, suddenly looking up to find myself in the desert with the body parts of my fallen men around me. The trucks are belching black smoke and cackling flames. Greene has come to and is screaming inconsolably. I can't hear him. I can only see the ravaged stain of pain on his face. He's almost white with it and a river of blood surrounds him. My gear and clothes are soaked in it. My vision spots white and I look up to see the smoke of another rocket coming straight for us.

A loud *smack* breaks me from the waking nightmare, sending shockwaves throughout my body. I tune back in to the present and find a red-faced Cole staring at me, his snack spread out in a wave on the floor. My fingers grip the edge of the table. I take a deep breath, offering up a weak smile.

"Sorry, kid. Was I ignoring you?" I get to my knees and rake up the food with shaking hands. Cole hiccups above me and a tear streaks down his cheek. "We'll get you cleaned up and I'll make you another snack. Does that sound good?"

I get to my knees, tossing the food in the trash and the bowl in the sink. I wipe the tear from his face and there, just for a second, he leans into my hand and closes his eyes. The earlier panic melts away and a seed of connection is born between us. I didn't get to bond with him while he was in Livvie's belly. I didn't get to see him when he was born. I hadn't even quite wrapped myself around the concept of being a father. But touching him, seeing him, having a moment with him, makes our bond real for the first time. That simple wonder is enough to wipe away the cold sweat and the remaining dregs of fear.

He opens his eyes and smiles at me. I smile back. "Yeah," I whisper. "I think that sounds good, too."

His second round of snacks taken care of, I hunt around the kitchen for fixings for dinner. There isn't much to speak of when it comes to food, and though I'd be satisfied with a sandwich and chips, Livvie needs a good meal to keep up her strength.

A few minutes later and I've still got nothing. My cooking skills range from MREs to microwavable noodles, but I don't see any of those in her fancy cabinets.

"Next time I tell you not to sell your car for a motorcycle, maybe you'll listen," my approaching mother snaps.

I unbuckle Cole from where he's happily tossing his

snack and watching it tumble to the ground with maniacal laughter.

"It's not just a motorcycle, woman," I hear my dad growl. "It's a ticket to freedom from your constant nagging."

"I can't wait until you drive that monstrosity on my driveway. I'll show you exactly where you can stuff your nagging."

My mother flounces into the kitchen in a wave of AquaNet and attitude, where she immediately pounces on me. "I've given you plenty of time, Benjamin. Plenty of time. Now, your father is under some misguided impression that we should give you two more time to settle after everything that's happened, but I'll not be kept from my only grandson one day longer. Or my future daughter-in-law," she adds with a pointed look.

Cole smashes his hands on the table in agreement, and my mom descends upon him with a sound of delight. Dad follows with the twins and I look to the ceiling for strength.

Dad turns to me and says, "I kept her away as long as I could, but there comes a time in a man's life when our stamina just isn't what it used to be."

Livvie chooses that moment to return and blushes prettily at the entrance to the kitchen. Her hair falls around her shoulders in dark red waves. She smiles shyly at my dad and says, "Hey, Mr. Hart, Mrs. Hart. I'm sorry if you felt that you had to stay away. I-I would have come sooner, but—"

"No buts," Mom interrupts. "Lord knows I raised Benjamin for eighteen years and then some. I know just what a pain in the ass he can be, and quite frankly, I'm glad I can finally wash my hands of him and have him be some other woman's problem."

Mom smiles at me, and I wrap an arm around her shoulders and pull her to my side so I can press a kiss into her hair. "His stamina is just fine," Mom also informs me, as though it were something I need to be made aware of.

Livvie hastily changes the subject. "Why don't y'all join us for something to eat?" Though I doubt she knows what she's getting herself into. Hanging around occasionally when we were kids is entirely different from becoming a part of my crazy family.

"What are we having?" Mom asks.

I nod to the stove. "I was making omelets."

"Gross," Mitchell says. "Ben can't cook for shit."

"You watch your mouth, Mitchell Hart," Mom says sharply. "It just so happens I brought stuff to make lasagna. I figured the two of you could use a good home cooked meal."

"You don't have to cook for us, Mrs. Hart—" Livvie starts.

"I won't hear a word about it, girl. Why don't you

boys help your father cart in the groceries? I'm going to sit for a spell and get to know my grandson."

"Careful," I tell her. "Make sure to watch out for his chest. Don't pick him up by the armpits. Always lift from the neck and butt."

"Oh, my," she says as she picks him up. "What a handsome little boy!"

Livvie sits next to my mom at the kitchen table. "He knows it, too, I think. He's a little flirt."

"They mentioned it on the T.V. About his heart condition. Is he going to be okay?"

"He's just fine. He had his second surgery a few weeks ago and will have to have another within the next few years."

"Will he need some sort of transplant?"

"Hopefully not," Livvie says. "If all goes well, his third surgery should take care of everything. He'll have to be careful, and he'll always be on medication." She runs a finger over Cole's hand. "But he's just as happy as any other baby. Maybe tires a little bit more easily, and we have to be extra careful about germs and all that, but he's a strong boy. He's a fighter."

"Oh, absolutely," Mom says. Mitchell ambles in, his arms loaded down with grocery bags. She speaks to him without even looking first, "Mitchell James, don't you even think about setting those bags down on the floor and wandering off on that damn phone. You unload those groceries on the counter there and put the bags in the trash."

Mitchell groans and changes direction.

Livvie looks at my mom in awe. "I want to be you when I grow up."

My mom winks at her proudly. "You stick with me, honey. You've got one of ours now. They're a handful."

"So I've learned," Livvie says, looking at me.

I hold my hands up. "I haven't done a damn thing."

"You know he moved himself in with me." *Not this shit again.*

Mom nods her head. "Good. That just shows that I've taught him well."

Livvie groans. "I give up. I swear arguing with your family is like arguing with a bunch of rocks."

"Stay around us long enough, you're bound to pick up the same trait. It comes in handy with dealing with these guys."

"I don't know how you did it with the four of them."

"Wine," Mom answers and they share a laugh.

Dad nudges me on the shoulder. "You gonna take the next week off? If so, just let me know so we can get you covered at the shop."

"I will if that's all right with you. I'd like to keep close, at least until we're sure this is over."

"They got some leads?"

"A few. We'll see if they pan out."

"Good to hear, Son. And feel free to take as much time as you need."

"Thanks, Pops. I appreciate it."

He nods to me, then turns to Mom and says, "Alright woman, the men folk are hungry. Are we gonna eat or what?"

OLIVIA

After spending the day surrounded by Ben's family, I come to the decision that letting him have his way is the easiest way to handle the situation. After all, I'm the one in the wrong here. I'm the one who kept his son a secret from him. He just wants to protect his child, and that's understandable, I reason. Once the threat passes and things settle down, we'll be able to set up a more acceptable situation. One that doesn't involve a living, breathing temptation sharing my bed.

With Ben's family still happily chattering away in the kitchen, I take Cole upstairs to put him down for a nap. I'm drifting in and out myself when I hear a knock on the door. I ease myself out from under Cole's body and tug a spare afghan around me, careful not to jostle my shoulder.

When I reach the foot of the stairs, I see Ben at the front door and beyond him Sofie and Jack. *Oh, crap.*

Sofie and Jack in the same room is bad by itself, but

adding Ben to the mix is a surefire way for things to blow up now that they aren't bound by social niceties.

I wince as soon as Jack's eyes come to me. "Explain."

"Well, come in. Don't make Sofie stand outside."

Jack glances behind him, looks Sofie up and down, and turns back as though he didn't see her. I resist the urge to roll my eyes. I don't know what it is between those two, but they need to get over it or get back together before I wring both their necks.

When Jack doesn't make room, Sofie pushes her way inside. She immediately comes to my side. "Hi, Cole's dad! So nice to finally see you in the picture." She waves to Ben, who's closing the door behind a still-steamed Jack. "But I didn't realize he came with a party. What's going on?"

"Why don't you come in the kitchen? I'll make everyone something to drink. Ben's mom made lasagna and there's enough for a football team. You can make yourselves a plate."

Ben stops me by the entrance to the kitchen with a hand at my waist. I look up at his face, steadily ignoring the way my body reacts to his closeness.

"I'm going to go check on my parents. You okay here?"

"Yes, I'm not a child."

He presses a short kiss to my lips and I raise a hand to his chest—to pull him closer or keep him at a distance,

I'm not sure. His guerrilla-style tactics are hell on my resistance.

I ignore that and the looks on Jack and Sofie's faces as I pull out tea and some extra plates. They might not want to eat, but I'm suddenly overcome with the urge to stuff my face, if only to keep from their inquisition.

"Uh," Sofie starts. "What the hell was *that*?"

"I don't want to talk about it," I say around a bite of garlic bread.

"Too bad," Jack says. "A few days ago, the two of you were barely speaking and now he's walking around your house like he owns the place. He's my friend, and I love him, but what the fuck?"

"Keep your voice down, Jack."

Sofie nods. "I have to say, I agree with Jack."

I narrow my eyes at my supposed best friend. Jack is supposed to be the enemy, and she should be on my side. What the hell?

"About time you agreed with me on something."

"Don't start." Sofie turns back to me. "Spill."

I rub the dull ache in my temple. "I was the one who was shot here. Shouldn't you guys be giving *him* a hard time?"

Jack stops his furtive study of Sofie and looks back at me. "Don't pull the injured card. I didn't put up with a year of your wishy-washy bullshit for things to change and you not even tell me."

"It's not wishy-washy bullshit, Jack. Ben is just here so he and Cole can get to know each other. I feel safer with him here since the shooting. That's all."

"Oh, so he knows he's Cole's dad now?" Jack asks quickly.

I study him suspiciously for a beat. "Yeah. The news blabbed all about it while I was in the hospital and, you know...he was there, so..." I trail off, once again feeling like crap and not liking the way all of that went down.

"I'm glad you're okay," Sofie says, placing a hand on my shoulder.

"We're fine, really." I glance back up toward my bedroom, where Cole sleeps peacefully. "I just hope we continue to be so lucky."

"I'm going to go have a talk with Ben," Jack says before grabbing his tea and bee-lining for the huddle of people outside.

"By 'talk with Ben' he means he's going to go grill him about his intentions." Sofie's eyes linger on Jack a touch longer than necessary.

I groan. "Okay, I am over this conversation, Sof."

"That's too damn bad. You gotta catch me up here. So he found out he's the baby-daddy at the hospital and what now? He's shacked up here?"

"I don't know, really. He says he's here because he's freaked out about me getting shot. My plan was to have him be a part of Cole's life. But he seems to think we should just pick up where we left off."

"And you don't want to?" she asks, picking apart a piece of garlic bread.

"I have enough on my plate right now, learning the whole Mom thing and then going back to work. I don't know if it would be a relationship out of necessity or based on real feelings. Does he just want to be with me because I'm the mother of his kid? It's completely out of order. Not to mention that there is some lunatic going around shooting at me. I'm still trying to find out the cause of all this mess." I gesture with my bandaged arm and wince at the tenderness. "A relationship with Ben isn't part of the plan."

Sofie's eyes trail back to Jack, who is talking to Ben outside. "Yeah, well, love doesn't always follow the rules, Liv."

"Even so, I don't have time for a relationship right now. I go back to work in a few weeks, and I just need to focus on Cole."

Cole, thankfully, interrupts the inquisition just as Ben and Jack walk back inside.

"I'll get him," Ben says, already starting up the stairs.

Sofie gives me a pointed stare, which I steadfastly ignore.

"Hey, little man," the monitor cackles.

Oh, sweet baby Jesus. All the female things inside of me turn to mush.

"Rise and shine, sleepyhead." A chuckle sounds, followed by a few plaintive cries from Cole. "I know, I know. You don't know who I am, but we're going to get to know each other. I bet you're hungry. Let's get you changed, and we'll hunt down your mom and go play with your new family."

Sofie makes more eyes at me, but I'm too distracted by the sweet-as-hell conversation between them to notice.

"There you go, all clean. See? That wasn't so bad. We may get the hang of this after all."

When I hear footsteps coming down the stairs, I book it to the living room, not wanting to be caught listening to Ben's conversation. Sofie and Jack follow closely behind. Ben rounds the corner to the living room with Cole lying on his bare chest, bundled up in a camouflage sleeper outfit.

"He's all changed, Momma."

I hold out my hands and Ben passes him to me. As my arms are full of squirming baby, I am unable to resist when Ben places another swift kiss on my lips. Then he turns to grab something from the kitchen and leaves me staring after him like I don't have any sense. I catch Sofie's knowing look before retreating to the rocker to feed Cole, only to find Ben's mom, Sheila, at the backdoor with his father and brothers, giving me a knowing look of her own.

Somehow, my life has spiraled straight past normal and into crazy town.

246

CHAPTER SEVENTEEN

BEN

IT IS AN IMPOSSIBLE TASK, and that is saying something considering some of the shit I've had to do over the years. I stare at the mountain of products before me and vow to just grab one if I can't make a decision in the next five minutes. You'd think a man who held the lives of twenty other Marines in his hands could handle picking out a pack of fucking diapers, but you'd be wrong.

"Ben?"

I turn my head and find my cousin Chloe and a big, hulking bastard walking up to me. I frown, because I don't recognize him. "Chloe? What the hell are you doing here?"

Her face breaks into a wide smile and she throws her arms

around my shoulders. "Visiting the family," she answers after a lengthy hug. "I didn't know you were back in town, too. Aunt Sheila must be slacking on the inter-family gossip."

"Must be." I shift my attention to the guy now standing behind her. I jerk my chin and extend the hand not holding a pack of diapers. "Hey, man. I'm Ben."

"Gabe."

"Nice to meet you."

Chloe glances pointedly at the package in my hands. "Got something to tell me there, Ben? Your parents didn't have any more surprise anniversary babies, did they?"

I choke out a laugh. "No, thank God. I think the twins were more than enough. No—uh, this is actually for me." I clear my throat. "For my son."

Her eyes widen. "When the hell did you have a baby?"

Gabe puts a hand over Chloe's mouth and gives me a sympathetic look. "What she means is congratulations. That's great news, man."

"Thanks." Apparently, this guy knew how to deal with Chloe's outbursts—something that was a constant source of amusement amongst the rest of our family.

Chloe glares at Gabe and jerks his hand away from her mouth. "You know I can speak for myself, right?" She rolls her eyes then looks back at me. "The reason I ask is because I saw you not too long ago and you most definitely didn't have any plans of having kids—nor were you currently even dating anyone. Last I heard, you and Olivia were still dancing arou—ohhhh!"

I look down at the perfectly innocent pack of diapers then back up at her. "Yes, his mom is Livvie. It's—it's a pretty long story."

"I heard my mom talking about something that had to do with her when I was at her house the other day. Is it true she was shot a few weeks ago?"

"That's part of the long story, yes."

Chloe gasps. "Oh, my God, is she okay?"

Gabe interjects before it can become a full-blown discussion in the middle of the grocery store. "Actually, we're about to have dinner at Chloe's place if you want to bring them by. We'd love to have all of you over."

I give Chloe a pointed look. "Maybe then you'll explain the rumor I heard about you on some island last summer."

Chloe blushes and Gabe looks rather smug.

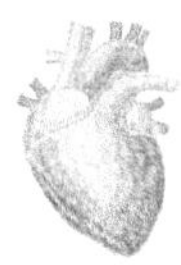

Livvie brushes a hand down her dress and winces when the movement jolts her shoulder. I shift Cole to my other hip and wrap my arm around her waist to support her weight, even though I know she'll manage just fine on her own. She looks up, her lips forming a little '*O*' of shock. When I kiss those lips, it surprises us both.

The moment shatters when Chloe opens the door to her apartment. Her lips pull into a knowing smile when she sees the three of us. I glance back down at Livvie and find her cheeks stained red. A part of me that has long since withered away comes to life, warming me from the inside out.

I urge Livvie forward when Chloe gestures us in. We find Gabe in the kitchen, whipping up something that looks like Heaven and smells even better. Chloe walks past us and leans in to give him a kiss.

"Move over," I tell him. "That smells so good, I might have to kiss the cook, too."

The girls laugh and Chloe says, "Sorry, Ben. He's all mine."

Livvie settles down onto a dining room chair with Cole in her lap. Chloe appears with an ancient set of blocks that must have weathered both of our families combined and dumps them in front of Cole on the table.

As Chloe sits down to chat with Olivia, I leave them to commune with Gabe over beer. Both to escape the feelings that caused me to impetuously kiss Livvie again and to get a feeling for Chloe's new boyfriend.

"Beer?" Gabe asks from the fridge.

"Sure, thanks." I accept the cool bottle gratefully. "What's for dinner?"

"Salad, stuffed shells and homemade brownies for dessert."

"That sounds amazing, man. Thanks again for inviting us over."

"No problem. Chloe's gone on and on about her infamous family, so I couldn't wait to get up here and meet all of you." He finishes stirring some sauce in a pan and turns to me. "I was sorry to hear about your girl. Did they ever catch the bastard who did it?"

I shake my head. "Not yet, though not for lack of trying. My buddy Logan is a cop here. Thankfully." I take a sip from my beer. "No leads yet, but we'll find them."

If it was the last thing I did, I would find whoever threatened my family. That was for damn sure. I may not have a clue as to what the fuck I'm doing with my life or how I'm going to be a dad to a kid when I could barely hold myself together, but I could at least keep them safe. I had to.

The phrase *my family* reverberates through my brain as I take another drink. Olivia laughs in the other room, and my eyes automatically flit to her. I remember the night we spent together and the way she'd laughed when I tried to convince her to make love with me just one more time, even though her body was still shaking from the last orgasm.

"So," Gabe begins as he plates the shells. "I hate to ask

this, but Chloe will eviscerate me later if I don't at least try to get some information out of you."

I can't help but smile. It's good to know she has him wrapped around her finger, though I do feel sorry for the fact that he has to face the little tyrant. "Sure, what's up?"

"How did you not know you had a kid? You sure surprised the hell out of Chloe. And trust me, I've given significant time and effort to the plight."

"We've been on-again, off-again for a while now. I was in the Marines until a few months ago. Anyway, I deployed a while back and we hooked up just before I left. I didn't have access to internet, and the mail service was spotty at best where we were. And I..." I look over at Cole, who's gnawing on a block. "I wasn't in the best shape after that last deployment, for a lot of reasons, and when I saw her, with the baby and all, it was like I shut down. I won't forgive myself for that."

Gabe looks like he wants to say something, but Livvie chooses that moment to holler into the kitchen, "Hey, we're starving here. Are you ladies going to keep clucking, or are we going to eat?"

I help him finish the rest of the food, but the actions don't distract me from my renewed guilt.

After dinner, I walk Olivia and a sleeping Cole back to the car.

"That was nice," Olivia says. "It's been a long time since I've been able to see Chloe. And Gabe seems like a good guy. They make a cute couple. The way they met was so sweet."

"He'll do," I tell her.

Olivia buckles Cole into his seat, and I set his bundle of things next to him. Though it's only been a short time since we've been going out together as a family unit, we've already gotten things like this down to a rhythm. I find myself watching the street for a white SUV as Livvie buckles herself in next to me.

As I make the short drive back to Livvie's house, I scan her yard for odd shadows. Her security system is top-notch, Jack made sure of that, but ever since I moved myself in, I've kept an eye out. Just in case. After the past ten years, it's become second nature to keep an eye on my surroundings. The break-in and the shooting have left a bad taste in my mouth and make the hairs on the back of my neck stand on edge. Even though Logan's co-workers covering the case think both are isolated incidents, I know better than to let my guard down.

Her house is quiet and seemingly safe when we enter. She smiles at me then takes the baby upstairs to put him down. I lean against the back door while Hank runs excited circles around the kitchen. As I wait for Olivia to make her way back downstairs, I cycle between wanting to push her away and never letting her leave my sight.

CHAPTER EIGHTEEN

OLIVIA

I FELT his charged stare all through dinner and it's left me
unsettled in my own skin. I escape to the bathroom after
settling Cole in for the night to splash some water on my
face, though it does little to cool me down.

I take a few deep breaths and tell myself not to be such
a child. We have a kid together, for Christ's sake. I'm going
to have to face him for at least eighteen more years. We
should be able to do things like have dinners and go on
outings without there being this kind of tension between
us. I resolve to ignore whatever lingering feelings I may
have because even if Ben can trust me after my lie, who's
to say he even wants a relationship now?

I repeat these things to myself after freshening up as I

walk down the hallway toward the stairs. I'm so caught up in resolving to ignore Ben that I don't realize he's come upstairs until he's right in front of me.

My feet freeze and my eyes round. My traitorous heart beats an unsteady rhythm in my chest. "Hey," I whisper, because all other words have failed me.

He rocks back on his heels and hooks his thumbs in the pockets of his jeans. "Thought you got lost," he says.

"No—uh—I was just in the bathroom." I shake my head to clear the confusion. "Are you going to bed?"

He takes a step toward me, and I find myself backing up toward the wall. "No, I was coming up to talk to you."

"Me?" I'm completely mortified to find that my voice is little more than a squeak.

"I think it's time we had that talk."

I shake my head. "I don't know if that's such a good idea."

"I'm thinking we're past letting you make decisions about things that concern me for a while. Don't you?"

My cheeks heat. "Look, about that—"

Ben puts a finger on my lips, halting my confessions. "I think it's time for me to talk for a bit." When I nod, he lowers his hand. "I was in a fucked-up place, for a long time, Liv. Truth be told, I'm still in that place. If you were smart you'd be running away from me right now."

Even though I had suspected that something had happened to change the person I once knew, he'd never out-and-out confirmed it. I bring my hands to his cheeks and pull his crystal-blues up to face me. "I don't want to run away from you, Ben."

"You don't deserve to be saddled with a man like me. I knew it when we were together that night. I knew it the first time I kissed you, and I know it now. If I were a good man, I wouldn't be here right now, but I'm not. I want you, everything else be damned."

"Do you—"

He traces the gentle curve of my cheekbone with the tip of his finger and says, "I don't want anyone else. What I want is to spend every day I have with you. Every mundane moment. I don't want to keep letting you slip away."

Thoughts slow to a pathetic crawl and every nerve ending is focused on the soft pass of his skin on mine. "What are you trying to say?"

"I'm saying that you've brought me to my knees, Spit-fire. I tried to get you out of my head and I couldn't. I don't think I want to."

Despite my confusion and the emotional whiplash of the past few weeks, I have to admit that I've missed him, too. So much.

His fingers delve underneath the thin material of my shirt, pushing my bra out of the way as he cups one breast in his big hands. My knees weaken and he wraps his available arm around my waist. He presses my back against the wall.

I gasp for breath that sounds ragged in the darkness of the secluded hallway. "Are you sure that's a good idea?"

"Really?" His teeth catch my earlobe, and he sucks it into his mouth and nibbles. "I'm sure it's probably a bad idea. But don't you remember how *good* the last bad idea we had was?"

He catches my lips in a searing kiss, one that is in no way playful, or loving, or soft. This kiss dominates me, reminds me of all the times I've fantasized about doing exactly this. It ignites a fire inside me that burns away every misgiving I have.

He starts to edge us toward my room, hitching my thighs around his hips as he walks so our lips never break contact. Somehow, we make it to my room without tumbling to the floor in a heap of limbs and lust.

When he reaches to turn on the lamp on the bedside table, I grab his hand to stop him.

"What's wrong?" he asks, pausing his investigation of my bra clasp.

"I would just rather have the light off."

Ben makes a confused sound and flicks on the lamp. "Is something wrong?"

"No, nothing's wrong. I just don't quite look the same."

Understanding dawns and he lays me down on the

bed, climbing between my legs so his face is even with my stomach. "Every inch of you is perfect." His hands travel from my thighs to the hem of my shirt. "Every inch. Do you hear me?"

I squirm in his hold. He'd seen my body pre-baby and mostly obscured by shadows. It's completely different now; the months hadn't dulled the stretchmarks, hadn't taken away the new curves. I'm no supermodel. "I—"

He doesn't even give me a chance to protest. "No. I've spent the last year dreaming about you. About touching you. Tasting you. Seeing you. All of you. Don't hide yourself from me."

My chest warms. It feels like I'm on the edge of a precipice. Taking this step will change everything. Again. "Ben. I'm scared." Of what I'm feeling. Of the future.

He climbs up my body and holds me in his arms, tipping my face up with a hand cupped under my chin. "Don't be. I'm here. What we have is more important than any imperfection you may think you have. It's more important, stronger, than what we're up against." His free hand grips my hip and pulls me closer. "This body grew my son. It nearly died for him. Twice. You have no idea how beautiful that makes you to me. How gorgeous you are. All of you."

He seals this proclamation with a drugging kiss. The first time we were together, it was like we were ravenous, trying to fit in all the taste and touch we could into the short time we had. Now, we have all the time in the world to explore.

And based on the meandering way his hands have begun to map my body, Ben plans on making use of each and every second.

His fingers inch up my stomach, taking my shirt off as he goes, all the while being careful of my arm. He dips down my body to press kisses to each new section of exposed skin. Baring myself this way to him makes me feel vulnerable and exposed.

As he slips my shirt over my head and looks down at my naked body, I'm hit by the sudden irrevocable realization that once we go down this path, there will be no turning back for me.

I can't believe I'm in this place again. Fragile, vulnerable, and essentially at his mercy. They were right when they said only fools fall in love, because that's what I am for this man. A fool.

"Stop," he whispers.

"Stop what?" I manage through a gasp.

His hands slip between my body and the bed to loosen the clasp of my bra. "Stop thinking so much."

"I'm not—" His lips close over my nipple and my sentence is drowned by my own moan.

I've been ready for this ever since he had me undress to change my bandage. Hell, I've been ready since the first time, if I'm being honest.

Now I'm naked from the waist up. He sits up so he's on his knees between my legs. Then he crosses his arms in front of his body and grips his shirt, sliding it up, baring his beautiful body like a veritable feast for my eyes.

I rear up and wrap one arm around his back, cupping his head with the other to pull him down to me. Part of me is screaming that I need to think this through. Is he still upset with me? Is it smart to stir the already-muddy waters? The other part of me completely submits to the kiss, surrendering control to his every whim. I need this, need it so much that I give myself over to his kiss.

It helps that Ben is a phenomenal kisser. That he can, with one press of his lips against mine, make me forget everything but the soft rub of his tongue or the simple taste of him. Bad decision though it may be, I can't summon the strength to complain.

His hand curves around my jaw and the other trails down my neck, tickles the skin on the undersides of my breasts, then brushes the marred skin of my stomach with the backs of his fingers. My breath catches in my throat at that simple touch.

He breaks the kiss and looks me straight in the eye. The hand that was cupped around my jaw presses against the bed as he uses it for leverage to hold himself up. The one on my stomach slips down to the button on my jeans and his nimble fingers unbutton and unzip, then slip underneath.

My lips part as his fingers slide over my folds. I hear the rumble of his growl in my ear and I whimper, "Ben."

"Are you wet for me, baby?" His fingers delve between my legs and the sound of his satisfaction makes my pussy clench in anticipation.

Then he presses against my clit with his thumb and moves in such ways that causes my breath to catch in the back of my throat. If I learned one thing after our night together, it was that Ben knows me almost better than I know myself. He understands from the pitch of my sighs and the restless way my fingers grip the sheets that I'm about to come. He watches as I twine the material around my hands and undulate against the play of his fingers. My desire reaches a fever pitch and he catches my low moan with his lips, his fingers flicking an insistent rhythm until I tremble against him in relief.

My muscles are so deliciously relaxed that I don't realize Ben has even moved until I feel the rasp of my jeans sliding down my legs and the cool air curling around my now-exposed skin. My panties disappear along with my pants, and I don't have a moment to adjust to my complete nakedness before his hands are spreading me wide and his mouth is on me.

The wet slick of his tongue against me sends a shock of pleasure along my nerves, short-circuiting any second thoughts I may have had. He presses against my legs as the flat of his tongue devastates me. He places one leg over his shoulder and uses his free hand to add the thick length of his fingers.

My hips lift, unbidden, and I moan through my second orgasm. I nearly scream through it, but Ben lifts and kisses me as his fingers help me through the after-shocks. His taste and mine mingle through the kiss, and I shudder underneath him.

His breath becomes ragged and a sense of urgency now underlies each of his movements. His fingers tremble as he undoes the button and zipper on his pants, so much that I knock his hands away to finish the job. I push his pants down his thighs with impatient fingers, dragging the cotton of his briefs along with them. He's still wearing his customary black combat boots, so I don't even consider shucking them the rest of the way off. That will take way too long, and I want him inside of me. Now.

His legs are pinned by the confines of his jeans, so his range of movement is significantly limited. The thick length of his cock springs free, and my mouth waters at the same time my pussy tightens. It's been so long since I've even wanted to make love to anyone that my sudden and significant response to him surprises me. Though, it shouldn't. The few moments it takes for him to slip on a condom feel like an eternity.

I scramble to pull him on top of me, needing the heavy press of his weight to assuage the need burning inside me. He spreads my legs and settles between them in a smooth movement, his lips taking mine for another kiss as he drives inside me.

We groan in unison and I remember how much I love the feel of him, the fullness of him. The rough material of his jeans abrades my calves from where I have them wrapped around his legs. He hooks his hands underneath my shoulders so he can hold me in place for each hard thrust.

He shoves his face in my neck and bites the skin there as I clench around him. Then he loosens a hand to press between us and I arch my neck in response. "Baby," I manage between heaving breaths. "Don't stop, that feels so good."

Ben, the bastard, slows his movements in response, thrusting deep, holding, pulling out, then thrusting again even more slowly. "You want it?" he asks.

"Please," I whisper.

"Are you gonna give this a shot?" he murmurs in my ear.

"What?" My voice hitches as he sits up and presses my feet into his chest so the head of his cock is hitting just the right spot.

"I'm here. You gonna be here with me?"

"Yes," I gasp.

"Gonna give this a chance, Spitfire?"

I clench around him and relish the sound of his gasp in response. I adjust my legs so they're wrapped around his waist and push up to roll him on his back. My hands clutch at his shoulders as I start to ride him. He slides his own up my waist to cup the weight of my breasts, his thumbs flicking over the hard tips of my nipples.

With each of my movements, he flexes his hips up to meet me and I nearly see stars the pleasure is so intense. My back arches, but he abandons one breast to cup my neck and force my gaze back to him.

"Watch me when you come, baby. I wanna see those gorgeous eyes."

It's just as beautiful as it was the first time. Just as all-encompassing, soul-shattering, and heart-breaking. It builds me up just to tear me down and starts all over again. In the end, my muscles are quaking with the need for release. I want to give in, but part of me is holding back, afraid.

His fingers and hips speed up, noting my heavy breathing and the fast pace of my hips.

"C'mon, baby," he growls. "I want to watch you. I need to feel you come on me."

The orgasm builds and my breath catches in my throat. He holds my legs still so he can take over again, meeting me with deep thrusts. The combination of his hard cock pulsing inside of me, the delicious tugs of his fingers on my nipples and the throaty commands he whispers in the darkness throw me over the edge with a savage force.

"That's it, baby," he says. "Oh, yes, just like that. I feel you around me. Yes, lay on me. Let me help you through it."

He pulls me forward so I'm splayed across his chest, a languid heap of satiated flesh and bone. His hands grip the globes of my ass as he grunts. My orgasm rolls through me as he works himself to the end. His groans reach a fever pitch and end on one long, low note which sends shivers down my spine.

As the moment fades and reality returns, even after everything he's said, I start to worry that my exhaustion will overtake me and I'll wake up to another empty bed.

Ben shifts us so we're lying on our sides facing each other. "You're overthinking it already," he tells me. Then, after a few seconds with no response from me—because, well, he's right—he mumbles, "Give me ten minutes. I promise we'll go again—and again, if I think you fuckin' need it—until you're not able to think at all."

CHAPTER NINETEEN

BEN

"You promise we won't be gone long?" she asks, her hands fiddling with the hem of her dress.

I glance over at her out of the corner of my eye and smile. "Stop worrying so much. Cole will be fine. Mom's raised a couple kids. She knows what she's doing, I promise."

"I hate to put her out this way. Melissa normally sits for me, but I told her I wanted to let your family get to know him and all."

She checks her phone for the millionth time and I slip my hand around her leg and squeeze her thigh. "Stop worrying so much. He's going to be fine. Mom has both of our numbers and she'll call if anything's wrong."

"I know, you're right. It's just that your paranoia is rubbing off on me, I guess."

"Well tonight isn't about that. Tonight it's just about us. Plus, I've got something to show you that I think you'll like."

"Are you going to tell me what it is?"

"No. Not ruining the surprise."

"I don't deal well with surprises," she says, finally caving in and resting her weight against my side. I resist the urge to grip her tighter in satisfaction. About damn time she started giving in to me.

Chill bumps cover her legs as I brush her inner thigh with my fingers. Ever since we had sex again, I haven't been able to keep my hands off her. "You'll like this one," I assure her.

Her breathing deepens the higher my fingers go and I start to wonder if I'll ever make it to where we're going, without wanting to stop and find that spot on the side of the road again where we could make full use of our night alone together.

The road curves and the lights reflecting off of the dark ink of the lake come into view. Her leg stiffens underneath my hand and she sucks in a deep breath. She turns to look at me, lips parted and eyes wet with tears.

"What are we doing here?" she asks.

I pull into the driveway, headlights illuminating the empty porch and the swing I'd had installed with her in mind. I'd left the living room lights on so the place looks like home. Or at least my best guess of what she would think home would look like. I resist the urge to fidget as I wait to see her reaction.

"Closed on it today," I say quietly. "It's mine. I wanted to share it with you. I know how much he meant to you and I wanted to spend the night with you here. I wanted Cole to have the same memories you had, and even those that you didn't, when you grew up here. I had a great childhood, so I can't imagine not having one filled with the people you love. I know giving him a family, roots, is important to you. Whatever happens between us, I want you to know he'll always have that."

When she doesn't say anything, I get out of the truck and rub my hand on my neck. Maybe it was too much. Fuck, I've probably gone and upset her. I move around the truck to the passenger side door and open it up to let her out and apologize. I'm barely able to get a word out before she vaults herself into my arms, her hands wrapped tight around my neck.

"Thank you," she whispers brokenly. "Thank you so much, Ben."

The knot in my stomach eases and I wrap my arms around her waist. "You're welcome."

She sniffles and pulls back, wiping her eyes. "That's some surprise."

"I just thought you'd like it."

"It's perfect." She takes my hand in hers and drags me to the entrance of her dad's old lake house.

"Now don't expect much from the inside. I haven't had time to furnish it, so it's pretty bare bones right now."

"I've learned that it's not the things inside the house that makes it a home. It's the people and the love they share." She stops inside the doorway and turns to face me. "That's what you've given me here. I don't know how to thank you for it."

I step closer and pull her to me. "You don't have to do a thing. Just enjoy it with me."

Her hands cup my neck and bring my mouth to hers. She brushes against me all heat and softness. I linger on the sweet taste of her until I remember that I didn't bring her here for this and break away.

She looks disoriented. "What's wrong?"

I rub a finger over her lips. "Nothing, I just didn't bring you here for this."

Her face falls. "You didn't?"

That surprises a laugh out of me and I smile. "No, but don't think I won't take care of you later."

Instead of biting back at me like she normally does, she melts into me with a breathy, "'Kay." A part of me likes that even more than her attitude, that she trusts me to lead her anywhere.

I lead her through the empty, shadowed house and to the backyard where the overgrown path leads down to the lake. Her hand is clasped firmly in mine as we make our way down the dock, where I've set up a blanket on the sand. Haloes of light from the torches surround the spot and she gasps when she sees the setup.

"I thought it was the least I could do for missing out on so much. I know it doesn't make up for the past year, but I thought I'd try."

"I don't know what to say. It's beautiful."

"I'm glad you like it." I tug on her hand and lead her down to the blanket. "I figure since we haven't actually been on a real date that we're long overdue."

She glances at me with a smile that makes me forget my earlier resolution to keep my hands to myself. "Are you saying that this is a date?"

"We've done everything else out of order, I didn't want you to miss out on this, too."

That adorable pink shade tinges her cheeks. "You're being ridiculously sweet right now. Quick, do something possessive or arrogant."

"I'm afraid I can't do that. I save that for the second date."

She stretches out on the blanket and my eyes catch on her skirt riding dangerously up her thighs. "Are you saying you want to go out on a second date with me?"

"Let's just put it this way," I nip at her lips and deepen the kiss until she's breathless, "consider yourself unavailable, just in case any other guys come sniffing around you. I won't go as quietly as little Chad did."

"No talk about Chad tonight. Rule number one. No talk about shootings, or burglaries, or surgeries. No talk about me at all," she declares.

"Sounds like a plan." I ease back on the blanket, draping her over me so that we can look up at the stars. For the first time in a long time, the anxiety that buzzes under my skin is as quiet as the night around us.

"We can talk about you instead."

I groan. "Let's not ruin the night, Liv."

"Oh, uh-uh," she retorts, all sass again. "I've put up with you butting your nose into my life since you got home. I want to know what you've been doing. Where you're going. I know you're sensitive about it, but I want to know about your hearing. You don't have to tell me about what happened, but I just want you to know that you can talk to me."

I fight the urge to put some distance between us. "It doesn't make for good first date conversation."

"It does for us. I want to be here for you, like you've been for me. I know you try to be the big, strong man, but there is obviously something bothering you. You can lean on me, too, you know. I'm stronger than I look."

"I know you are, Spitfire, but there are a lot of things you can't know. A lot of things that I will never tell you." Her hand finds mine and pulls it to rest on my stomach.

"We were clearing a hill, trying to gain some territory. A lot of political bullshit that doesn't matter. Anyway, our guys were getting smoked and we got called out. Our convoy was ambushed by rocket fire. I managed to save one of the guys before I was knocked unconscious. When I woke up with the worst headache of my life, they told me I'd never hear out of my right ear again and that, aside from the guy I pulled out, I was the only survivor. And I don't even know if he made it. He was in critical condition last I heard, while I was in the hospital. It was crazy over-crowded so I couldn't find out much else."

"I'm so sorry you had to go through that, Ben." Her hand tightens around mine.

"Don't be. It's what I signed up for. It was my job."

"I'm so glad you made it home safely, though."

"Sometimes I'm not so sure," I murmur.

She sits up and leans on an elbow. "What does that mean?"

"Nothing."

"No, tell me."

"Look, there's no way you can really understand what I've been through. To work with these men, train with them for months and then watch your men die while you live... It doesn't feel like honor. I don't feel like a special snowflake. When I think about the fact that they died and I lived, I don't feel lucky. I feel like I should have gone down with them."

She's silent for a moment before clearing her throat. "This may make me sound like a horrible person, but I'm glad you made it. If you hadn't, Cole would never have had the opportunity to meet you. To get to know the good man that *I* know you are."

"I told you this wasn't good date conversation." I laugh hollowly.

Livvie presses a kiss to my jaw. "This is the best date I've ever been on because it's with you."

"I'm sorry, what'd you say?"

She looks up at me and says, "I said this is the best date—"

"I'm just kidding. A little deaf humor to lighten the mood."

Her elbow makes sweet love with my rib. "That's so not funny."

"Sorry, sorry. Too soon." She settles back down by my side and I search for a topic that doesn't relate to me. "Have you had any luck with your bio parents?"

"Actually, Sof says she stumbled onto something. She's supposed to email it to me at some point. After all that's happened though, I almost don't care. I'm just happy to have my two guys happy and healthy. Right now, that's all that matters to me."

She shivers against me. "Why don't we head inside for a bit," I suggest.

"Thanks for this. It was nice."

I ball up the blankets and pull her to me. "The night's not over yet," I whisper against her lips.

Then she shivers for a completely different reason.

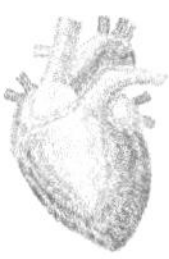

It almost feels like we're teenagers again, sneaking away from the group of our combined families to neck underneath the lights of the Ferris wheel. I wasn't worthy of her first kiss, and I'm sure as hell not good enough to have her look at me the way she does, but like the greedy asshole that I am, I take it.

I lay her down on the bed, a sexy sprawl straight from every dirty fantasy I've had about her over the years. Her chest heaves with shuddering breaths as I dip underneath the material of her dress. I find her wet for me, drenched, and I worry for a second that I'm going to end it before we even get started, so I pause to kiss her. Which doesn't do anything other than fan the fire.

We break apart and I bury myself in her neck. Her hips rock under me and she takes my hand in hers to lead back down to the place between her thighs. My fingers stroke her deep, her walls clenching around me. I love how turned on she gets, how loud she can get, just for me.

"I wanna hear you this time," I tell her, nipping her ear lobe for emphasis. "There's no one around here but you and me. I wanna hear you every time you come for me."

"Ben, I can't..."

"Yes, you can." God, and there she goes. Her muscles tighten—both inside and out—and her skin blushes *everywhere*. She wraps her arms and legs around me, using them to slide herself up and down my fingers as the convulsions reach a climax.

As she goes slack around me, I quickly roll on a condom. When I get her pregnant the next time, it won't be left to chance. She looks up at me, the corners of her lips pulled into a pleased smile, and the thought of her full with my child strikes a hell of an attractive image.

I fit my body between her thighs and guide myself to her entrance, sliding inside on one smooth thrust, causing both of us to moan. Her nipples draw up tight, flushed pink and brown even in the shadowed room. I can't resist the impulse to take one into my mouth, teasing it with the flat of my tongue. She clenches around me and I release her to breathe deeply.

"It gets better every time," I choke out.

Her hands lift to my cheeks and she kisses me. "It's always good when it's with you," she tells me, her lips moving against mine.

"Fuuuuck," I murmur against her, caught in the slow, wet glide. I pull back to give myself some breathing room, regain some portion of my sanity, but her hands catch at my hips and she arches hers up to meet me.

"Keep going. You feel so good." Her voice catches as I sink back in, tipping my hips in search of the spot that makes her go crazy. "So good," she whispers.

"We've got all night, baby. I promise I'll make you feel a whole lot better."

She giggles through another moan. "Oh, God, I don't think that's possible."

I take that as a challenge. My vision flashes white as I set a steady rhythm, thrusting up to meet her hips and gliding out slowly. Her hands clutch at my back, her nails digging into my skin.

I want to draw it out, make it last, but I can't kid myself. I've been gone for her for a long time. To combat the pending orgasm I can feel drawing my balls up tight, I slip a finger between us to bring her to the edge. Her legs weaken, falling open in response, her body melting beneath mine.

"Shit, shit, shit," she whispers. "I'm gonna come."

"Oh, yeah?" I slow my pace, watching as she tightens up, her mouth opens and she lets out a voiceless scream, offering up her throat to me. "God, baby, yes."

I let go, following her over. My arms give and I levy my weight over her, trying not to crush her. Rational thought is drowned out by the buzzing in my ears.

I manage to get up and dispose of the condom in the

bathroom and slide back into bed next to her. She turns to me automatically and fits herself to my side, resting her head on my shoulder and wrapping a thigh around my legs.

"Is that a picture of me?" she asks, propping herself up on an elbow and peering at my nightstand.

"Uh—yeah. It is."

"Where in the world did you get that? How long have you had it?"

"Since last year," I reply sheepishly. "I kept it with me in Afghanistan. Nicked it from your brother's car before I left."

"You've kept a picture of me with you that long?"

I swallow thickly. "Yeah."

She relaxes back down on top of me, her hands tightening around me. My world contracts down to this house. This room. This moment.

"I love you." The words come from a place I don't let anyone see. The place that I've kept wrapped up tight since I left.

When she doesn't respond for a second, I start wrapping us up in the sheets thinking she'd fallen asleep. Then she looks up at me, emerald eyes twinkling, and says, "I love you, too" and I know she does. A woman like Livvie doesn't give herself easily. To anyone.

That's really what I meant when I told her that Chad would go crazy over a woman like her.

She's special and now that she's mine, there's no way in hell I'm going to let her go.

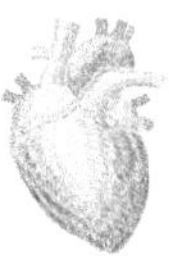

Livvie eventually agrees to let me stay at her place, though I think it's out of sheer exhaustion for the most part.

From that moment on, I don't leave their side. I take her to her physical therapy appointments. I take Cole to his checkups and quiz every single doctor and nurse I can get my hands on about his condition. I help Olivia feed, change, and clothe him. When she has her own appointments, I'm the one who watches him.

One morning a few weeks after our date at the cabin, I find her downstairs, a cup of coffee cradled in her hands. "Mornin'," I say.

Her eyes flit between me and the cup. "Good morning."

I make my own cup and sit next to her at the island bar. She shifts uncomfortably. "You're up early."

She nods. "I have a meeting at eight with the principal from my school to discuss going back to work next week."

The hot coffee burns my tongue. "Next week?"

Livvie hops up from the chair. "Uh huh. Thankfully they've held the job for me after Cole's diagnosis and this catastrophe. I just want things to get back to normal as soon as possible."

"*Normal.*" I repeat.

"Yeah." She returns with creamer and a toasted bagel. "The doctors have given me the go ahead to go back to work. If I have to spend another day cooped up in this house, I'm going to go crazy, Ben."

I take a calm sip of my coffee. "Like hell you're going back to work next week."

Livvie looks at me with a mouthful of bagel, her eyebrows raised. Her jaw works as she swallows. "I'm sorry," she says after a moment. "What are you talking about?"

"In case you forgot, someone tried to kill you less than a month ago. They *shot* you. If you think I'm letting you go back to work before they've even caught the fucker, you're crazy."

She sets down her bagel carefully and splays both hands on the counter. "I can't let this guy ruin my life. I've given my arm plenty of time to heal so that I can get back into working order. Cole's healed from his surgery and ready to go back to daycare. I don't want to let this affect our lives more than it already has. If I do that, if I go into hiding, then he wins."

I nod. "He'll also win if you aren't being safe. Were you even going to tell me?"

"I'm telling you now. Besides, this is my decision, not yours."

"I'm going to make it my business if your decisions put you in danger."

Livvie growls in the back in her throat. "I can't put my life on hold for things that may happen. If there's one thing that Cole's illness has taught me it's that nothing is guaranteed in our future. We have to live each day to the fullest."

"You can't live it if you're dead."

"I can't talk to you right now. You're impossible." She tosses her uneaten bagel in the trash and dumps her coffee in the sink.

A desperate feeling claws its way up my throat, but I force myself to calm down, to reason with her. "We need to talk about this."

"We can talk when you're ready to be reasonable about it. Ordering me around isn't being reasonable. I'm glad you're back in our lives, but I do have to get back to mine at some point."

I swallow my retort. "The point is," I say through my teeth, "it's not safe for you to go back to work right now."

She acts like she doesn't hear me. "Okay, then. I should be back sometime this afternoon. It shouldn't take long."

Livvie starts heading up the stairs, but I grab her hand

and turn her to face me. "Don't think that means that this discussion is over, Olivia. We're going to talk about it when you get back."

She waves a hand and I take that to mean that she agrees.

Cole and I are sitting downstairs watching a movie when she flounces into the living room. I immediately take notice of the tight-as-sin pencil skirt and the white button up. The shirt is hanging from her wounded side and it's untucked over the skirt.

Her cheeks are stained red. "Can you help me button, please?"

I lay Cole down in his vibrating chair and rise to my feet. She can't look me in the face as I slowly do up the buttons on her shirt. By the time I reach the top, we're both breathless.

"Thanks," she says faintly.

I lean in, brushing her ear with my lips, then my teeth. "About this conversation that we're going to have later. If you need extra *convincing*, be prepared to take it without any lip."

"Don't think you're going to be able to change my mind with sex."

"I don't think anything," I say with a smile, having finally gained the upper hand. Her body sways towards me as I walk to the playpen to pick up Cole.

I'm pleased to hear that her voice isn't so self-assured when she follows. "You sure you're going to be okay with him? If you need anything, you can call mine or Jack's cell. His cardiologist's phone number is on the fridge in case you have any questions. She's available 24/7."

I rub the back of my hand across her check. "Don't worry. We'll be fine."

She releases the breath she was holding. "I know you will. I'm just always nervous about leaving him." She grabs her purse and gives Cole a kiss on the head. "I should be back soon. Yes—" she cuts me off before I can respond, "I promise I'll be careful. I'm only heading there and back."

"You better," I whisper to her back as she walks out the front door.

I try to keep myself busy after Cole goes down for a nap. His third of the day. Unlike a completely healthy child, he tires easily. Which is okay with me, because it's given me a lot of time to bond with him. My new favorite thing is letting him fall asleep on my lap while I watch a movie or play video games.

When the door opens and she steps through, the relief is all encompassing. As is the irritation. She bounds into the living room—as much as she can with her injured shoulder—with a huge smile on her face.

"They said I can come back on Monday. The temp they had filling my class moved to Arizona. I can't wait to get back to my students."

"So you're still determined to go back, huh?"

Her smile dims a little. "Yes, and there's nothing you can say that will change my mind. I've been away for far too long as it is. They can't hold my job forever."

"Fine, but I have some conditions."

A laugh bubbles through her lips. "You sound like my dad."

"The conditions are," I talk over her, "that someone will drive you to work and pick you up each day. And you're to stay in public places at all times."

She crosses her arms and heaves an exaggerated sigh in my direction. "In fact, I think I had this exact conversation with him when I went off to college. You remember, right? He asked the dean if he could be my roommate in the dorms?"

Ignoring her, I say, "I'm being completely serious, Olivia."

"Yes, Dad," she answers with a smile.

I sigh. "This isn't a joke."

"Relax. It will be fine."

"I'll feel better when Logan's caught the sonuvabitch," I admit.

She snakes her arms around my waist and I hope to God that she's right, because I know just how bad it can be when it goes wrong. And I can't fail Olivia and Cole. Not this time.

PART THREE

CHAPTER TWENTY

OLIVIA

"THE CARNIVAL?" I say, my voice ending on a surprised note. The bright lights wash over my face. I turn to him and can't help the slow rush of excitement that buzzes along my nerve endings. "What are we doing here?"

Cole bounces happily on Ben's hip, also entranced by the sights before him. "To celebrate you going back to work. Plus, I figured I might as well get started on date number two."

"Oh, so you've decided that I was right. It *is* time for me to go to work."

He wraps an arm around me. "I've decided that I still like fighting with you, Spitfire. Sometimes, I may do it just to see you get all riled up."

"I think date two is getting off to a rough start."

He leans down to me, his lips whispering across the shell of my ear. "Then wait until you see what I've got planned for you later."

I ignore the resulting warmth that spreads through my chest as we join the growing lines of people at the ticket counter. Ben contents himself with Cole's gibberish conversations, and my heart simply melts as I watch them together. Most of the time, it's like they're in their own little world and I'm merely afforded the privilege of the show. I don't mind much. Since they've been spending so much time together, I've noticed how different he is around the baby.

Out of everyone, Cole is the only one Ben devotes one hundred percent of his focus to. No matter how over-whelmed he gets or how huge the tantrum is, Ben is ever patient and attentive. They're inseparable, and I could have never in a million years thought I'd be so lucky.

We reach the counter and I reach to get my wallet from my purse, but Ben bats away my hands and pays for the bracelets that will serve as our entry tickets. I roll my eyes at his impish grin as the attendant attaches mine.

The scent of fried food and boiled peanuts permeates the cool night air. We immediately stop to get a cup of the salty goodness, sharing it as we wander through the booths of wares and stalls of games. Ben hoists Cole on his shoulders and grabs my hand so I don't get lost in the crush of people. For a moment, I forget everything that's torn us apart—and the things that we have yet to discuss about our strange situation. Relationship? Whatever it is, I vow to forget about it for one night and enjoy it.

Even though Cole can hardly balance, we help him atop a miniature horse and lead him around in circles. Ben keeps him steady with one strong hand and I stand outside the gate, taking pictures of the two of them. I find myself doing that a lot these days—taking pictures. Ben laughs every time I do, insisting it's unnecessary. But having no real mementos from my childhood makes me all the more determined to make sure Cole has more than he could possibly need. Overcompensation is the watchword for parenting, I've learned.

The boys return, smelling a might earthier than they did before, but both have identical grins stretched across their faces. "We've got a happy baby, Momma."

I can't help but smile back. "I see that."

Ben straps Cole back into his stroller and turns to face me. His face is awash with the cheerful lights from the carnival rides, his smile easy, free, and unspeakably alluring. It's the look of the man he was before he deployed for the last time. Before he took on the unbearable burdens he now shoulders on his own.

"Where to next?" he asks, breaking me from my thoughts.

There aren't many places Cole can go, but I spot a

carousel across the way and point to it. "How about that?"

Cole spots the swirling lights and makes high-pitched sounds of excitement as we near the carousel. Ben throws an arm around my shoulder and pulls me close to his side. I turn, lean up and press a kiss to his stubbled cheek. He pauses in the middle of the crowd to meet my lips for a more passionate embrace.

By the time we make it over to the carousel, I'm giddy with happiness. I lift Cole from his stroller, choose an aquamarine seahorse and strap Cole on. Ben watches from a crowd of onlookers. I gesture for him to take pictures, but he shakes his head. The carousel starts moving, so I gesture more violently. He finally relents and points his phone towards us with a beleaguered expression.

We go around one turn and make it back to Ben. I manage to get Cole to pay attention for a few seconds while Ben snaps off a round of pictures before we're out of view.

The ride winds down to a stop, and I pull an over-excited Cole off the seahorse. We buckle him back into the stroller and set out through the crowds.

"I hear there's a petting zoo somewhere back near the horses," I tell Ben.

"Let's grab something to drink first. Those peanuts made me thirsty."

Ben deftly guides the stroller through the masses until

a loud sound from behind startles the both of us. Ben whirls, throwing his hands up, eyes wide and feral. I flinch at his reaction and turn to search for the noise.

A couple of kids howl, waving sparklers and fisting handfuls of bottle rockets. Their parents intervene, grabbing arms and jerking them backwards while spewing stern words.

I slip an arm around Ben's waist and whisper, "Are you okay?" I can feel the heavy beat of his heart in his chest and his breathing is shallow. His throat bobs as he swallows thickly.

"Yeah." His voice is hoarse. He shakes himself then returns the hug. "Yeah, I'm fine."

We both turn back to the stroller to make our way towards the concession stand. I lean down to offer Cole some consoling words—the noise surely had to startle him, too—but the stroller is empty. My mind blanks and my stomach drops somewhere in the vicinity of my feet. I look at Ben, thinking maybe he somehow grabbed him in the commotion, but he's looking off in the distance, his jaw tight.

"Ben, where's Cole?" I gulp for breath, but it doesn't help.

His head jerks to me sharply, and he turns the stroller to confirm that my nightmare is real. I twist, looking wildly through the ever-moving crowd of people, but there are so many around us I can't even see the edge. The world reels away and the lights are no longer bright and cheerful. The crowd around us is no longer happy and friendly, but terrifying and sinister.

"Cole!" I screech, searching blindly.

Ben leaves the stroller and strides away, pushing through the people too slow to get out of his way. His eyes scan the immediate vicinity, but there's no way he can see through the mass of people.

I spot a uniformed officer and sprint to him. "Someone took my son."

As the officer speaks into his radio, I fumble for my phone. I scroll through, find the photo Ben took while we were on the carousel and show the officer. "This is what he's wearing. He was in the stroller, but some kids set off some fireworks and we turned away for one second and he was gone. He's not even a year old yet; he doesn't even know how to unbuckle the stroller."

The officer has me send the photo to his phone and he distributes it to God only knows who. I remember to tell him to get in touch with Logan and then I mentally check out. Fear and hopelessness feed a sucking black hole inside of me where my heart used to be.

I watch numbly as Ben talks with the officer and a small crowd of them gather around the stroller. I'd fooled myself into thinking the shooting and the break-in weren't related. I was an idiot to think we were finally safe in our own little family bubble. If nothing else, the catastrophic events of the past year should have taught me to expect the worst.

I go to Ben on auto-pilot, reaching out for a hold in a world which has begun to spin unsteadily underneath my feet. He turns to me, his face a mask of pain that pinches the areas around his eyes.

"Anything?"

I don't even need to hear his answer.

The look on his face says it all.

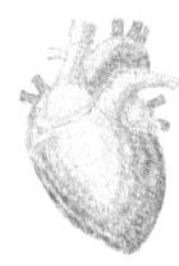

I let myself into the house. Grimly, I go into my bedroom and unpack Cole's baby bag. It's a mindless, numbing task that I do without any real thought. I take my time, losing myself in the motions, hanging what was clean or unused back in the closet and separating Cole's little clothes into two piles, one to put away and the other to wash. I spend a lengthy amount of time crying into his favorite stuffed dog, the one we found in the dirt ten feet away from his stroller.

I feed Hank, start a load of laundry, then I call the school. I'm sure someone has already told them, but the empty house feels like it's pressing in around me and I need something to do to keep my mind preoccupied.

The receptionist answers, a temp that had started

working there a few weeks before I'd taken off. "Lindsey, hi. It's Olivia Walker. I just wanted to let you know that I won't be able to come into work this week after all. I'm sorry for the inconvenience."

"I wouldn't let you even if you begged!" Lindsey McIntosh exclaims. She'd had her own fair share of drama, I recall numbly. According to the rumor mills, she'd even been married to a genuine rockstar, until recently. "Sweetheart, I've been watching the news for the last hour, and I can't believe you even considered it. No one would ever hold you to that. You don't worry about a thing. I'll take care of it."

"I'm sorry," was all I could think to say. What else *was* there to say?

"You don't have a thing to be sorry about. You don't worry about any of it. We'll cover you until things are settled. Get some rest, you sound dead tired. Call me when you have word."

"Of course. The detectives on the case were able to get a license plate and they've put out an APB and an Amber Alert. Ben, Cole's father, has some contacts, so he's doing whatever it is guys do in an emergency..."

When I trail off Lindsey clears her throat and says with false cheerfulness, "It's good you have him on your side then. And we are all willing to help in any way we can."

"I can't tell you how grateful I am, thank you."

With that taken care of, I look around for something

else to keep my mind and hands busy. If I had even the barest second to think about things, I would fall into a blind panic. My eyes land on a stack of bouncy toys I had yet to open and put together. Cole would like them when he gets back, I think. He is much more active these days, and I'd been meaning to set the toys up in his room for him to experiment with.

That's where Sofie finds me four hours later, except I haven't managed to do a damn thing other than cry a river of tears as I cling to his toys.

"Oh, sweetie," she says, falling to her knees beside me and enveloping me in her arms. "Where's Ben?"

I wipe my face with her proffered tissues. "He's with Logan and Jack and the police, I think. There wasn't much I could do, they said, so they told me to go home until there's word." I hiccup through my tears. "I couldn't stay there and listen to them talk about statistics and have all their eyes on me, wondering. No doubt grateful they weren't in my shoes, that their kids were safe. I couldn't stand to watch Ben shut down right in front of me after we'd finally grown so close. I thought being here would make me feel better, but Sof, I don't think anything will ever make me feel better."

CHAPTER TWENTY ONE

OLIVIA

I SIT on the couch in a drugged stupor. Sofie had fed me sleeping medicine, but even though she'd passed out hours ago, I wasn't able to succumb to sleep. So I sit, waiting, feeling oddly numb and my brain is so sluggish I can't manage to form a coherent thought.

The door opens and I can see Ben walking in, his head low. If I could feel, hope would have stirred in my chest, but it's probably a good thing that I can't, because when he looks up, the ravaged look on his face would have dashed those hopes right away.

"They're interviewing all of the carnies now. They're still working on people that were there or that may have seen something."

My voice is raw and scratchy. "So they don't have anything?"

"They will, Liv. Logan was still there when I left."

"Ben, I don't know what to do. What am I supposed to do here? I don't think I can handle this."

He brushes the rain off of his hair and I spot his hearing device as he shucks his jacket and boots. I remember his story about what happened to him overseas, the nightmares he's prone to having after rough days. He's been through things like this before. I don't even know how he's handling it—if he's handling it at all.

He comes to sit beside me, pulling me into his arms. "We'll get through this together, Liv. We won't stop until we find him."

"He's out there all alone. He could get sick. I can't lose him, Ben. It would kill me."

"We aren't going to lose him. I won't let that happen."

I shake my head, because what can he do? "I just don't—"

"Stop. You need to get some sleep. We've got the press conference tomorrow. They're going to want to have you say something on camera. They've got everyone in the surrounding counties mobilized." He squeezes me tighter. "We're going to find him, baby. I promise you."

He holds me on the couch until I succumb to a fitful sleep.

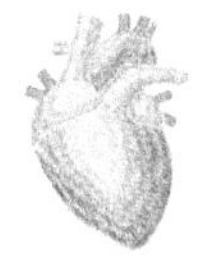

"Baby, you have to eat something."

Ben offers a bowl of some mushy looking cereal, but the mere sight of it causes bile to rise in my throat. "No, I can't."

"You have to."

With a hand covering my mouth, I say, "I'll try later, Ben. Okay?"

He nods, watching me warily, but doesn't press the issue, thank God. Simply getting dressed and looking presentable is just about all I can do. And I wouldn't have been able to do that much if Ben hadn't dragged me out of bed and Sofie hadn't been there to pour me into a dress.

What does it matter how I look when my heart's been ripped out of my chest?

The house where I raised my son doesn't feel like a home anymore. The walls my brother and I finished painting a creamy beige aren't comforting. They feel hollow and cold. Empty.

"Livvie," Sofie says softly from the doorway. "It's time."

It's uncharacteristically overcast for the Sunshine State, but the weather feels fitting. No day without Cole should have sun. I know for sure that any light in my life had been robbed from me the moment he went missing.

As I stand in front of a room of reporters and policemen, I feel as though I could shatter at any moment.

"Do you need anything?" Ben asks in a low voice as we're filed into the conference room at the police station to address the press.

"Just hold me. I don't think I can face this without you."

His arm is a steel band around my waist. "Don't worry," he says, "you won't have to."

The sensible black dress Sofie picked out for me clings to my sweat-slicked skin. Not even the slowly whirring fan stirs the thick, muggy air and even though we're inside, I can smell the coming rain. I concentrate on the sticky feeling of the dress against my flesh, the heat from the camera lights that glare into my eyes, and the pregnant, gray clouds that threaten to burst outside the window. Anything but the real reason why we're here. Doing so will cause me to break—again—and there's only so much I can do to hold myself together at this point. The distraction and Ben's closeness are the only things keeping me together.

I note the familiar faces in the crowd. Jack and Sofie stand front and center. He has his arms around her and is murmuring something in her ear. A surprising sight considering the two of them still can't stand to be around each other for more than ten minutes at a time. They look good together, like they fit. She leans into him and he holds her steady, and I wonder if maybe there's hope for them, at least.

Logan is there, too, dressed in his police uniform and scowling magnificently. Beneath his stoic façade, I sense an inner turmoil. I know he blames himself, and I want to tell him that none of this is his fault. There's no way he could have known any of this would happen. But the words would feel false, because like him, I also blame myself.

My stomach churns as my mind wanders. No matter how much I try to pretend otherwise, this is really happening, but I don't want to acknowledge it. My brain simply can't compute that he's gone. My baby is missing, and I'm helpless. Completely and utterly helpless. There's a room full of people to attest to the fact that someone broke into the sanctity of my life—again—and threatened my son. Except this time, they were successful.

Beside me, I can feel the tension rolling off Ben in waves. Anyone that doesn't really know him wouldn't be able to tell from the outside, but I can see the ghosts in his eyes. The shadows of despair shimmer in their depths and if I weren't numb from the anxiety medication I had been forced to take, the sight of Ben so shuttered and closed-off again would have brought me to my knees. If I could feel anything, it would be the insidious, sucking pit that is sorrow.

"Only a few more minutes," he murmurs.

I stare at the police chief as he updates the public on

the atrocities committed against my family. He entreats anyone with any knowledge of my baby boy's whereabouts to come forward and directs the viewing public to a tip line and anonymous website, one I've already had Sofie hack and monitor. He ends with a plea to those on social media to share Cole's photo and information. My heart calls out to every mother in that moment. Every mother who's ever worried about losing a child—I hope they see this, and I hope they have it in their hearts to spread the word and help me find my baby.

We had so little time together. I glance at Ben, who is still staring into the camera as if to challenge it and everyone watching to defy the chief's orders. Ben especially has had so little time with Cole. Because of me. I wipe away the traitorous trail of grief from my cheeks. Maybe this is what I deserve for not trying harder. My penance for being a horrible person. I deserve this, but not Ben. Not a man who has spent the last decade of his life fighting for his country, sacrificing his time, mental health and future for something greater than himself. If nothing else, I deserve this pain for lying to Ben and stealing away the precious time that was rightfully his.

I didn't want to give the kidnapper the satisfaction of seeing my tears, but I had been instructed by the negotiators that it was important to make them realize Cole was a person. That his family cares for him.

Ben must sense the change in my emotional state

because he glances away from the cameras and back at me. The look on his face doesn't change, but he shifts closer to put an arm around my shoulder and pull me into his strong, reassuring side. I press my face into his chest and take a moment to allow his strength to reassure me.

"Are you okay?" he asks.

I sniffle. "I'm okay. I'll be okay."

I don't know what I would have done if I had to face this by myself. I'd been kidding myself to think I could have done this on my own. No matter what the future holds for Ben and me, I'll always remember he was there for me when I needed him most. Even when he was hurting, too. A far cry from how he responded a year before.

The reassuring scent of him and the strong band of his arm around my waist distracts me from the words I know he's speaking into the camera. The pleas to the kidnapper to return Cole home unharmed. Outwardly, Ben is steady, determined, but I can feel the tremble that racks his body and the deep, unsteady breathing that belies his calm demeanor.

My silent tears soak his shirt, but I close my eyes and take a cleansing breath. When I look in the camera, I know I'm not as steady as Ben or as easily able to hide my emotions, but I do what I was told to do and speak from the heart. I implore them—whoever 'them' may be—to bring my baby home. I hold up his picture.

The cameras cut back to a view of the both of us then

back to the police chief. As soon as I'm out of view, I burrow back into Ben's arms as my body is racked with shudders of fear and shock. The adrenaline I experienced since waking up to realize Cole was still missing is finally abating. I can feel the lethargy stealing over me. I sink more heavily into his side, using his strength to keep me upright.

Once the chief declares the press release concluded, the reporters start filing out and we're urged back down the hallway to the sanctity of one of the conference rooms. Perhaps sensing our need for a few minutes alone, the officer escorting us excuses himself with a few quiet words and closes the door behind him.

I focus on the sound of the whirring air conditioner and hug my arms around my waist as if that would contain the roiling pressure building in my chest threatening to break free. I don't know how to process anything that's happened.

My father, the shooting and now this?

From my position in front of the window I watch as the flock of reporters disperses and the blue-black clouds above finally break. Thick drops pelt the metal roof of the police station and a darkness descends, painting everything a dull gray.

Hands grip my sides and turn me away from the window. I look up into Ben's face and see my grief reflected in his eyes. Until that moment, I'd been able to hold everything back. Having practically raised myself prior to my teenage years, I was used to taking care of everything for myself. That modus operandi continued even after the Walkers adopted me, as I never wanted to be a burden on their family.

But seeing a man like Ben vulnerable and overcome with emotion touched something inside of me that I'd kept hidden away for far too long. I feel my face crumple and run hot with fresh tears. Ben's mask of indifference dissolves and he jerks me into his chest, his arms going around me and holding me closer. His comforting scent surrounds me and his chin comes to rest on my shoulder. The ragged sound of his breathing and the rapid beat of his heart fills my ears.

A keening wail bursts from my chest and I scream into the rapidly dampening cloth of his shirt. My fingers find their way under the material of his shirt, and I grip the warm skin of his back to anchor me through my sobs.

Ben curves over me as if to absorb my pain into himself. His hands rub across my back as he relays soft words of consolation. I can't make out anything he's saying, but I can hear the rumble of it from his chest and the gesture soothes me.

I almost can't handle the overwhelming sense of despair and emptiness. There are so many things I wish I could change, so many mistakes I'd made and so many things we'd yet to experience. Now, I don't know if I'll ever be able to make up for them or experience them. Not only did this person steal my flesh and blood, but they also stole my future happiness. Without my son, there is no happiness.

With the spending of my tears into Ben's shirt, I also cry away the last of my energy. The past twenty-four hours had only been one horror after another. Combined with lack of sleep and food, I barely have the energy to hold up my head once the first wave of grief passes.

Ben smooths a path up my back and neck to cup my face in his big, warm hands. My watery eyes reach his, and he dips his head to kiss the trail of tears away from my cheeks. His tender act warms me from the inside out, chasing away the chill that today's trauma has wrought.

No one has ever made me feel as at home as Ben does. In truth, he ruined me for anyone else when I first laid eyes on him at thirteen; I was just too scared to take the chance on him. None of our past matters now. The only thing that matters is how safe his arms make me feel.

"I'm sorry," I whisper, my voice warbled and scratchy. "I didn't mean to break down all over you."

"Anytime, baby." I can hear the emotion in his voice and my arms constrict around his body, pulling him closer.

"I always seem to ruin your shirts."

"I don't care about the damn shirt," he says gruffly.

Then he embraces me, assuaging the hurt in one of

the only ways he knows how. His touch is insistent, focused. He rubs his hands with a practiced precision that has my mind going fuzzy and blank, which is a welcome turn from the blind panic I've been in all day. I accept his comfort greedily, taking everything he has to offer.

We stay there, locked in each other's arms, until someone knocks quietly at the door. Ben steadies me with a firm grip on my elbows, his eyes searching mine.

"We'll find him. I promise you that on my life, Olivia."

I don't answer. Instead, I press a kiss against his chest and am reminded of all the terrible things he's had to endure over the years. The loss of friends, men who were akin to brothers, innocent families he's had to watch be tortured and ruthlessly murdered. The many times he's had to fight for his life. He's spent a lifetime training for atrocities like this. He hides his inner turmoil well, as he was taught to do. I look up, and he rubs a hand over my hair.

If there's anyone I can trust now, I know it's him. We'll get through this together.

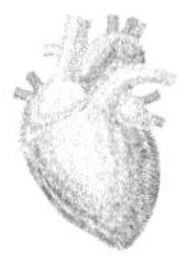

Logan and Ben pow-wow with the police while Sofie makes it her number one priority to get me home, fed, and keep me relatively sane as we do the only thing we *can* do:

wait. She even allows Jack to tag along, though the tension between them is so thick, I still notice it even through my stupor.

As we pull in the drive to my cute two-story bungalow, I wonder if this little house I called home for so long, the place I'd hoped to raise Cole in, would ever feel safe again. An ominous weight settles over my chest as I unlock the front door and swing it open to an empty room.

The bouncer is still a mess of parts on my living room floor and the scent of the dinner I'd burnt lingers in the air. Hank winds around my legs, even more anxious than normal, so I let him out the back to work off the nervous energy.

Sofie and Jack busy themselves with straightening the mess in the living room while I plop down on the couch, unable to do more than watch listlessly as they clean. They make every effort not to pay any mind to one another, but even I can see they're both forcing themselves not to watch each other.

Jack takes a load of toys upstairs to the nursery, and Sofie plops down beside me after grabbing my computer from the coffee table.

"What are you doing?" I ask from my curled position on the other end of the couch.

"The police chief said we should share this everywhere we can. I'm going to put a call-out to every friend, family member and classmate on all twenty-three of my friends' lists. I'll do the same on yours." She looks at me, her face illuminated by the glow of the computer screen. "I'll hack into Jack's and do his, too. Maybe even spread it to some of my friends to do their thing to make sure the news coverage is spread far and wide."

For as long as I've known her, Sofie has been brilliant, if not a little nerdy. She can do things with computers that make my already-limited skills look like child's play. In fact, after high school graduation, she went on to university to study things I couldn't even begin to understand. Jack always used to say she could take over the world with the way she knew how to handle men and a computer.

Jack returns with a plate of sandwiches and a big glass of sweet tea. He sets them on the table beside me and says, "Eat."

There's nothing I want to do less than eat, but I know I haven't had anything in twenty-four hours and I have to keep up my strength, so I do as he asks. I choke down bites of it with the refreshing glass of tea as Sofie clicks away on her computer and Jack scowls at her from his perch on the recliner.

With each hour that passes, the sucking hole in my stomach grows until I feel like I'm going to be swallowed by it. When darkness falls, Sofie has exhausted all of her resources and Jack has taken to pacing the length of the couch as we wait for word from Ben and Logan.

I almost jump out of my seat when I hear the lock clicking on the front door and Logan's smooth voice trailing through. I immediately jump to my feet and race to the door, hope surging to my throat.

The look on Ben's face tells me all I need to know, however, and my knees just go out, making me fall against him. I sense Logan heading to the living room, presumably to tell the others the news—or lack thereof, rather. Ben murmurs to Logan to let the others know they can head home until tomorrow.

Ben gathers me close to his chest like he did in the conference room, only this time, I'm too raw to cry out my pain. I feel like I have nothing left. I'm completely empty inside. As the others talk to Logan, Ben leads me up the stairs to my master bathroom.

His once light-hearted face is completely somber as he undresses me. When I am standing before him naked, he turns on the shower and adjusts the temperature. I watch listlessly as he sheds his own clothes, too numb to react in any way whatsoever.

He pulls me underneath the warm spray and I mold to him, drawing what strength I can from his embrace. The water sluices over us both, washing away the grime and sweat. We take turns lathering up a washcloth and rubbing it over each other.

Ben still hasn't said a word, but I'm starting to learn that this new Ben doesn't need to talk a lot to get his point across. Regardless, what little energy I had was completely sucked out of me when Cole wasn't with him when he came home. I slip into one of his shirts that somehow showed up mixed in my laundry. The smell manages to calm my jangled nerves somewhat. I brush my teeth as he tugs on a pair of briefs.

He slides into the covers and holds them open for me. I join him, snuggling into his shoulder and plastering my body against his. I fall asleep to the cadence of his heartbeat with the hope that the next day will bring good news.

CHAPTER TWENTY TWO

BEN

WATCHING Olivia shuffle around her house like the life has been sucked out of her hurts just as much as not knowing where our son is. Every other day, I woke up wrapped in her scent, wrapped in *her*. Her legs and arms twined around me like she was afraid I would somehow disappear again.

But not today.

Today, I woke to a cold, empty bed, and as I watch her make half-hearted attempts at conversation, I feel the same emptiness clawing at my chest. Guilt burns heavy and hot in my stomach.

I find her in the downstairs bath, hands sheathed in

yellow rubber gloves as she scrubs the tub with a sponge. "Baby, why don't you sit down for a while?"

She doesn't look up at me when she responds, "No, I'm okay. I need to keep busy or I'm going to go crazy waiting. Has Sofie heard anything?"

"No, not yet." I hate this helpless feeling. I've been running from feeling like this ever again.

"Okay. I'm almost done here, I promise."

She doesn't notice when I leave. Yesterday, she was vulnerable, open to using me to support her when she was breaking down, but her defenses have shored up overnight. Her self-reliance is something I've grown to love and admire about her over the years. As someone who has had a stable, supportive family, I can't imagine what it was like to grow up without one, then have what little you *did* have ripped away from you. Time and time again. And now this.

My phone chirps and I answer it automatically, "Hart."

"It's Logan. No updates, but I just wanted to check on the both of you. How are you holding up?"

I glance back at the open door of the bathroom and see Olivia now scrubbing the grout. "As good as we can, considering. Did you check on what I asked?" A weighted silence answers me on the other end. I grip the bridge of my nose with two fingers. When he doesn't respond, I prompt, "Logan?"

"I'm looking into it, but it may take some time."

"That's not something we have much of at the moment."

"I've got a lead I'm following, so I should have something for you soon. Keep your head up, man. We'll find him."

I end the call without saying goodbye as my stomach clenches. I can't help but feel like I should have stayed away when I had the chance.

Sofie and Jack are busy arguing in the living room, so I use their distraction to slip out to the backyard with Hank. Olivia has since moved on to distract herself with the upstairs bath.

The storms the day before sapped the heat from the region and as a result, the air is refreshingly cool. I sink down on the glider on the back porch and stare blindly into the yard as Hank investigates every bush and tree trunk. I'm a miserable combination of anger, despair, and regret.

The tenuous relationship Olivia and I had managed to cultivate after years of hit and misses won't survive this latest devastation. I'd taken the one chance I had at happiness—however short—and wanted to run with it. Now, it seems as though it's going to slip through my hands again.

The nine months I'd been deployed after our night together were some of the worst I'd ever had—and it wasn't my first, so that's saying something. The years of devastation had only made everyone involved meaner, more determined and even worse—more desperate.

Coming back from that, I was in no shape to be any good for her. Learning that she had a kid when I was gone only devastated me all the more. The only thing I could think when I laid eyes on them the first time was that I had missed out on my chance. I was too blinded by all I had lost to realize that everything I wanted was right in front of me.

And now it may be too late for any of it.

Around me, the world is still turning; the birds sing in the trees and I hear the laughter of children playing in the backyard down the street. I note these things and wonder if I'll ever be able to enjoy the simple things I liked so much again.

Even if we find Cole, they'd be better off without me.

"Ben!"

The scream shakes me to my core and I jump to my feet and rush back inside. I find the three of them huddled around Livvie, who is holding my cell phone. Tears are streaming down her face and my heart stops in my chest.

"Yes," she says. "We're on our way."

The phone falls from her limp fingers to the floor and she doesn't notice, as she's already running toward the door. I scoop it into my fingers and race after her. By the time I reach her, she's already in my truck, buckled and backing out of the drive. She barely notices me, only stopping just enough to let me hop in the passenger's seat.

Jack waves from the driveway and shouts, "We'll meet you there!"

Beside me, Livvie whips through traffic with the agility of a seasoned racecar driver as she whispers, "Come on. Come on."

I don't want to ask her what the call was about. I'm almost afraid to know.

We make it across town in record time. She brings the truck to a screaming halt, not bothering to turn it off as she flings the door open and jumps out. The press must have already got wind of the news because they huddle around the entrance like buzzards scenting a fresh kill. I pocket the keys and follow her into the police station, barely breathing as the wings of hope beat in my chest.

Inside, the station is quiet save for the rustle of papers and the soft murmur of conversation. It ratchets the hooks of anxiety ever tighter around my lungs. Livvie spots Logan standing outside of the conference room about the same time I do. She reaches for my hand and I take it, grateful for the small measure of comfort.

The length between us feels never-ending, but when we reach Logan's side his face brightens with a smile, and I nearly drop to my knees. The relief is all-encompassing. She spares Logan a glance and inhales deeply before opening the door to the conference room.

I let out a breath I didn't know I am holding when the air is rent with the squalling of a very unhappy baby. I never thought I'd be so happy to hear someone cry.

Livvie lets out a sob, lets go of my hand, and falls to her knees in front of the female officer holding a very unhappy Cole, who notices his mother for the first time and holds out his arms. She accepts him into her embrace and he makes happy sounds, though he's still sniffling. Her shoulders shake as she cries into his hair.

Logan puts a reassuring hand on my shoulder, and I realize silent tears are streaking down my own face. I clear my throat and wipe them away as Jack and Sofie arrive—for once, not arguing.

Sofie bursts into tears the moment she sees Livvie on the floor and Cole looking around at all the adults in confusion. She nearly collapses, but Jack is there in a moment, supporting her with an arm around her waist.

Cole looks up at me and gives me a gummy smile. His little hand reaches out to me and he says quite clearly, "Da-da."

Relief is both welcome and crushing. I gather him in my arms and take comfort in the fact that my fuck up didn't cost him his life.

CHAPTER TWENTY THREE

OLIVIA

A FEW HOURS later we reconvene at the house once the media furor has died down.

"They found him in an empty car—a white SUV—at the gas station over on Seventh Street. Someone recognized the description from one of Sofie's social media call outs and reported the car to the police. They went out to check and found Cole asleep in the back seat."

I rub my hand over a sleeping Cole's back. "A white SUV?" My mind flashes back to the day we were attacked at the doctor's office and the few glimpses I'd manage to get of the car they were driving.

"It's possible," Logan says, knowing where my mind was going. "We ran the plates, but they turned out to be stolen. From what we can gather, they were heading out of town. The back was full of suitcases, baby toys and clothes."

"So, this couldn't have been a ransom—not that we have tons of money in the bank. They were truly planning on taking him. Keeping him," I finish on a whisper, and my body is racked by shivers. I lean down and kiss his forehead. I can't seem to go a few minutes without touching him in some way. He's gotten more hugs and kisses in the past few hours than in his entire life, and I've always been very affectionate.

"That's what the evidence points to," Logan says gently. "But something must have spooked them because they abandoned the car. The witness who found it works across the street. They didn't see anyone drop it off, just that it had been there for over an hour and he recognized the car from the description Sofie gave."

I flash Sofie a grateful look, but she's fast asleep on the couch opposite me with her head cradled in Jack's lap. While I was in the oblivion of sleep last night, she had been trolling every website and imploring every hacker connection she's made over the past five years to help find Cole. I'll never be able to repay her for that.

"What about prints?" Ben asks.

Logan shakes his head. "No luck there. There were too many in the car and none that matched anyone in the system. We believe that since they abandoned the car and didn't take Cole with them, he should be safe. Even so, I think it would be best if Ben continues to stay with you to keep an eye on things. I can also have a car stationed outside your house until we're certain they've fled the area."

"I doubt I'll even sleep tonight, but that sounds great, thank you." For the foreseeable future, I want to keep Cole as close to Ben and me as possible.

Logan nods. "I need to get back to the station. Take care of yourself."

Ben stands to walk with him to the door, and I lift Cole up to take him to the portable play pen. At least I can move it around to keep him in sight while he sleeps. As I'm pulling the blanket over him, I catch a thread of Logan and Ben's whispered conversation in the doorway.

"Did you find him?"

"I have a lead on his last place of residence, but no one's seen him in months, so it's possible he's moved on."

I hear Ben's heavy sigh and my heart slows to a heavy thud in my chest. *What in the hell are they talking about?*

"Thanks, man."

The door opens and I heft Cole's pen so it's shadowed behind the couch. My hands are trembling with a combination of rage and shock, and I can't believe there's something Ben is hiding from me that could possibly help find who took Cole.

He appears in the doorway, a hand rubbing his neck with his eyes downcast.

"Was that about Mason?"

Ben's head jerks up and he says softly, "No."

"Then what *is* it about?" After the horrors of the past few days, the last thing I want are more secrets—or more surprises.

"Livvie not now." His face is hard and closed-off, and it sparks to life the dregs of anger that have been building since this whole mess started.

"No!" I yell. "I've had enough of wondering what's going on inside that head of yours. And bullshit that it doesn't have to do with Cole. You wouldn't be asking Logan to check in on someone right now if it didn't have to do with Cole."

"I'm telling you right now, Livvie, this isn't something I want to discuss, so drop it."

"After what we just went through, what we've been building, I think you owe it to me to explain. Let me in, *something*."

He doesn't answer; his facial expression doesn't even change. My sinuses begin to tickle, but I force myself not to cry—again—even though I want to. I stand in front of him, feeling like I'm wide open, baring my soul for him, but he doesn't give me anything. And that hurts so much worse.

His expression hardens further. "I told you what I

could give you a long time ago, Liv," he says, his voice rough. "I told you what I was capable of. Either way, this business," he gestures with a finger in a circle, "has nothing to do with you."

He gives me one last hard look then brushes past me.

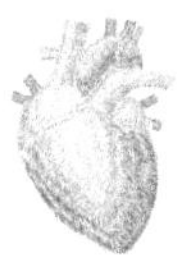

I wake later that night to an empty bed. I'd gotten so used to Ben's warmth that the cool sheets beside me make me frown. Sliding from underneath the comforter, I grab my robe from the rocking chair, slipping it on as I take the stairs down to the first floor. Hank barks outside, and the sound leads me to the back porch where I find Ben. I stop in the doorway, the cool night air swirling around my bare legs.

Ben is sitting with his head cradled in his hands, wearing a pair of sweats sans his customary black T-shirt. Normally, the sight of his bare body would send my hormones into overdrive, but this feels wrong. This feels like the Ben from the night of the break-in, the one who has a penchant for leaving. A hollow feeling takes up residence in my stomach.

"Ben?" I pause in the doorway, unsure if I want to even have this conversation. Maybe it would be better all-around if I were to just turn right back around and pull the covers over my head like a child who's afraid of the dark.

He turns to look at me, his face pale in the yellow cast from the porch light. He clears his throat. "I've been thinking... Maybe this wasn't a good idea."

My heart stops. "What wasn't a good idea?"

"Us," he says. "I don't think it's a good idea for us to keep seeing each other. I still want to be a part of Cole's life, be his father... but, aside from that, I think it would be best if we were just friends." He licks his lips and looks at me as though I should happily agree with his statement and go on my merry way.

"After—" My voice breaks, so I clear my throat and lick my lips before I continue. "I told you after you came back that we shouldn't pursue any kind of romantic relationship." My voice raises a few octaves. "*You* were the one who convinced me it would be okay, that this would work. *You* were the one who came on to *me*. *You*—you know what? I'd like you to leave now."

We finally have our son back safe and sound and he's leaving me—us—again?

I turn to the kitchen and stalk back upstairs, paying no mind to the awful racket I'm making. My temper reaches a boiling point when I see his clothes strewn all over my room. I lose a growl at the sight and stalk to my closet where his giant duffle bags have taken up residence.

I hear him enter the room, but I ignore that. Instead, I

grab his duffle bags and toss them on the bed. I go to my dresser and open each of the drawers he's taken over, tossing his things on the bed. Dresser finished, I do the same with the toiletries in the bathroom and the clothes hanging up in my closet.

Nearly two years, I think. Two years of waiting on this man and his wavering sense of duty and complete inability to commit to anything. I am so done with all of it.

I had thought before about whether or not there was a time limit on love. No, I realize, there's not, but there sure as hell is a limit on the amount of shit one person is willing to take to be with another. And I have had more than my fill. In fact, I'm full to bursting.

Ben watches solemnly and silently from the doorway as I throw a fit of epic proportions. If I had just a hair of Walker blood in me, I would have done the outrageous thing and thrown all of his crap out of the window. Instead, my motherly instincts force me to at least toss his things in his bags. When every last trace of him is gone, I drop each bag at his feet and give him my fiercest look.

"I have errands to run tomorrow. If you'd like to keep Cole while I do, I can drop him off at your parents or wherever else you need me to. Around noon, if that works for you, and I'll pick him up tomorrow night around six."

He only nods, and his lack of response and the fact that he can shut down so easily when my heart feels like it's withering in my chest pisses me off even more.

I charge past him and back down the stairs. I can hear him behind me, lifting his bags and following. The sound of his steps down the stairs echo with finality.

I reach the front door and hold it open for him, but he stops walking and turns toward me. "I know I'm no good for you, Livvie. I told you that when this first started. The only thing I ever wanted to do for you was keep you safe and be there for you. I just realized that I can't be the man you need, the man you deserve. It's better that we let this go now before it's too late. If it weren't for me, he would have never been taken in the first place."

It's then that the pieces click together. "You think that Cole getting kidnapped was your fault?" Now, I hurt for him instead of me.

His face is hard. Unreadable. "I told you that you wouldn't understand. You don't know what it's like to lose people that you're responsible for. I can't let my failures or my weakness be the reason that he's hurt again, Livvie. If I hadn't been distracted by those fuckin' fireworks, this never would have happened."

"Ben, we were both there. There were a million people around us. It wasn't your fault. The person that kidnapped him is to blame, not you."

"I'm not going to argue about this with you, Liv."

"Then stay. Don't go."

"I can't." His scent lingers as his steps recede into

darkness. Tears pool and fall down my cheeks as I close the front door behind him.

CHAPTER TWENTY FOUR

OLIVIA

In retrospect, it was a good thing I had so much to do before going back to work again. Thank God the school board was understanding, considering the circumstances. Had they not, I would have been single—again—*and* jobless. Focusing on returning to work, getting all of the paperwork completed and lesson plans organized is just what I need after my horrific break-up with Ben.

Could it be called a break-up if it had never really started in the first place? Can you break up considering our fucked-up way of "dating"?

I push the thought and resulting self-doubt from my mind. The last place on my list was to visit the accounting department at the school board to turn in the last of my paperwork. Then I can pick up Cole from Ben's parents' house, where he is due for dinner. They'd invited us a few days ago, but—no, I stop that train of thought right in its tracks. This makes the third time Ben has walked away from me, and I am determined it will be the last.

I get a text from Sofie and my cell rings just as I'm pulling up to the school board office. I throw the car in park and dive into my purse to retrieve it. I recognize Ben's mother's number and my heart leaps into my throat at the thought that something could be wrong with Cole.

"Hello?" I answer breathlessly, putting the phone on speaker so I can make sure everything's okay with Sof.

"Hi, Olivia. This is Sheila Hart."

I try to control my instant panic. "Yeah, hey, Sheila. Is everything okay?"

"Yes, honey, Cole is fine. Everything is fine."

I heave a sigh of relief and open up the text message. "Good, that's good. Was there something you needed?"

Back when we were all younger, Mrs. Hart had been like the local mother hen, mothering all of the neighborhood children. When my father died, she was one of the first people to come and cook up a storm to feed all of those visiting with their condolences. She reminded me a lot of my mom, Celeste, which only made me miss her all the more.

Now, I don't know how to handle her. It reminds me too much of what I've lost.

I rub a hand into my eyes and hope I can get through this unscathed. Based on how her son essentially made me crash and burn, that's unlikely. Sofie's attachment to the text takes me to an outside link. Based on the URL it looks like some sort of news report.

"You need to do something about this, girl. I'm at the end of my rope."

I blink at the empty parking lot in front of me then rub a hand over my brow. When I said mother hen, I meant it. She's the nosiest, most busy-body woman in the county—probably the state. So I ask cautiously, "What do you mean?

"I mean, I've had it up to here." The word *here* is emphasized and I can picture her, clear as day, gesturing with one hand above her head. "...With this boy and his nonsense."

Considering she has four men she noses after, I say, "Which boy?"

"It wasn't that long ago that I thought maybe, just maybe, you'd be able to help pull him out of this funk, but he seems bound and determined not to let that happen."

My heart sinks when my suspicions are confirmed. She can only mean Ben and I really, *really* would rather not talk about what's going on between us with her. Though it was inevitable, really.

I decide to shoot for honesty because, well, honestly, I

don't have the energy left for anything else. "You know Ben," I say simply. "He won't change unless he makes his mind up *to* change. There's nothing I can do or say that will pull him out of any funk unless he wants to be pulled out of it. And you and I both know whatever he's dealing with goes a lot further than a funk."

She sighs, the rasp of it amplified through the speaker, and I wince as I go through the papers I need to turn in. "I just thought that I finally had my son back. It's been so long since I've seen him so...happy, that I'm willing to do anything to help him stay that way. You're a mother. I know you don't understand now, but you will."

I press my fingers against my eyes. "I understand where you're coming from, Sheila, but Ben clearly said that he and I weren't going to work out, and I'm tired of beating my head against a wall."

"It's their father," she tells me. "All four of my kids have his bullheadedness."

I highly doubt that, but I wouldn't dare say a word to her. In an uncharacteristic show of emotion, I whisper, "He hurt me and he didn't have to."

"Oh, honey."

"I tried to give him a chance, the way he wanted me to, and clearly, that's not what he really wants. And I'm tired, so tired, of giving and not receiving."

"If you could just give him one more chance--"

The page loads and I start reading the link, which does turn out to be a news story. Sheila talks in the background, but her voice turns into a buzz and my stomach rolls.

Local drug dealer and son die in car accident

Police were brought to the scene of a horrific traffic accident this weekend after witnesses describe a high speed chase occurred. According to police reports, Thomas Thurston and his newborn son were fleeing the scene of an apparent drug deal gone wrong when they drove headfirst into oncoming traffic. Both Thurston and son were pronounced dead at the scene.

The driver of the pursuing vehicle, Mason Smith, suffered minor injuries. Once interviewed by police, it was determined that Smith was intoxicated. He is now in custody.

Thurston is survived by his wife, Lucy, and their daughter Amy, 5.

Attached to the article is a photo of the wife and daughter. The girl looks...she looks like me.

"Hello? Olivia, are you there? Hello?" comes Sheila from my phone.

A knock on my car window makes me jump. I look up and find the woman from the news article. Only she's a good twenty years older and someone that I considered to be a friend.

Melissa knocks on the window again and opens the

car door before I can lock it. She nudges her way in and presses a gun against my temple.

"Hello, Amy."

BEN

I thought cutting Olivia loose would make me feel better, but fuck if it doesn't make me feel like shit. Lower than shit. Lower than I felt when I ignored the last couple of emails from Scott. But nothing could make me feel worse than putting Cole in danger.

I'm lying on the couch with my arm thrown over my eyes in an attempt to ignore my mother's glares at me from across the room. Cole is sitting on my chest, pretending to drum out a beat as he watches my brothers play some music game or another. Mom makes a sound of derision and stalks from the room.

I was going to beg off the dinner with my family tonight, but my house was too quiet. I would take the chaos of my parents' house over facing my own demons any day.

Mitchell comes over and takes Cole to sit between them, and I watch with a smile pulling at my lips. A knock sounds at the door, so I leave the boys to their antics to answer it.

Logan gives me a grim look and says, "Can I come in for a minute?"

I open the door and move so he can enter. "What's up?" I ask, though from the look on his face, I'm afraid to know the answer.

"We got something off the prints from the break-in at Olivia's house."

I rock back on my heels and rub a hand over my face. "That's good, man, but you should be telling Livvie this."

"I tried calling her cell a few minutes ago, but I didn't get an answer. There was something else, and I wanted to make sure to tell the both of you in person."

Despite what happened between us the day before, I grab my cell and try to call Livvie myself, but she doesn't answer, which surprises me. I know we didn't part on the best of terms, but it's not like her to ignore a call from me, especially considering the fact that I have Cole and it could be an emergency. I try again with the same result.

"She isn't answering for me, either," I tell Logan. The back of my neck starts itching, and that's always a sign something isn't right.

"What was it you needed to tell us?"

"Ben!" my mom shouts from the other side of the house.

I glance in her direction then back at Logan. He opens his mouth to speak, but another shout from my mom cuts him off.

"Sorry, man. Come on in. Let me see what she needs and then we can sit down and talk."

We find my mother in the kitchen clutching the house phone, her face sheet-white. I immediately go to her side and say, "Mom, what's wrong? Are you okay?"

Her eyes find mine. "I was just on the phone t-talking to Olivia."

Relief flashes through me. "Good, is she still on? Logan needs to talk to her, too. It was about the case."

A sheen of tears fill her eyes. "I was on the phone with her and she said to hold on for a second. Then--then I heard a scream," she whispers. "And the phone went dead."

The ground shifts under my feet, and I have to grasp the kitchen counter to find purchase. A high-pitched ringing fills my ears. Logan comes up beside me and puts a hand on my arm. I shake it off, but it allows me to refocus.

"What did you have to tell us, Logan?"

His face is solemn. "The prints we got from Livvie's house came up with a match. Ben...dammit, Ben, they matched the prints we lifted from the car where we found Cole."

"Were you able to get a name?"

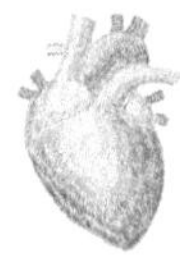

My ears are ringing—with rage or with his high-pitched screams, I'm not sure. My hands and face are coated with his blood, but I don't care. Rivers of it rain down the sloped linoleum floor. If it weren't for the grip on my boots, I would have slid to my knees with my next punch. The crunch is as satisfying as his unanswered pleas for help.

"Where is she?" I don't recognize the sound of my voice. The guttural tone and pitch of desperation sounds a lot like madness.

His eyes widen—what little they can around the blood, sweat and swelling. One is already swollen shut, so it can do little more than twitch. His chest shudders with breath, but he doesn't answer.

Impatience has me getting to my knees, soaking my pants in his blood. I straddle his legs and grip his tattered T-shirt with my left hand, twisting it to hold his weight. His good eye darts to my face as he spasms underneath me. I get a warped sense of satisfaction from the fear in his eyes.

"Listen up, motherfucker, or I will do what I have been dying to do since I got here and put an end to your pathetic life. You have one last chance to tell me where she is, or my friend Jack here will take that gun of his and start with your feet, working his way up to your knees, your balls, your gut. Then we'll leave you here to die like the coward you are. It'll be painful. In fact, I may just have him do it anyway, just for what you put my family through. You deserve much worse."

Mason Smith's face drains of color and he nearly goes slack in my arms. I jerk him back to consciousness. When his eyes meet mine, I tighten my hold on his shirt and force my voice to calm. "Now, are you going to tell me, or do I need to let Jack have you?"

His breath rattles between us for a moment. In that pause, I can feel everything I've done wrong over the past year bubble up in my chest. My regrets, my failings. I want just one chance to rectify all the mistakes I've made. The moment intensifies, and I don't realize I'm not breathing until my chest starts to ache.

"The old lady." He wheezes until I loosen my grip on his shirt. "Melissa."

My hand goes slack and Mason thumps into a mass of bruises and blood on the dirty, cracked floor. I fall back on my heels and look dazedly at Logan and Jack behind me. Jack is slumped on a tattered chair, his hand running through his hair. Logan is on his phone murmuring to put an APB out on Melissa's car, pointedly ignoring our little beat down inside the trailer.

"Livvie said it was a white SUV." Jack's voice is hollow. "I never thought—I didn't even think to consider Melissa. She has one."

I leave Mason on the floor and pull Jack up. "No one did. Focus. We have to find them before she gets hurt."

"What about him?" Jack nods to Mason, who is huddled on the floor in a pile of his own blood.

Logan holds up his cell phone and walks back into the room. "I've got a car coming around. I'll stay here until they get here. You guys go."

"You gonna be okay with this?" I ask, knowing he put his ass on the line, letting me get to Mason first before calling it in.

He jerks his chin. "You don't even have to fuckin' ask."

I look at Jack and say, "You know Melissa best. Where would she take Livvie?"

His face falls. "She could be anywhere."

CHAPTER TWENTY FIVE

OLIVIA

I CHOKE on the smell of fumes. Well, that and the tape covering my mouth. The gas Melissa pours on me stings my eyes and I struggle to breath.

"Shit, girl. I swear you fuck everything up wherever you go," Melissa says, dropping the gas can and slamming the door shut.

Ignoring her, I search in the back seat for something to saw through the bindings around my increasingly chaffed wrists.

We'd been driving for a half hour before she stopped to douse me in fuel. I tried to keep track of where we were going, but she took no discernible direction and she talked nonsense the entire way. I'd long since stopped listening as I was so fucking pissed yet terrified at the same time.

She turns again, throwing me against the door and I scream against the gag. She'd wrenched me like a rag doll when she threw me into the car and I felt something give in my still-healing shoulder. When I get out of here, she's so not going on my Christmas list.

I manage to work the tape off by licking my lips repeatedly until it peels off, one side hanging off my cheek. "Where are we going?" I ask.

Melissa turns to me, all traces of the sweet woman I'd known have vanished and are replaced by malice. "Back to where it all started. Back to where you tore my life from me. If it weren't for you, I'd still have Tommy. I'd still have my Sam. If it weren't for you *none of this would have happened*!"

My eyes catch on the speedometer which is inching towards eighty. The long stretches of back roads don't worry me, but the close turns and pinched sections spell certain death if I can't wrest control of the car from her.

"Why couldn't you leave me alone? I was finally happy. I had a family I loved, that loved me. What did I ever do to you?"

"You ruined my life."

She's certifiable. My skin crawls, knowing that I left her alone with my son, that she had her hands on him.

"I never did anything to you. I was just a kid."

She turns back to me and her backhand connects with my cheek. "Shut up." We take another sharp turn and my freshly bruised cheek strikes the window with a snap. My vision flashes white and my ears start to ring. Over that, I hear her say, "I tried to give you a second chance. I wanted to see what you were up to. I thought maybe we could even be friends. Family. But when I overheard you telling your dad that you wanted to find me, I knew I needed to take matters into my own hands."

That would explain why she wormed her way into our lives. Like a disease, infecting everything she touched.

"And my dad? You dated him just to get close to me?"

"Henry. He was sweet. I felt bad about him."

My fingers pause in their attempt to work a pen from between the seat cushions. "What do you mean you felt bad about him?"

"Well, he stumbled on that article, like I'm sure you did. I couldn't have him go blabbin' to you before I was ready. Especially not when you were carrying my grandson. I figure it's only fair that you repaid one baby with another."

I swallow around the knot in my throat. "Is that why you tried to kill me and tried to kidnap Cole?"

She slows a bit to take a corner. "You're hardly fit to take care of a child, Amy."

"My name is Olivia," I growl. "And you will *never* have my child."

I lurch forward, my freed hands reaching for the wheel and jerking it to the side, jerking the car to swerve dangerously off of the road.

The car skips over the knotted ground and careens into a fence, the force throwing me into the front seat. My head smacks against the dashboard and something cracks. Melissa screams, or maybe it's me and things go black for a while.

When I come to, it's because the sound of a car horn is blaring nonstop. I blink, blood dripping into my eyes, and find Melissa conked out, draped over the steering wheel.

I try to sit up, but my ribs protest and I let out a long, low moan. Shit. Something is definitely wrong there. I push myself up, slowly, and slither into the back of the car. The front, from what I can see, is completely shattered and pinned against the fence. The back driver's side door is free and I'm able to wedge it open, though it makes a God-awful squeak that causes Melissa to jerk in front of me.

I pause a few seconds to make sure she isn't going to raise like the dead. When she doesn't, I scoot out the door, but my foot catches on the frame and I stumble to the damp ground, wrenching another scream from my throat. My leg is caught in the doorway and when I turn to free it, I find Melissa's cell on the floorboard.

After I manage to snag the cell I slide backwards along the ground, mud caking my jeans and soaking me to the core. I dial Ben out of instinct, fingers trembling, and use a tree with my free hand to get to my feet.

"Melissa, what *the fuck* did you do with Olivia? Listen to me bitch, if you—"

"Ben, wait, it's me. Please don't hang up," I beg, my voice breaking.

"Olivia? Where are you? You okay?"

"I-I don't know where we are. She just started driving. God, Ben, is Cole okay?"

"He's fine, baby, focus. Find a street name, if you can. Look around."

"I don't know. I don't know where we are. Oh my god, Ben, she's so fucking crazy."

"Goddammit, Olivia. Fucking find a street name right now!"

I do as he says and relay the only sign I can see. "Please hurry, Ben."

"We're on the way, baby, sit tight." Then the line goes dead.

I turn back around to check on Melissa and find her coming at me, blood dripping from her hair, a vicious gash on her hairline and her eyes wild. She screams as she charges, wielding the gun she used to get me in the car.

"This is the last time you'll fuck things up for me, Amy. The last time. Get back in the car!"

My body decides that it's had it and it takes every single last store of energy I have to make the short trek back. Hopefully it was enough to bide Ben some time. Hopefully he'll get here before it's too late.

I'm thankful for the numbness spreading through my chest. It would be so easy just to give in at this point and let it completely overtake me. How much can one person take?

She shoves me back into the back seat and I screech, my vision going dark for a second. The door slams behind me and I sit up to find her digging in her pockets. She pulls out a lighter and then the gas suddenly makes sense.

"This is for Tommy and Sam," she shouts, dumping the remaining fuel on the car. "It should have been you."

She flicks the lighter and sets the car on fire. I watch unable to move, shock from the pain and adrenaline having sapped all my energy. Smoke furls in from the windows and fills the interior in a shocking amount of time. I see her face split in an evil smile before it, too, is engulfed in smoke. Sweat beads at my hairline and mixes with blood. Both sting my eyes as the smoke stings my lungs.

Something cracks. The front window maybe? There's a veritable feast of accelerants to feed the fire. Please dear God let someone get here before then. I curl on the seat, as low as I can get, to find fresh air.

Over the crackle and *woosh* of fire, I hear the squeal of

brakes and my heart lifts. Someone screams and the black part of my soul hopes that it's Melissa.

A male voice catches my attention and I force my eyes to open. I see Ben standing in the open door, and I'm half-convinced I've died and gone to heaven. He leans into the car and I can make out the ruddy streaks of blood on his shirt. The sight causes me to frown. This man needs a near constant supply of shirts. His face comes into view as he kneels next to me. I hear a woman screaming and the muffled sounds of a scuffle. Warm hands cup my cheeks and I refocus on his face.

"Jesus Christ, Spitfire. It's going to be okay. Look at me." His voice sounds real, a feeling of absolute calm comes over me and I know he's right. Everything is going to be okay.

"She's bleeding. We have to get her to a hospital," Jack says from somewhere behind Ben.

But he's already wrapping his strong arms around me and lifting me into his embrace. I try to voice my fears about Cole, but the horrors of the past few weeks converge and I give up the fight against the darkness consuming me. The echo of Melissa's shouts follow me into oblivion.

BEN

I carry Olivia from the car to the emergency room, though because I'm not family, I'm not permitted to be with her during the evaluations. Jack goes in my stead and keeps me updated as they admit her and examine her wounds. While I wait, I make a call to check on Cole and find my mother nearly frantic with worry. I manage to calm her down with the news that Olivia was found safely and promise to call back when she wakes.

Logan still hasn't quite explained to me how the small-time drug dealer and Melissa were related, but I can't seem to muster the energy to care. The only thing I can focus on is the fact that Olivia nearly died for the third time due to my own stupidity and selfishness. I wasn't about to let there be a fourth. In fact, she won't be leaving my sight for the rest of her life.

Three hours after I carried her lifeless body into the emergency room, I still haven't been permitted to see her. But I don't care. They're going to have to pry me out of the waiting room with a crew of firemen and the Jaws of Life if they want me to leave.

Jack made a few trips, but none of them brought the news I wanted. The doctors sedated her, so it wasn't likely she'd wake any time soon, Jack said. He even suggested I go back to my parents with Cole and get some sleep. I ignore the suggestion until he takes the hint and leaves again.

When at last they let me into her recovery room I find myself unwilling to enter, afraid of the truths I may see in her eyes. Jack comes out and holds the door open for me so I have no choice but to face my mistakes. My shortcomings. My failures.

"She's awake, but groggy," Jack says. "She's asking for you."

I pause at the entrance to the hospital room with Jack at my side. "I want to apologize to you."

"You don't have anything to apologize for, man."

"Yeah, yeah, I do. I've let her down so many times. But I want to tell you, to promise you, that it won't happen again. You have my word."

Jack nudges my shoulder with his. "If it does, I'll have your ass. Now go."

For the second time, I walk to her hospital bed and gaze down at her slumbering form. I take the chair already placed on her uninjured side and hold her free hand in both of my own. I bow my head over it, like a man seeking absolution. And maybe I am, in a way.

I must have fallen asleep because when her hand jerks in mine, I shoot straight up to find her eyes open and on our clasped hands.

"Baby," I mumble, sure I'm dreaming.

"Ben?" Her voice is scratchy with sleep, so I grab her a glass of water and hold it to her lips.

I wait as she swallows, and for her to open her eyes again. She blinks rapidly and winces against the bright light.

"So, this is what it takes," she says and I frown.

"What do you mean?"

"This is what I have to do to keep you in bed next to me, isn't it? I have to say, the school pays me pretty well, but the insurance is shit. I don't think I can afford to keep landing in the hospital just to keep you around."

I'm nearly weak with relief. "It's not funny, Olivia. She could have killed you...again. For a while, I thought she had."

"We Walkers are made of pretty tough stuff." She coughs, and I offer her another sip of water. "What happened?" she asks when she's able to talk again.

"We don't have to talk about this now—"

"No," she cuts me off. "I want to get it over with so we can finally move on." She pauses and seems to consider something before continuing on, though her voice is now laced with a tremor. "She was my mother, my biological mother.

I caress the soft skin of her cheek, thankful she didn't suffer another round of head trauma. "Yes," I tell her gently. "She was. How did you know? Did Jack tell you before I got here?"

"No," she answers. "She did. She blamed me for my biological dad's death. He and my little brother were killed in a car accident. How did she find me?"

"You'll have to ask Logan for the specifics, but he believes she's been watching you for a long time." The mere thought of how close she came to dying makes me want to throw something. "We think your pregnancy may have set it off, maybe even caused a psychotic break. That'll be up to the courts and the psychologists to decide. Whatever it was, she tracked down your family, your dad, you, and bided her time. But you don't have to worry now. She'll be going away for a long time."

Tears leak from the corner of her eyes, and I wipe them away with a knuckle.

"I just can't believe it, after all this time." She hiccups.

I nod. "She couldn't handle their loss, so she put you up for adoption."

Livvie closes her eyes and rests her head against the pillow. "Cole? Is he with you?" she asks, her voice still heavy with grief and sleep.

"He's still with my parents. My mom is keeping a hawk eye on him."

She smiles softly. "Of course she is," she says around a yawn. "Did she tell you that she called me, trying to convince me to take you back?"

"She did?"

Livvie nods.

"Was she convincing enough, or do I need to grovel?"

She levels a pensive look at me and narrows her eyes as though deep in thought. The moment seems to suspend for an eternity. "We'll save the groveling for later, but first I want you to tell me what you were hiding from me. All of it. Otherwise, we're never going to work, Ben. Secrets," she sighs, "secrets don't do anyone any good. And whatever you're holding inside, I just know it's eating at you. Let me help you," she pleads.

I swallow thickly. "Logan was looking into that guy for me. My friend? From my convoy that I saved but was critical...I was having Logan take a look, to see if he had any luck, because I sure haven't. I need to know that he's all right somewhere. I just *need* to. All of my guys can't be gone."

He pauses and takes a deep breath. "I'm sorry I didn't tell you about it. I just couldn't. I feel like he's one more person who I turned my back on. The things I've done... it'll be a long time before I ever come to terms with what happened, if ever. I can't promise you that I'll ever get over the things I've been through, but I *can* promise I'll try. Every day, I'll try. For you. Because the only thing that got me through the worst of it was imagining coming back to you. Seeing you."

Livvie lifts a hand and cups my cheek. "Thank you for telling me. I hope you know that I'm here for you, whatever you need. All I want to do is to share my life with you.

I want you to be the one by my side. And I want to be there for you."

I press a kiss to the palm of her hand. "Thank you."

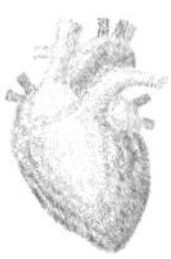

I look up from the laptop in surprise as the doorbell rings. After the kidnapping, I wanted to give Olivia some time away from everything. I couldn't think of a better place than my—our—lake house.

"Who is it?" I ask as she peers through the peep hole.

"Logan. Were you expecting him?"

I set my laptop down on the countertop. "Yeah, I forgot to mention that he'd be coming by. He wanted to check on us, but I told him to wait a few days so that we could unwind. You don't mind, do you?"

Livvie smiles, reminding me of the fact that we haven't touched in what feels like fucking years. Now I'm regretting letting him come over. "Of course I don't mind."

Logan enters the living room, his watchful eyes falling on Olivia and I see him smile for the first time in a long time. "Damn, girl," he says, "you look good even all wrapped up in bandages."

She blushes and pulls him into a hug. "It's so good to see you, Logan. I'm glad you came by."

"I had some time," he says, shooting me a sly look.

We'd both known that he wouldn't be getting any commendations for looking the other way when I beat the shit out of Mason Smith. As it turned out, he would be on unpaid suspension for a long time—if they even let him back on the force, but Livvie didn't need to know that yet. I wasn't going to keep it from her—I didn't want to keep anything from her anymore. But, she deserved a break.

"Why don't you come say hi to Cole? I think he's gotten bored with us."

"How's the little guy doin'?"

Livvie picks him up from the playpen and brings him over to Logan. "Much better."

"I just wanted to check in and make sure y'all were doing okay," Logan says.

"We're doing great, thanks to you. And you're more than welcome to come by any time. We'll probably be here for a while." Livvie looks to me and I nod.

"I'll be taking you up on that."

Logan slaps me on the back and offers Olivia a smile. Which was more than she'd offered me in the past few weeks. Not that I didn't understand.

After they were released from the hospital, I managed to convince her to come with me to the lake house. Ever since she'd been focused on Cole. If he wasn't in her arms, he wasn't far away.

That night I rock Cole to sleep as Olivia finishes her shower—and I try to distract myself with something else, anything else. So I take to singing cadences—songs we'd use to keep time during PT—to help him sleep. I hope to hell he can't understand anything I'm saying and that Olivia doesn't happen to overhear. Military men can be… colorful.

As I lay him down to sleep, I brush a hand over his eyebrow and smooth down his blankets. "Sleep good, little man." I rest my hand on his chest and feel the reassuring beat of his heart under my palm. "I love you," I tell him, like I tell him every night. Every chance I get.

I hear a sound behind me and find Olivia wrapped in a towel in the doorway. *Fucking Christ.* My eyes feast on her bared flesh. I can feel myself grow instantly hard. I'm damn near frozen to the spot, barely able to breathe.

When she drops the towel, my heart leaps into my throat. She smiles, backing away and I follow, like I know I always will. If it takes years to convince her of that fact, I'm determined to make sure she knows it.

Her skin is pale in the darkness and she takes measured steps toward my bedroom. My feet thud heavily with each labored step. I find her slithering onto the bed, her ass round and firm right in front of me. I reach the foot of the bed and slide my hands over the softness of it, unable to resist touching her. She lowers down to the bed and I hover over her on all fours.

"Gonna let me in?" I ask.

She turns over to face me, pulling my neck down to

meet her lips and that's answer enough. Her fingers snag the button on my jeans and flick it open. I hiss in pleasure / pain while she unzips and then draws out my straining cock. Her slim hands work it up and down slowly and I fear we may end before we've even gotten started.

I possess her mouth in a deep, drugging kiss as I shuck my jeans and tangle with her heat. I spread her legs wide and ease inside. She wraps her legs around my waist and sucks me so deep I almost go off right then. With each slow, smooth thrust, she lifts her hips to meet me until we're rocking in tandem. Each time her internal muscles grip me, fighting my backwards glide and pulling me back in.

Soon, she's breathless beneath me, her muscles going hard and her limbs tightening around me. She calls out to God and curses me in the same breath as I bring her through her orgasm. Then, when she's arching beneath me, caught in an endless storm of pleasure, I bring my finger back to her clit and send her over again with me right behind her.

Soon after, when we're both exhausted and limp, she turns in my arms and says, "I don't know what to do now."

Fear has my throat closing up. "You don't need to do anything. In fact, it would probably be good for my health if you could stay in this bed for a couple years at least."

"That's not what I mean. I just...the past year has been

a whirlwind. I don't know what to do without all of the drama."

"So like a woman," I mutter. "I'm sure you'll learn to like the boring life eventually."

I feel the vibration of her laugh against my chest. "I don't know if that'll ever be possible," she says.

"I know what you can do."

She looks up at me and I can see the love in her eyes. "What's that?"

"You can let me take care of you. Let me love you."

She smiles. "I can live with that."

EPILOGUE

BEN

There are good days, and there are bad days.

Today happens to be a very good day.

Though I'm still haunted by the loss and horror I experienced, I try to take each day as it comes and enjoy the hell out of the good things. My little boy taught me that.

It started when I almost lost him.

Now, we're celebrating his second birthday and the successful recovery from his third, and hopefully final, surgery. My mom has him sequestered on our front porch watching the birds flit around the lake. His little squeals pierce the humid afternoon and remind me to look forward to many more just like this.

Cole's future looks bright. As the surgeries to treat those with HLHS are relatively new, no one knows exactly what the life expectancy is. In fact, we're incredibly lucky to have the technology and excellent cardiology staff on call to give Cole the best chance possible.

In the meantime, there are days for swinging at the park, watching the birds, and enjoying a good time with family.

"Sofie, Jack 'iss!" Cole yells.

Every person in attendance turns toward Cole and follows his outstretched hand. Sofie and Jack are clutched in a passionate embrace down on the beach on the edge of the forest. Hoots and calls from the crowd cause them to break apart. Sofie pushes away from Jack and rushes by everyone and into the house, her face as red as Olivia's hair.

Olivia turns to me with wide eyes from where she's setting out the cake. She mouths, "Oh my God," and does a little happy dance.

I roll my eyes. It was about damn time they made a move.

Though I'm not really one to talk. It took me nearly ten years to realize what I was missing with Olivia.

I move through the crowd of our friends and family until I reach her side. I cup her jaw in my hands and dip her backwards for a long, thorough kiss. She breaks apart, breathless, and I look into her eyes. "Have I told you today that I love you?"

She leans into me. "Only three or four times."

"Not nearly enough." I kiss her again. "I love you."

"Momma, Daddy, 'iss!" Cole shouts.

Gravel crunches in the driveway and I turn to see the newest arrival.

Livvie grabs my face and turns me back to her. "Now, I don't want you to be mad, but I did something and I'm not sure you're going to like it."

My brows furrow. "What did you do?"

"After you told me what happened in Afghanistan and explained who you had Logan looking for, I did a little looking myself and had Sofie help me out." She moves in closer and touches her forehead to mine. "I wanted to give you something that I know you'd never give yourself."

I release a breath and bring my hands up to place them on her wrists, still holding my head to hers. "Livvie," I say more calmly. "What did you do?"

The car comes to a halt and a young guy gets out with a service dog. It's not until he reaches the steps to the deck that I see his prosthetic leg. My face goes slack as I recall the day I nearly died saving his life.

"Scott?"

Livvie urges me toward Scott as he bounds up the stairs with a smile stretching across his face.

"No-Heart!" Scott exclaims, throwing his arms around my back. "God, it's good to see you, man."

My reply is choked with emotion. "You too," is all that I can manage before I break down like a little fucking sissy in front of everyone. "Lookin' good, man."

He steps back and shows me his new leg. "Yeah, with my own peg leg."

Cole comes closer to look. "Oohhhh!" he says.

"Scott, meet my son, Cole. Cole, can you say hi to my friend, Scott?"

Scott crouches down and extends a hand. Cole is more interested in touching the shiny new leg. Scott angles it so that he can see more clearly.

"You like that? I've got a brand new leg."

Cole smiles and pulls down the collar to his shirt. "New heart!" he says proudly.

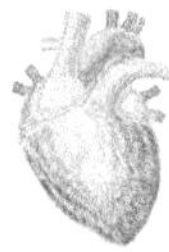

"You didn't have to do that," I tell Olivia later.

"Yes, I did," she replies, dressing in one of those pajama sets with short shorts that I love so much. The sight of her bare legs nearly distracts me from my goal.

"I was going to get ahold of him."

She sits next to me on the bed, smiling at me in a way

that I know means she's trying to hold back a laugh. "I love you, baby, but we both know if I hadn't, it would have taken you years. I had Sofie. Come on...you know Sofie can put the FBI to shame when she wants to. Besides, this is a new chapter in our lives. I thought it was time that we put the past behind us so we can move on."

"A new chapter, huh?" My hand finds the skin of her thigh. "What makes you say that?"

She presses her lips against my jaw. "Well, I figure you have to marry me now that you've gone and knocked me up again."

I jerk towards her, my face going slack in shock. "You're..."

Olivia smiles at me, bringing a hand to my cheek. "Pregnant. Yes."

My arms go around her, pulling her close to my chest where I'm determined to keep her. "Have you been to the doctor? Is everything okay? His heart?"

"Yes, I have, and they can't tell that yet, but the chances are slim that this baby will have the same defect," she says.

A weight eases from my shoulders. "That's good."

"Just as long as you promise to be there with me."

I cup her cheek in my hand. "Forever. You're my little spitfire and you always will be."

Yep, there are good days and there are bad days. For a guy like me, there always would be.

Now I know I can endure the bad days and fight for the good ones.

Continue the *First to Fight Series* with...
VALOR! Keep reading for a sneak peek of Ben & Livvie's happily ever after novella.

VALOR EXCERPT

OLIVIA

THE LIVING ROOM walls tell the story of our lives.

There's the thin stripes of color near the dining room where I've been testing out paint colors, but haven't made a decision yet. Ben tells me I should just choose one because they're all the same shade of beige, but each time I make up my mind, I have second thoughts. Is beige too boring? Too Suzy Homemaker? Is the green-tinted beige too risky or will I get bored with it in two years? Sometimes I drive myself mad thinking about these things.

In the corner, by the TV, there's a little framed section where Cole and Phoebe had gone chuck wild with the crayons one day and drew a dinosaur and a butterfly, respectively. Or at least, that's what they said they were.

Instead of painting over it, Ben had decided to frame them and wouldn't listen to my pleadings otherwise. Looking back, I'm glad he didn't listen to me. Now that the kids are six and four, and have mostly outgrown those kind of antics, the memory is a sweet one to look back on.

In the entryway by the front door, there's a tumble of boots, my flats and sandals, and the kids' shoes that have left scuff marks near the baseboards. I keep meaning to scrub them down, but there never seems to be any time for those things. Besides, with my kids it would only end up scuffed again the second I turned my head.

There are a cluster of portraits I had done when Phoebe was a newborn. It was probably the happiest time of my life. The terror of Cole's kidnapping was far enough in the past that I was able to keep it tightly under lock, and the joy of sharing my life with Ben and our children was enough to blot out any shadow of darkness. Cole's heart transplant had taken spectacularly and he'd been out of the woods for a couple months by the time Phoebe was born.

The pictures hang over our fireplace mantle in a grouping of three, two smaller ones on each side and a larger one in the middle. Cole is on the left in a sweet little button-up shirt the color of cornflowers. He's smiling so big you can see a mouthful of teeth still a little oversized for his boyish face and one only halfway grown in. He looks so much like his dad, seeing the picture makes my heart squeeze. On the right is Phoebe with a capful of strawberry blonde hair, her almond-shaped eyes relaxed in sleep, and her plump pink lips pursed with attitude. Her hair and her creamy pale complexion are about all she gets from me. She's her father's daughter through-and-through, with boundless sass and stubbornness in equal measure, even as an infant.

The center portrait is of the four of us. I take a step closer with my morning coffee—decaf because it makes me jittery otherwise—clasped in both hands as I wait for it to cool. Wrangling two kids to sit still for the photographer hadn't been easy, especially for Cole, who always had to be careful because of his heart condition, but it had been worth it.

Ben stands next to me with an arm around my shoulders. He has Phoebe propped up on his chest, still fast asleep. Cole stands in front of me, allowing me to rest my hands on his shoulders. We're all wearing shades of blue and green and on the backdrop of a gorgeous Florida spring afternoon, we look stunning.

The perfect apple pie family.

My dream come true.

I hear a thud above my head and smile to myself. Cole is awake. Due to wreak terror on anyone in the vicinity. I wait for a second, studying the lights twinkling on the mantel over the fireplace. Then, turn back to the kitchen for another cup of coffee as a second thud sounds.

Phoebe, never one to be left out, follows close behind as they both stomp down the stairs to begin their day.

"Mo-om," Cole shouts as he reaches the bottom. "Do I have to go to a stupid wedding? I hate weddings." He says it like he'd rather eat a plate full of Brussels sprouts. "They're all about love. Gross."

Phoebe hefts herself up to the breakfast bar next to her brother and rolls her eyes at him. "They are not. It's a grown-up party with food and dancing."

"Thank you," I say to Phoebe, as I butter toast and plate up eggs for their breakfast. "Besides, this is Scott's wedding. You love Scott."

"I like playing video games with Scott," Cole says around a mouthful of toast. "That doesn't mean I want to go to his wedding. All people do is kiss and be all gross."

Sighing, I instruct, "Don't talk when you have your mouth full."

"Plus, there's going to be cake!" Phoebe adds brightly. "A big, huge cake."

I give her a stern look. "One piece."

Her happy expression falls. "But Mo-om."

Pointing my spatula, I say, "Don't 'but Mom' me. One piece. I need you two sugared up like I need a hole in my head. Cole, did you take your medicine?"

He rolls his eyes. "Yes, I took my medicine. It's not like I haven't been doing the same thing for the past forever."

Making a face, I exchange the spatula for orange juice.

"You two can play for a few minutes while I finish getting ready, then you'll have to put on your fancy clothes. There will be no dirtying them up once they're on, do you hear me?" They're too busy stuffing their faces to answer, so I repeat myself, "Do you hear me? Yes, ma'am?"

"Yes, ma'am," they both intone.

"That's better. Now, finish your breakfasts, then stay inside the fence while you play. No killing each other, but if you do draw blood, then go find your father because he's the one with the first aid training."

I kiss their heads, pausing for a second to inhale the scent of children's shampoo, then take my mug of coffee and head upstairs. With my free hand, I snag a NERF gun and a Barbie doll, then toss them in their respective rooms. Somehow, the toys never seem to find their way back to their designated space, but today, I have other things on my mind.

The sparkling lavender dress I'd bought special hangs on a hook on the back of my closet door. I'm not quite the size four I used to be, but the shape was flattering and accentuates my breasts, and the pale purple compliments my light skin and red hair. I'll admit, I half had Ben's reaction in mind when I bought it, hoping he wouldn't be able to take his eyes off me.

The thought lingers as I strip off my robe and step into the shower, adjusting the spray until it's near-scalding. I let the warmth soak through me and allow the tension to seep from my muscles. Today is a happy day. Faith and Scott deserve all the love and joy in the world.

I hear the bathroom door open and close and spin around with a head full of suds, hoping the kids won't be interrupting. "Kids?" I call out, my eyes closed against the soap. I swear I can't go five minutes without one of them interrupting me once I shut the bathroom door. It's like they have some sort of internal alarm.

The shower door opens and I sense someone stepping in. "It's me," comes Ben's deep voice. I shiver, despite the hot water pounding down on me. It doesn't matter how long we've been married, being close to him still does something to my body. His hands close around my breasts from behind and I nearly choke. "You don't mind if I join you, do you?" he asks.

Soap glides down my chest, making my skin extra sensitive, especially when his fingers tweak my nipples. I clear my throat. "Of course not." Knees weak, I lean against his hard body, feeling the light scrape of hair against my back.

"Turn around," he says gruffly.

Eyes still closed, I let his hands guide me around, then I lean into him as he washes the rest of the soap out of my hair, then works in conditioner. The brush and sway of my body against his works me up until I'm practically panting. With two full-time jobs and two very active kids, the only times we have to be together are stolen moments like these, so having him this close to me makes me forget I should be getting ready for the wedding. Instead, all I can think about is having him inside me.

It's that simple. I can't remember a time in recent memory when I look at him and don't want him. It's a blessing and a curse.

"Ben," I plead.

"Shh, I've got to get you all cleaned up. But first I'm going to get you a little dirty."

Turning him down doesn't even cross my mind. "You've got to hurry, the kids—"

Ben kisses me until I'm quiet and forget what I was saying.

He grows hard against my belly and I lift up on my tiptoes to feel him, but he's too tall and too focused on driving me crazy to satiate the growing ache between my legs.

"Ben, please."

He takes my mouth then, either to shut me up or because he's also incredibly turned on. I'm not sure I care about the motivation. His taste is a familiar comfort, one I seek greedily.

We spin around until I'm pressed against the wall of the shower and he lifts me up into his arms. All I can think is *Oh God, Oh God,* because even after all these years, no one knows my body like he does. He's not even inside me and I'm already close to tipping over the edge.

Carefully, he brushes the water out of my eyes until I can open them and see his face for the first time. He's got lines around his eyes that weren't there a couple years ago and laugh lines fanning out from his lips. It's a kind face, but it's his gaze that tells the stories of the horrors he's seen. Sometimes I can still see the shadows of the memories that haunt him, but right now, all I can see is the hunger for me.

Then a bang comes at the bathroom door. One that doesn't sound like it comes from a six-year-old boy, but it's his voice that follows. "Mom? Dad? Phoebe threw dirt in my eyes and it stings. Mom! Dad!"

We both groan in unison and I rest my head against his shoulders while he sets my feet back down. So close. We both smile a little in regret as we quickly finish our washing off.

"Go to your bathroom and start rinsing your face. Be very careful, I'm coming out and I'll help you," I shout back.

Ben halts me with a grip on my arm. "We'll finish this later," he says with a wicked grin.

I'm smiling as I dab myself dry with a towel, then dress in a robe.

"I'll be looking forward to it," I say.

MILITARY SLANG GLOSSARY

COURTESY OF BEN HART

- Dicks of Death – The little disgusting beef links found in bean MRE's. You only eat these if you're about to die. Even then, I wouldn't recommend it.
- A-10 Warthog – the prettiest ugly little shitkicking plane on the planet. Built to carry the GAU-8 Avenger 30mm gatling gun. Basically you don't want to be against one in a fight.
- Clusterfuck – when everything is messed up or going wrong.
- Chest Candy – ribbons and awards on your uniform.
- Fast movers – the really, really fast jets. Vroom.

(Cole's favorite, though I'll have him switched to the A-10 in no time.)

- Gunner – Man guaranteed to fuck you up with whatever heavy artillery we have at hand.
- Groundhog Day – Because deployments are endless, repetitive, and would be better with a side of Bill Murray.
- Helo a.k.a. Whirly Bird – helicopter.
- JTAC – The most badass of the badasses that control combat aircraft and air support. The definition of makin' it rain.
- Jodi – the asshole your wife / girlfriend is screwing while you're in combat. Normally followed by a Dear John letter.
- Monica – derogatory name. A.K.A. pussy.
- MRE – Meals Ready to Eat. If you can get your hands on lasagna or chili mac, you're gold, but stay away from the bean burritos and seafood gumbo.
- RPG – not the role playing game. The rocket propelled exploding kind. Guaranteed to fuck up your world.
- ROE – rules of engagement. When we can and cannot fuck you up.
- TBI – traumatic brain injury. Headaches for badasses.

ACKNOWLEDGMENTS

Thank you to my family, my mom, my brothers, my in-laws for humoring my crazy dream.

To my Knockouts for being beside me every step of the way. A special shout-out to Ella Stewart, Hayley Picknell, Mandy Sawyer, Melissa Fisher, and Joy Lynn for your eagle eyes. To my beta readers for their patience and enthusiasm. Thank you to Elle Vanzadnt for being there for the years it took for me to actually finish a book.

Mia Searles, you are an amazing woman and friend. I appreciate your patience and support more than you can possibly imagine. Thank you to Alana for getting me into this crazy mess in the first place. I wouldn't have had the courage if it weren't for you.

Vanessa from PREMA Romance. You are a legit goddess. You made Warrior shine. It wouldn't be the book it is today if it weren't for you. Your insight is priceless.

Afton, I finally finished Warrior so that I can start on your "favorite book". I love you!

To all of those either dealing with or loving someone

with PTSD, thank you for your courage and your strength. I hope you find peace.

ABOUT THE AUTHOR

 **Nicole Blanchard** is the New York Times and USA Today bestselling author of dangerous romance from antiheroes to aliens. She and her family reside in the Sunshine State along with their menagerie of animals. Nicole is represented by Katie Monson at SBR Media.

Visit her website www.authornicoleblanchard.com for more information or to subscribe to her newsletter for updates on sales and new releases.

ALSO BY NICOLE BLANCHARD

Battleboro Fire & Rescue Series

Storming His Heart

Shielding His Heart

Saving His Heart

First to Fight Series

Anchor

Warrior

Valor

Box Set: Books 1-3

Survivor

Savior

Honor

Box Set: Books 4-6

Traitor

Operator

Aviator

Captor

Protector

Armor

Friend Zone Series

Friend Zone

Frenemies

Friends with Benefits

Box Set

The Lost Planet Series

The Forgotten Commander

The Vanished Specialist

The Mad Lieutenant

Journey to the Lost Planet (Books 1-3)

The Uncertain Scientist

The Lonely Orphan

The Rogue Captain

Return to the Lost Planet (Books 4-6)

The Determined Hero

The Arrogant Genius

The Runaway Alien

Saving the Lost Planet (Books 7-9)

Dark Romance

Toxic

An Immortal Fairy Tale Series

Deal with the Dragon

Vow to the Vampire

Kiss from the King

Standalone Novellas

Bear with Me

Darkest Desires

Mechanical Hearts